Tania turned and saw that Rathina had risen to her feet. She was standing tall in the prow, staring hard into the east, a look of alarm and concern on her face.

"Rathina? What is it?" Tania called. She followed the line of her sister's eyes but could see nothing—nothing but the smooth, dappled jade green face of the sea.

"Danger!" Rathina called. "Danger blown on the wind!"

"I can't see anything," Connor called, twisting his head to scan the horizon. "What kind of danger?"

"Someone is calling on the Dark Arts," Rathina said. "We are being followed!"

"Are you sure?" Tania was on her feet now, balancing herself with a hand on Connor's shoulder. "There's nothing there, Rathina."

"It is coming nonetheless," said Rathina, moving down the vessel. "It is upon the water." She looked at Tania. "Do not doubt me, sister. I know the taint of the Dark Arts in the air. We are pursued."

Also by Frewin Jones

The Faerie Path
The Lost Queen
The Seventh Daughter
(also published as The Sorcerer King)
The Immortal Realm
The Charmed Return
Warrior Princess
Destiny's Path
The Emerald Flame

The ENCHANTED QUEST

Book Five of The FAERIE PATH

FREWIN JONES

For Rob Rudderham,

". . . rub sandman dust in sleepy eyes to see . . ."

With special thanks to Shannon Peet for the fireflies.

HarperTeen is an imprint of HarperCollins Publishers.

The Enchanted Quest

Series created by Working Partners Limited

www.harperteen.com

Library of Congress Cataloging-in-Publication Data

Jones, Frewin.

The enchanted quest / by Frewin Jones. — 1st ed.

p. cm. — (Faerie Path ; #5)

Summary: Princess Tania must travel outside of the Immortal Realm to seek a cure for the plague afflicting her people, while joined in spirit with all of the children of Aurealis to weave a web of protection over the realm of Faerie.

ISBN 978-0-06-087160-4

[1. Faeries—Fiction. 2. Princesses—Fiction. 3. Voyages and travels—Fiction. 4. Sick—Fiction. 5. Fantasy.] I. Title.

PZ7.J71Enc 2010 2009024096

[Fic]—dc22 CIP

AC

Typography by Al Cetta

11 12 13 14 15 CG/BV 10 9 8 7 6 5 4 3 2 1

❖

First paperback edition, 2011

Faeries tread the Faerie Path
A trail that leads from Faerie Realm
A ship upon the Western Sea
Dark sister's hand upon the helm

Into Alba, into Erin
Enchanted quest to undertake
An ill to cure, a truth to learn
A life to lose for true love's sake

The Story So Far . . .

A savage plague is sweeping through Faerie—the Immortal Realm that has for thousands of years been free of illness. Suspicion over the cause of the outbreak falls first on Tania's mortal parents, Clive and Mary Palmer. It is believed that they brought the deadly illness through from the Mortal World. Oberon gathers the Conclave of Earls at the Summer Palace of Veraglad to decide a course of action. Clive and Mary Palmer are banished, and half-Mortal Tania is put under close guard. The earls command that the ways between the worlds must be closed forever—and that Tania must choose between Faerie and the Mortal World one final time.

Against the wishes of the King, Tania steps secretly into the Mortal World with her sister Rathina at her side. Her intention is to bring family friend Connor Estabrook back into Faerie in the hope that he can help her defeat the disease with his knowledge of modern medicine.

However, Tania has enemies at court: Lord Aldritch of Weir speaks against her and brings a "Healer" to find the source of the sickness and to affect a cure. It is not until Princess Eden, using her Mystic Arts, learns that the sickness comes from Faerie itself that suspicions toward the Mortal World ease and Tania is free to find a cure for the plague.

But Tania's relationship with her beloved Edric is under severe strain. He is meddling with the Dark Arts, and when she rejects his unexpected proposal of marriage, he tells her that he intends to return to his childhood home of Weir as a captain of Lord Aldritch's court.

Brokenhearted, Tania begins her quest without him and she, Connor, and Rathina seek the submerged Lost Caer, where she and her companions learn that, in the long-ago times, the people of Faerie were mortal and winged. They also discover that this is not the first time the plague has fallen upon them.

A mysterious entity calling herself the Dream Weaver tells them of a time before the Great Awakening when Oberon traveled into the west in search of the Divine Harper and made a covenant that gave the folk of Faerie the gift of Immortality in exchange for their wings. This covenant was broken when the Sorcerer King of Lyonesse temporarily took the throne of Faerie from Oberon. The breaking of the covenant has allowed an ancient enemy—a being known only by the name Nargostrond—to return. Nargostrond is working his evil again in the land, and now, to end the plague and to defeat him, Tania, Rathina, and Connor Estabrook must travel across the Western Ocean and seek the mythical land of Tirnanog . . . before it is too late.

Part One:

Wingèd We Were Before Time Was . . .

Princess Tania stared silently out over the Western Ocean. The air was full of whispering and hissing as the oil black waves slunk in along the beach, staining the rippled sand. It was an ugly, brooding night and the sea churned restlessly under the starless sky.

It was difficult to believe that she, Rathina, and Connor had ventured beneath those sinister waves—able to breathe and walk freely on the seabed as easily as they might wander the gardens of the Royal Palace. While they had been tracing the pathways of the submerged and ruinous Lost Caer, the rust red evening sun had dipped beyond the horizon. Now night flooded the Earldom of Weir.

They had emerged from the deep as dry as if they had been walking the sandy dunes. Tania was hardly able to comprehend what she had learned beneath the ocean, hardly able to take it all in.

The wind blew cold from the distant mountains, troubling the grass that bristled along the dunes.

Tania shivered. She was still wearing the clothes she had picked up in the Mortal World: a black T-shirt and loose black trousers. She had not even thought to bring a coat—but when she and her two companions had started this journey, they had not realized how far from home it would take them.

Surf lapped around her ankles, cold and clammy, like dead fingers plucking at her skin. She felt exhausted, as though their time under the sea had drained the life out of her.

She crouched and cupped her hand in the rolling water, now feeling its wetness. How could that be? She did not understand.

Looking up, she saw Rathina and Connor standing together watching her. They too were in Mortal clothes: Rathina in a red blouse and white combat trousers, Connor in jeans and a blue denim jacket.

"Is the night not chill enough, Tania, that you must freeze your blood thus?" asked Rathina, her dark hair blowing across her face.

"It's wet," Tania said, offering up her hand to them. "The sea is wet now." She stood up, wiping her hand on her hip.

She glanced past them, looking for the line of old standing stones that marked the Road of Faith and that had led them under the waves and down to Caer Fior, the legendary lost castle of Faerie. They were invisible now, swallowed up by the night.

"Maybe the water is only different *between* the lines of stones," said Connor. He looked at Rathina. "Is that how it works? Is there something in the stones that changes the molecular structure of the water around them?"

Her hazel eyes widened. "Seek no knowledge of these things from me, Connor Estabrook," she said. "I am no lore master and no practitioner of the Mystic Arts, neither." She shook herself as though icy fingers had run down her spine. "I have learned things this night that confound my senses and fill me with foreboding." She looked at Tania with haunted eyes. "Who or what is Nargostrond—and why does his name strike me with such a terrible dread?"

"I don't know any more about it than you do," Tania replied heavily. "The name means nothing to me at all."

"If I understand it right," Connor began, "everyone in Faerie had their memories wiped clean when Oberon came back from doing his deal with the Divine Harper. But I guess you must all have some residual memory of Nargostrond left in your subconscious."

Rathina's forehead creased. "Your words are meaningless to me."

Connor tapped his head. "The name Nargostrond is in your brain whether you're aware of it or not. You know it because your father knew it—it's been kind of passed down to you. That's why it gives you the creeps. The psychiatrist Carl Jung called it the collective unconscious."

"And are we Faerie folk still Immortal?" Rathina asked, looking at Tania. "When the covenant was broken, did we become Mortal again? Will I sicken and die as Mortals die? Will all my people become nothing but dust blown on the wind?"

"Not if I can help it," said Tania, hoping she sounded convincing. "But where do we go from here? The Dream Weaver said we have to sail across the Western Ocean to find the land of Tirnanog and speak to the Divine Harper to get the covenant renewed. That means we need a boat of some kind. Why didn't she tell us where to find one?"

"And why can't she talk to us now that we're back on dry land?" asked Connor, shaking his head in bafflement. "The rules that this place run on are completely crazy. This whole world would benefit from a big dose of honest-to-goodness *physics*. I mean, does Einstein's theory of relativity work here? And how about the basic laws of thermodynamics? Does this place even *have* them? And how come we were able to breathe underwater?" He laughed halfheartedly. "That's totally ridiculous!"

Tania could see that, despite Connor's flippant comments, his face was pale. She got the impression he was finding the uncanny nature of Faerie harder to come to terms with than he may have expected. She hoped he wouldn't end up regretting his decision to stay. Feeling himself adrift in a world he couldn't make sense of might really mess up his mind.

"How could we have survived otherwise?" Rathina asked. "We would have been three drowned bodies cast upon the beach, our quest thwarted hardly ere it began."

"I know that," Connor replied, his frustration showing in his voice. "I'm not saying the laws of physics would have *helped* us. But all this magic is doing my head in—I don't get how this universe works. I was brought here because Tania knows how to walk between the worlds. We were flown to Caer Regnar Naal in a ball of fire! We've just been breathing underwater. Don't you get how totally insane all that is?"

"There's no point in thinking about things like that," Tania said. "It'll drive you out of your mind." She stared into the sky, feeling the whole weight of the world bearing down on her.

"Yes, there *is*," Connor insisted. "You Faerie people seem to just accept the way things are without questioning any of it." He looked urgently at Tania. "But there has to be a logic to it; there has to be a way of making sense of it all. And I don't understand why no one here seems in the least bit interested in doing just that." His eyes glittered in the darkness. "You could use a few scientists around here to get to the bottom of things. And once this quest is done, that's exactly what I plan on spending the rest of my life doing. Figuring this place out!"

Tania winced, not used to such anger and aggression from him. But she understood why he was venting his frustrations on her, and she could hardly blame him. She had brought him to Faerie. It was her fault that he was trapped here—hostage forever in a world he didn't understand. She had convinced him to step with her between the worlds; she had brought him here in an attempt to cure with Mortal medicines a disease that had been created in Faerie. And while he was here, the ways between the worlds had been closed for all time. There was no way back—not for Connor and not for her.

"Your words disturb me, Master Connor," Rathina said gravely. "Have you not heard the tale of the boy with the drum? He so loved the sound it made that he determined to seek its source." She paused, her eyes deep and soulful as she gazed into his face. "He took a knife and ripped the skin of the drum from end to end, hoping to find within the cause of its merry beat."

"And he destroyed the drum in the process," Connor finished. "Yes. I understand. But if you use that logic, you'd never learn how anything works."

"Untrue, Master Connor," said Rathina. "You learn the art of music by *playing* the drum, not by setting a knife to it."

Connor shook his head and turned away from her. "You don't get it," he murmured.

"We're wasting time with all this talk!" Tania broke in. "Connor—I'm sorry, but you're going to have to stop freaking out. The plague is everywhere, and we have to find a way to cure it." She pointed over the whispering ocean. "The Divine Harper lives somewhere out there, and we need to get to him. Which means finding a boat." She turned to her sister. "Rathina, do you know of any ports or fishing villages near here?"

"If memory serves, the River Styr meets the sea no

great distance north of this place," said Rathina. "And the town of Hymnal lies at its mouth."

"Hymnal?" said Tania. "Why do I know that name?"

"It is the town where our mother made landfall after her voyage from Alba," Rathina said.

That was another revelation that had rocked Tania's world—that Queen Titania was not a trueborn Faerie but that she had been born Mortal in the land of Alba across the Western Ocean. She had sailed alone to the shores of Faerie to fulfill a prophecy made at her birth.

"Is it far?" Tania asked.

Rathina shook her head. "I do not know Weir so well," she replied. "I wish that our horses had not bolted, for I fear we have a long march ahead of us. Let us hope that we reach the river-mouth before all our strength is done." She turned and strode out along the flats of the beach. The footprints that she left in the sand were quickly filled with the rising tide.

Tania followed, but as she paused, turning to Connor, he seemed lost in thought.

"Coming?" she urged him.

He nodded and quickly caught up. "We'd have a better idea of where we are if we'd taken the map we found in Caer Regnar Naal," he said quietly, his head lowered.

"You know we couldn't have done that," Tania reminded him. "The King said we weren't allowed to take anything from the Hall of Archives."

"But he didn't say *why*," murmured Connor.

"Maybe not," agreed Tania. "But he told us doing so would bring evil down on us—and that's good enough for me."

Connor let out a sharp breath. "You know, I really don't respond well to orders that aren't properly explained to me," he said. He glanced sideways at her. "If I'm going to do what I'm told, I need to know there's a good reason for it."

Her eyes narrowed. "Meaning what?"

"Meaning that when I see a sign that says 'do not touch' I've got a tendency to touch just to see what will happen."

"That's not the way people think in Faerie," she replied gently, trying to check his hostility. "I can understand why you're getting annoyed with things here," she added. "It must be really scary." She looked into his face. "Would it help to know I had a bad time adjusting, too? I fought it for the longest time."

"And what happened that made you adjust in the end?" Connor asked.

"I found a kind of temple thing dedicated to Titania," Tania said. "There was a statue of her in it—and she looked exactly like *me*. That's when it finally dawned on me this wasn't a dream."

"So you found out you belonged here, right?"

Tania nodded, realizing her explanation didn't help him a whole lot.

"Well, maybe just now," he said, "while we were strolling about bone dry and *breathing* on the seabed—maybe that was the moment when I realized I *don't* belong here."

"I'm so sorry," she said quietly.

"Don't be," he said, his voice softening. "It's not your fault. I decided to stay. I made the mistake. And I have to find a way to live with it." He gave her a wry smile. "Maybe I can shake things up a little now that I'm stranded here," he said. "Stand aside Mystic Arts! Here comes rigorous scientific analysis, care of yours truly." He grinned but there was no humor in his eyes. "It'll be quite a challenge!"

Tania said nothing. Let him believe that if it gave him a sense of purpose. But she'd seen too much of Faerie to believe that its secrets could be laid bare quite the way Connor assumed.

They had been walking relatively slowly, and Rathina was some way ahead of them, her body a dark blur against the beach.

Rathina turned, lifting a hand, and her voice came floating back. "I see lights in the distance!" she called. "A town. It is not far."

"It must be Hymnal," Tania said to Connor. "Come on." She broke into a jog to catch up with Rathina. Connor was quickly at her side.

"We should be careful," he said. "Remember what happened in the last town."

She remembered it well. Arrows shot from cover—the fear and suspicion of a village already visited by the plague.

They came up alongside Rathina. Peering into the

darkness, Tania saw a huddle of pale yellowy lights on a ridge of raised land.

"Behold the town of Hymnal," Rathina said solemnly. "A glad sight on a bitter night. But how shall we be received by the people of Weir? I wonder. With friendship or with fear?"

Tania narrowed her eyes as she stared out at the dimly flickering lights.

"There's one way to find out," she said.

II

They moved warily through the night, alert for the first sight of the town's inhabitants, their ears straining for the deadly swish of arrows on the wind.

But they had misjudged the distance in the darkness, and the town was farther away than they had at first imagined. For some time its lights grew no brighter as they moved toward them. Altering course to keep the lights always dead ahead, they left the creeping tide and climbed up the shifting flanks of dunes and down the far side to find themselves among grasslands heavy with the salt smell of the sea.

It was marshy ground riddled with narrow water-filled ditches, tall brown grasses bending and swaying as the rushing winds eddied through them. Some small animal darted past—a hare perhaps—turning Tania's thoughts for a moment to her ailing sister, Cordelia.

They had to move slowly, and with every step Tania checked that the ground was solid before bringing her weight down. It would be all too easy to twist an ankle or slither into a ditch.

"Ah!" breathed Rathina, standing at the brink of a long black slot. "The River Styr, I believe."

Tania stood next to her on the grassy brink. The river was low but clearly on the rise, flowing swift and dark between reeking mudflats. The lights of the village were clearer now, set high atop a humpbacked hill on the far side of the river.

"Is it too wide to try and swim?" asked Connor.

Rathina stared inland along the curve of the river. "Swim, forsooth?" she said. "Do you not see the mire, Master Connor? You would be swallowed up, top to toe, before you set foot in the water. We must find a bridge."

"If the people here are anything like the ones we met in Faith-in-the-Surf, the bridge will probably be guarded," Connor said.

"We'll deal with that if there *is* a bridge," said Tania.

She knew Connor was right—but they had persuaded the other villagers of their good intentions and she was hopeful that she could do it again. Something else was worrying her right now.

It was not long since Lord Aldritch of Weir had stormed out of the Throne Room in Veraglad Palace, denouncing Oberon and denying his Kingship over the Earldom of Weir.

Would news of that renunciation have reached Hymnal yet? And if so, how would two of the daughters of King Oberon and Queen Titania be greeted? The last time Tania had been in Weir, she had escaped the clutches of Lord Aldritch only by fleeing his castle in the dead of night. How much worse would she fare now that Aldritch stood in open opposition to the King?

The river wound in a wide loop between its high banks, snaking off into the darkness, filling the night with strange guttural noises as the sea fed into it.

"There! A bridge," said Rathina, pointing to a distant black arch that vaulted the banks. "And unguarded, I think."

"But what's that next to it?" asked Tania, straining her eyes. Long gray shapes lay on the banks beside the bridge—shapes that she vaguely recognized, shapes that filled her with unease.

As they approached the bridge, the gray shapes became clearer. They were bodies draped with white silk. By the look of it, the bodies of seven adults and three children.

"This is wrong," said Rathina, her voice trembling as they stood over the shrouded shapes. "To be left without friend or family to watch over them till they are called to Albion. It is against all custom—against all virtue to abandon the dead thus."

Tania's stomach twisted as she remembered the baby boy whose death had been the first sign of the plague. She had spent a full night with his grieving mother, and the memory haunted her still.

Connor crouched and lifted a corner of one silk shroud. Tania saw a glimpse of yellow hair and an ash white face before she looked away. It reminded her too sharply of Cordelia's stricken face as she had lain sickening on her bed. And how were her other sisters and her mother and father faring? Were they still able to keep the plague at bay? Did any of them have that same deathly look about them yet?

"There's nothing we can do for them," Connor said, covering the face again and standing up. "Will they still get to . . . what was it . . . Albion? Will they still get there if they're left on their own?"

"They will," said Rathina. "But it will be a sad journey, and those who abandoned them thus will feel a wound in their hearts that will never heal." She sighed and walked away from the bodies. "The Rituals of Leave-taking are not solely for the dead, Master Connor," she said. "This pestilence eats like a canker into our very souls."

The bridge was of stone, rough-laid and clearly very old. The noises of the river were magnified under its arch. As they crossed, it sounded as though lost spirits moaned beneath their feet.

Tania was glad to get to the far side; things were bleak enough without their being haunted by river phantoms.

The main course of the Styr meandered into the eastern night, but close by they saw a spur of dark water that led off between banks that were supported by wooden stakes. It ran a straight course behind the hill.

"No sign of sentries or armed guards," Connor murmured, his head close to Tania's as they came to the steep trackway that led up to the town. "But maybe we should avoid the town altogether." He pointed along the straight channel. "That's got to be man-made," he said. "It probably leads to a marina or a harbor. There'll be boats there, for sure. Why don't we just take one and get out of here before anyone knows about it?"

"I think not," said Rathina. "The tide is low. I doubt that any seaworthy vessel could navigate these waters until the flood tide, and that is many hours away yet."

Tania gazed up at the dark mass of the hill. Few lights were now burning, and the town reared over them like a sleeping dragon, stone walls forming its backbone and peaked roofs and spires rising like spines and horns against the heavy sky. But for some reason the sight did not daunt her; perhaps it was the knowledge that this town had welcomed her mother hundreds of years ago. These people had befriended a young Mortal woman lost and alone in a land she did not know. Maybe Tania could hope for such kindness to be shown again—even in these grim times.

She turned to Connor. "We're going up there," she said. "I'm not going to steal a boat." She strode toward the steep path. "Besides, I'm hungry and cold and totally exhausted—we should try and find shelter for the night."

"Aye," agreed Rathina, following her. "An inn would be most welcome, if any will take three such curiously dressed strangers at such a time of wretchedness and despair."

Tania linked her arm with her sister's. "I don't know why," she said, "but I have a good feeling about this place. I think we'll be all right." She turned. Connor was still standing at the foot of the track staring apprehensively up at the town, his hands thrust deep in his pockets. He shrugged and walked quickly to catch up with them.

The town of Hymnal was a maze of narrow cobbled lanes and alleys that ran between half-timbered buildings leaning toward one another as if they were sharing outlandish secrets. Most of the dwellings were in darkness, although here and there a yellow lantern hung over a gabled doorway and the occasional mullioned window glowed with ruddy firelight.

"What time is it?" Connor asked.

"I don't know," Tania said. "I don't have a watch."

"The moon is rising," said Rathina. "The night is at the first quarter."

Connor moved close to Tania. "How does she know that?" he asked, staring up between the buildings into the opaque sky.

"I think everyone here can do it. They have a kind of intuition abut things like that," Tania said.

"But you don't?"

"No . . . not really. Not yet."

"But one day, huh?"

"I hope so." She knew what he was thinking: This was yet another thing that separated him from everyone around him.

The town was deathly silent. The footsteps of the three travelers echoed like the striking of drumbeats, and Tania was consumed by the impression that behind every wall people were huddling in sickness and fear.

There was no doubt that the plague had visited this place—the bodies down by the river were proof enough of that—and as Tania made her way between the hunched buildings, fear and dismay seemed to flow along with her through the deserted streets like a thick fog.

"What are we looking for?" whispered Connor. "A hotel or something?"

"Or *something* . . ." Tania replied.

"Are you sure this is such a good idea?" Connor asked. "It feels to me like we're walking into a trap."

Tania looked into his face. "Does it?" she said softly. "It doesn't feel like that to me at all." She took a deep breath, wishing to draw the essence of the town into herself. "I don't think we'll be harmed here."

They came quite suddenly upon a large round courtyard. Tania stepped onto the cobbles, her skin tingling as though the air of the town had come alive around her. There was something special about this place—she knew it instantly. In the center of the courtyard a stone fountain rose. Its wide granite bowl was filled with dark water, and from its middle lifted a fluted plinth with a single-masted, stone-carved boat on its top.

Words were etched around the rim of the bowl.

Tania walked slowly around the fountain, reciting the words softly.

"Drink, weary traveler, and take thy fill, for this water flows by Titania's will." A sudden rush of joy filled her heart. She looked at Connor and Rathina. "They built this to remember our mother," she said. "Isn't that amazing?"

Rathina ran her hand over the smooth granite. "I looked not to see such an honor to our family in the Earldom of Weir," she said. " 'Tis a good omen, I think."

Tania noticed that Connor was looking curiously at her.

"Is something wrong?" she asked.

"It's a bit odd to hear you refer to the Queen as your mother, that's all," he said. "When I think of your mum . . . well, I think of your *real* mum, you know? Back in London."

A shaft of darkness pierced Tania. There was no reproach in his voice, but she could sense the unspoken criticism. The truth was that she would never see her Mortal parents again. And worse, they would live out their lives never knowing her fate or the fate of Faerie.

"Do not grieve, my daughter—all is not lost."

The female voice sounded soft, insubstantial as mist.

"Mother?" A rush of emotion gripped Tania.

"Yes, Tania. I am here."

"Look!" breathed Rathina, staring into the water. "Do you see her? Do you see our mother, the Queen?"

Trembling, Tania gazed down into the still water. A silvery light glowed now in the depths, gentle and warm as candlelight. Gazing up at her was a face, green-eyed, framed with curling red hair, the cheekbones wide, the lips full and red. A face so like Tania's own that it was almost like gazing into a mirror. Queen Titania, mother to the Faerie half of Tania's split soul. But it was a face filled with fatigue and sorrow.

"I am glad of heart to see you, my children," Titania said from the mystical water-mirror. Her eyes turned to Connor. "And you, too, Master Estabrook—you who were brought here from your own world and sacrificed all to help us. Thank you."

"Don't mention it," said Connor, staring into the water. He looked at Tania. "How is she doing that?" he hissed.

"It was my wedding gift from Oberon," Titania explained. "In still water I can communicate across many miles." Her tired eyes turned again to Tania. "How goes your quest?" she asked. "It is two days now since Eden left you at Caer Regnar Naal—I had hoped to speak with you sooner."

"We found the Lost Caer," said Tania, leaning over the bowl, her hands gripping the sides. "But there's more—so much more. I don't know where to start."

"Reach down your hand and touch the water,"

Titania said. "Gently now—make not a ripple on the surface."

Breathlessly Tania lowered the flat of her hand toward the still surface. As she did so, she saw that Titania's hand rose to meet hers. They touched, palm to palm, finger to finger. The reassuring touch of her mother's flesh was startlingly real. Titania's hand felt warm and alive in the cool water, and Tania was profoundly comforted.

"May I enter your thoughts, Tania?" the Queen asked.

"Yes . . . of course . . ."

A moment later Tania had the sensation of something gentle and soothing moving through her mind. She had always known there were strong emotional bonds between the members of the Royal Family, but she had not realized that they ran quite so deep as to allow for such intimacy as this. She felt no pain or concern as her Faerie mother probed her memories. Quite the opposite. She sensed her mother's love stirring deep within her, vibrant and vital as the air in her lungs and the blood in her veins.

But suddenly she saw her mother's face grow concerned and then deeply alarmed.

"No!" Titania snatched her hand away, and the surface of the water shattered into racing furrows that crossed and recrossed one another.

"What happened?" asked Rathina.

"She saw everything I've seen since we left the

palace," said Tania breathlessly, leaning heavily on the granite rim of the bowl to try to see Titania in the agitated water.

Gradually the water calmed and the Queen's anxious face reappeared. "Daughter, I had not expected to encounter such things in your mind," came Titania's voice. "But I understand now all that has happened." There was a pause and her look of alarm faded. "You have come, then, to the town of Hymnal," she continued. "That is good, I hope. Even in these dark times you should not be harmed by the folk who dwell there. They keep a strong allegiance to the House of Aurealis, and in all of Weir only they share loyalty between the earl and the Royal Family."

"We need a boat," said Tania. "We have to sail to Tirnanog."

"Yes, I saw this in your mind," said the Queen. "But you need not depart these shores in the black of night. Go to the Inn of the Blessèd Queen. You will be welcomed there by the landlord, Elias Fulk. He will give you food and beds—and unless the plague has entirely corrupted his nature, he will find for you a ship come the dawn."

"I saw the inn," said Rathina, pointing back the way they had come. "I am sure of it! It is not far."

"Go find it," said Tania. She looked at Connor. "Go with her, please. I won't be long—I want to talk to my mother alone."

Connor frowned. "Talk about what?" he asked. "If

it's anything to do with the quest, I want in on it, too."

"It's personal, Connor," Tania said. "Please? Go with Rathina."

"Come," said Rathina, taking Connor by the arm. "I would warm myself by a fire. Tania will follow in good time."

Reluctantly Connor allowed himself to be led back across the courtyard and between two leaning buildings.

"You are distressed, Tania," said the Queen. "I felt it in you. Speak to me of it and perhaps I can give you comfort and ease."

Tania had hardly realized how the anguish had been building in her till this moment. She had been keeping her emotions under control—she didn't want to let Connor and Rathina know what was brewing in her mind.

"Why didn't the King tell me the truth about the plague?" she demanded fiercely. "Why did he pretend he couldn't remember about the Divine Harper and the covenant and everything?"

The Queen's face clouded. "Tania, your father the King remembered nothing of these things. Nothing!"

"Are you *sure*?" insisted Tania. "Are you absolutely *sure* he didn't know?"

"Tania, listen to me," came her Faerie mother's voice. "There are no secrets between the King and me—there can be none. All artifice and pretense are swept away in the Hand-Fasting Ceremony." Tania knew what that was: a mystic amber fluid was poured over the linked hands of a betrothed couple, and in that moment each could see clearly into the mind of the other. "If Oberon knew of the things you have learned, I would know them, too."

"I'm sorry . . . I thought . . ." Tania paused. "I don't know what I thought. But . . . I feel like I'm being *played*, you know?" Tears burned behind her eyes. "Everything's so horrible, Mother. . . . It's too hard. I can't do this on my own. I can't."

She leaned over the cold stone, her tears falling into the water, spreading rings through which the compassionate face of her mother gazed.

"You are not alone, Tania," said Titania. "You are never alone, my darling child."

"So why do I feel like this?" Tania gasped, her face hot, tears burning as they scored their way down her cheeks.

"Do not grieve, sweetheart." Her mother's voice was soft as feathers. "I know the hollow wound that gapes in your heart—but you have not lost him entirely. Trust me, you have not."

Titania's words allowed Tania to open up to her grief. Edric was gone. Her love. The one constant in the madness of the past months. She leaned over the water, her hair hanging, her shoulders rising and falling as violent sobs wracked her body. She could not speak: The pain in her chest was so intense that she could hardly even breathe. She felt ripped open, heart, spirit, and soul.

She had no idea how long her torment lasted, but

as her weeping finally abated, she heard a soothing voice from below her.

"Do not surrender entirely to grief, my child," Titania said. "Tomorrow is a glad new day! A clear path lies ahead of you, and who can say what wonders you will find at journey's end?"

Gathering herself, Tania lifted her head, wiping her sleeve across her face. The solace of the Queen's words filled her with new resolve. She was prepared now to face whatever the quest held in store. And perhaps her Faerie mother was right: Perhaps she would find wonders waiting for her on distant shores.

III

Tania arched her back, pulling strands of hair off her cheeks, feeling cool air on her burning skin. She knuckled her eyes then ran her hands down her face. She no longer felt disabled by her burdens. She could carry on. She could do her duty.

"How is the King?" she asked, gazing down into her mother's face.

"The King is weary, Tania," Titania replied. "As are we all. The strain of keeping the plague victims in the balm of Gildensleep is draining his strength."

The Gildensleep was a mystical cocoon of spun golden light within which those folk suffering from the plague could be held in peaceful stasis—fending off death for a while—sleeping in gentle oblivion. But King Oberon paid a heavy price for creating and maintaining the glimmering cocoons; only while he denied himself sleep could the Gildensleep cocoons exist. Tania had lost track of how many hours—how many days the King of Faerie had forced himself to remain awake.

"But there is good news," Titania continued. "Eden has worked hard and swiftly to bring the Gildensleep to all those who ail, and now we believe we have a way of making all of Faerie safe—for a while, at least."

"A cure?" breathed Tania, hope igniting that she would not need to embark on the quest the Dream Weaver had demanded of her. "Have you found a cure?"

"No, alas that is beyond us," said the Queen. "But we are gathering all those of the House of Aurealis into the Throne Room with the King. The Earl Marshal Cornelius, your uncle, is there and the Marchioness Lucina and their sons Titus and Corin. Hopie and Sancha are also with us, and soon Eden will return. When all are gathered, we will unite our powers to put the Realm of Faerie under a single cloak of Gildensleep. From Leiderdale in the south to Fidach Ren in the far north—all our people shall be protected."

A flicker of uncertainty showed in Titania's eyes. "At least that is our hope. But, heed me, Tania. If the cloak of Gildensleep is to be strong enough to cover the entire Realm, it will need the power of all the children of Aurealis. Alas, Cordelia is too ill to aid us, but we cannot do this without you and Rathina."

"You mean you want us to go back to Veraglad?" asked Tania. "But what about the Divine Harper?"

"No, your quest is vital; you must not turn from it," said Titania. "We can link ourselves with your spirits from afar, Tania, if you are willing."

"Of course!" Tania exclaimed. "Whatever you need."

"It will weaken you—you and your sister. It will drain you of strength. Not in a steady flow, but you will feel your power wax and wane as we call upon your spirits."

"That's fine; I can live with that," said Tania. "And I don't even have to ask Rathina! You know she'd do anything to make amends for . . . for . . ."

For causing so much suffering in the past. For loving Gabriel Drake and for letting him use her to harm Faerie. For setting the Sorcerer King free.

Tania gasped as a horrible realization dawned. She hadn't known the awful truth until this moment—but the seeds of this plague were sown when Rathina loosed the Sorcerer King of Lyonesse from his amber prison. This was all Rathina's fault! *She must be tormented by it!*

"I know what is in your mind, Tania," said Titania. "It's a fearful burden for your sister to bear, and it may be that the rest of her life will be spent in remorse. But do not cloud your own heart with thoughts of blame."

"I don't blame her," Tania said bitterly. "I blame Gabriel Drake—and I blame the Dark Arts that made him into a monster." She gripped the rim of the granite bowl till her knuckles were white. "But none of that matters now. I can't change any of it, but I can try and put things right—and I can make sure that Rathina is at my side when I do it."

"Well spoken," said Titania, a gentle smile of pride touching her lips. "Seventh daughter of a seventh daughter, you do not know yet what power there is within you. But I fear that your quest will test you to your limits."

"You do your part and we'll do ours," said Tania. She frowned as a thought struck her. "Will I be able to speak with you like this when I get to Alba?"

"No, that is not possible," Titania replied. "But the bond between you and your sisters is strong; you may be able to forge links with their spirits and ask for their aid in need. But do not look for mystical help. What skills we have will be poured into the Gildensleep; there will be little left to offer."

"I understand," said Tania.

"We hope to raise the shield of Gildensleep tomorrow," Titania said. "As soon as the sun fills the sky. Those it touches will fall into deep sleep. You must be away from Faerie by then, Tania, or you too will succumb to the dreamless slumber."

"Then we'll make sure we leave before dawn," Tania said.

"That is good," said Titania. "But one last word, my beloved child. I can give you little insight into the realms through which you must pass to reach the Divine Harper. But I can offer some advice to guide you in Alba. It is many centuries since I was a young woman in that fair land, but things may not have changed so very much. When you make landfall, seek out the home of my ancestors: the beautiful palace of

Caiseal an Fenodree. Any traveler you meet upon the road will know of it, I am sure. It is a white palace set in an enchanted lake. There you will find both an ardent welcome and, hopefully, aid in your further travels. And use these words to ensure that you are greeted as friends. Speak the words 'caraid clainne.' Remember them, Tania."

"Caraid clainne. I won't forget."

"I must go now. I sense that Eden has returned. We must foregather and brew the enchantments of Gildensleep. Farewell, Tania. The hopes of all the Realm go with you on your quest." The image of the Queen began to fade as the gossamer light dwindled. "Farewell." Her fading voice was like distant bells.

Tania reached down to touch the water a final time. The surface broke into rippled rings. The Queen was gone. Tania was alone in the courtyard and the night wind was cold on her face.

The carved wooden sign creaked in the wind that howled down the narrow street. The sign hung above a thick oak doorway studded with black crystal depicting a small ship with a single sail. A figure stood at the prow gazing forward. Carved upon the hull of the wooden ship were the words THE BLESSÈD QUEEN.

Tania lifted the latch and stepped into the inn. She found herself in a long dimly lit room, standing in deep shadow. Subdued firelight played on ivory walls crisscrossed with black timbers. The ceiling was low and hung with jugs and hunting horns. The walls held similar trophies: crystal harpoons with wooden shafts, hanks of tarred rope, framed pictures of seascapes and ships and leaping fish.

There was a scattering of wooden tables and benches—but the room was empty save for three figures sitting close to the roaring fire. A man was singing, his voice high and fluttery but tuneful nonetheless. Tania paused to listen.

"As I was riding through Weir so fair
I met a maiden raven of hair
I said young lady, will you marry me?
There's room at my side for a large family
Oh, no, said she, I will not marry you
You're a traveling man and you'll never be true
You'll never be true, for you are betrothed
And a jealous bride is the open road

"My mother is the road and my father the sky
But my love for you will never, never die
So come with me and lose all care
In a caravan through Weir so fair
I'll take you near, I'll take you far
Our only guide a shimmering star
So come with me, I'll give you my ring
And I'll teach you the song that the travelers sing."

There was applause as the song ended. Tania stepped into the light, clapping along with Rathina and Connor.

Hearing her, they looked up, their faces showing relief at her sudden appearance. Both Rathina and Connor had steaming bowls in their laps filled with a thick, aromatic stew.

The third figure, the singer, was a thin man with a friendly, wrinkled face and wispy gray hair. He wore a long white apron over a plain brown tunic and leggings that were tucked below the knee into gartered stockings.

"You took a fine long time to join us, Tania," said Rathina. "We were debating which of us should quit the hearth and seek you out."

As Tania walked toward the great stone fireplace, the warmth of the room enveloped her, seeping into her limbs, making her fingers and toes tingle.

The man stood up. "Princess Rathina and Master Connor have told me the tale of your journeying, both in Faerie and between the worlds, Princess Tania," he said, his aged voice like wind through reeds. "You are all most welcome. My name is Elias Fulk, and I am landlord of this inn. I apologize that your greeting could not be more merry." His eyes fixed on her face. "You are the very image of the Queen!" he said breathlessly, dropping to one knee and bowing his head. "It is long since your mother rested in this place, my lady, but we do not forget her—not even in such fearful days as have come upon us."

"Please," Tania said, embarrassed by this show of deference. "Don't do that." Hurrying forward, she helped him to his feet again.

"As your ladyship wishes," Elias Fulk said, stepping away from her as if the contact made him uncomfortable.

"The stew is great," said Connor, shifting along the bench so Tania could sit beside him. "I didn't realize how much I wanted some hot food inside me till Elias started dishing up."

A third bowl of stew was resting on a hearthstone.

Elias Fulk lifted it from the warm stones and placed it in her hands.

"Thank you," she said, enjoying the warmth of the wooden bowl in her palms. The rich aroma filled her head, thick and savory and cheering.

"What took you so long to get here?" asked Connor. "I was beginning to think you'd gotten lost."

"No, I didn't get lost," Tania replied, lifting the wooden spoon from the bowl. She glanced at the landlord, wondering for a moment whether it was wise to speak candidly in front of him. But then she remembered that the Queen had said he could be trusted. "There were a few things to talk over, that's all." She took a mouthful of the stew.

"Such as?" asked Connor.

"How is our father?" added Rathina. "And Cordelia—how does she fare?"

"I don't think she's any better," said Tania. "But they have a plan to cover the whole of Faerie in the Gildensleep. Our mother thinks it's possible—so long as everyone helps. Including the two of us."

"Name the way and it shall be done," said Rathina. "I would throw myself down a dragon's throat if it would ease the suffering of but a single child!"

Connor frowned. "You have *dragons* here?"

"Not that I've ever seen," Tania said, her eyes on Rathina. "Our mother thinks there will be enough power if she can draw on all of our spirits. I don't know how it's going to work, but she said it would probably make us feel weak at times."

"A small price to pay," said Rathina. "But when does she mean to throw the cloak of Gildensleep over the land? We must be away from these shores by that time."

"They're going to raise the Gildensleep early tomorrow morning." She turned to Elias Fulk. "That means we have to get away before the sun comes up. Is there a boat we could use?"

"I have my own vessel in the harbor, my lady," he said. "It is used by hirelings to catch fresh fish for the kitchens of the inn. You are most welcome to use her. The *Blessèd Queen*, she is named. A small vessel, to be sure, but tight-knit and bonny upon the water—if any of you have the skill to sail her."

"I know how to sail," said Connor, looking at Tania. "Remember? My dad had a twenty-eight-foot sloop that he kept at Essex Marina. The *Wee Tam*."

Tania nodded. She had been invited aboard the sailboat a few times when she had been younger. Yes, she remembered it well: the wind in her hair and salt on her lips, swaddled in a bright orange life jacket and clinging on for dear life as Connor and his father sent the *Wee Tam* racing through choppy waters.

"Tania, we sailed often together as children," Rathina added. "We had a yacht named *Magnifico*. You and I and Zara and Cordelia out on the water—do you not remember? The dolphins would leap and spin while Zara played the whistle."

Tania saw the grief cloud her sister's face as the

bitterness of Zara's death darkened the happy memory. Rathina dropped her head, becoming silent, her thick black hair falling over her face.

"I don't remember, I'm sorry," Tania said. The loss of the memory of her blissful Faerie childhood ached in her like a wound that would never heal.

"Elias was telling us that the plague has been in Hymnal for several days now," Connor said, breaking the silence. "The people have locked themselves away."

"These folk fear the plague greatly," added Rathina. "That is why the bodies by the bridge have been left unattended."

"Aye, it's a bad time to be sure," said Elias Fulk, nodding mournfully. "By the grace of the gentle spirits, my own family has been spared. But not a patron has set foot over my threshold for two days and nights now." His eyes glowed with firelight as he looked at Tania. "Is all of Faerie infected?"

"I think so," Tania said.

Elias Fulk sighed. "And it is at such a time that my lord the earl breaks faith with the House of Aurealis, as the princess your sister has just told me," he murmured. "Sad times, indeed, my lady, sad and galling times when friends should stand back to back against a common enemy."

Tania looked carefully at him. "Do you know the name Nargostrond?" she asked.

"Nay, my lady," he replied. "But it throws a shadow over my heart, like the wraith of a dreadful memory."

"For me also, Master Fulk," said Rathina. " 'Tis most like to waking from a nightmare, sweating and filled with dread but unable to remember the source of the fear."

"Collective unconscious," murmured Connor. "You all have it. Whoever this Nargostrond guy was, he certainly left his mark on you people."

"He must be a great necromancer to do us such harm," Elias Fulk said. "Greater even than the Sorcerer of Lyonesse." He reached out and touched Tania's arm with his fingertips. "I pray that your mission be blessed, my lady," he said.

"From your lips to the hearts of the good spirits," said Rathina. "Master Fulk, we are traveling to foreign lands on the morrow. I do not know how the people of Alba may dress themselves, but I doubt that it will be in such garments as we are wearing now—garments brought through from the Mortal World. In your household are there any clothes that we might borrow?" She glanced at Tania. "We do not know what manner of greeting we may receive beyond the ocean—and I would prefer that we move among the folk of Alba unremarked."

"I have daughters of an age with you and the princess Tania, my lady," Elias Fulk replied. "I will search out some hard-wearing traveling gowns. But I fear I have little to offer you, Master Connor. My clothes would be too small for you and there are no other menfolk in the house." He frowned. "In happy days I would knock upon a neighbor's door and ask for help, but none will answer tonight, I fear. I can offer a goodly cloak, oiled and snug—fit for the cruelest of weather. Wrap that around you and none shall perceive what you are wearing beneath."

"That's good," said Tania. "Thank you. That will be a big help."

"And I have empty rooms enough for three times your number, my lady," said Elias Fulk. "Sleep here in peace this night. I will awaken you before dawn and lead you down to the harbor where the *Blessèd Queen* lies at berth. Food and drink will I give you also, enough to last you many days." His gray eyebrows lowered in a frown. "How far is the land of Alba, my lady?" he asked. "If my memory remains true, Queen Titania was on the ocean's face for the passage of many long days before she saw the towers and spires of Hymnal on the horizon."

Tania shook her head. "No, that can't be right," she said. She looked at Connor. "Remember the map from the archives of Caer Regnar Naal? Faerie and the British Isles are almost exactly the same. If Faerie is England and Alba is Ireland, then it can't possibly take days and days to get there."

Connor frowned. "I've been on a ferry to Ireland," he said. "We went from Fishguard to Rosslare. I think it was about sixty miles. I know we're probably farther away up here, but it can't be much more than a hundred miles. On a good day a fast sailboat ought to be able to make that in twelve hours. Even if we have to tack against a hard wind, it shouldn't take us more than twice that." He looked at Tania. "If we leave at dawn tomorrow, we'll be there the day after, no problem."

"Then I shall provide food and drink for that time and more," said Elias Fulk. "May the good spirits of air and water protect you on your journey."

"Aye, sirrah," said Rathina somberly. "Let us hope indeed that their benison can traverse the wide waters that lie between. And let us hope that the Mortal folk of that land have a kindly way with travelers."

Tania nodded as they got up. "If not, we're going to have some serious problems," she said uneasily. "Without the help of the people of Alba this quest is going to be over almost before it begins."

"Morning Star, we touch hands in the pale mist
Morning Star, the night is done
The dawning sky is streaked with white and
amethyst
The Morning Star shines upon everyone

"We dwell in the balm of ageless summers
The snow-deep cold of winter's hoary rime
Gathering the flowers of four seasons
We break the bonds of your measured servant,
time . . ."

"Is it *you*?" Tania asked, speaking into a deep, velvet darkness. "It is you, isn't it? Dream Weaver?" She reached her arms out blindly and stumbled forward as the lilting voice faded away. "Don't go! I need your help. . . . "

She broke through a membrane of darkness and found herself suddenly in a familiar room.

It was night—but not the starlit night of Faerie. It was a Mortal night—a London night—and she was standing at the foot of her parents' bed in their room in Camden. Beyond the curtains she could hear city sounds. Small noises that went almost unheard when she lived among them—but they were sharp now in her mind after so long a time in Faerie. The rising and falling growl of traffic. The snap of heels on the pavement. Voices shouting in the distance. Doors slamming. Police sirens wailing from afar. A thickness gathered in her throat as she listened—who would have thought she'd miss the shriek of police sirens in the night!

The curtains were closed, but yellowy street light seeped through the cracks. The room smelled odd: the air was warm and stuffy and *sweet*, but sweet in the wrong way—sickly sweet. A single figure lay under the bedcovers, the face lost in shadows.

A sense of unease made Tania's heart beat a little faster. Tension was growing in her stomach.

A racking cough broke the stillness of the room. The figure moved restlessly under the covers. Breath rattled in a throat.

"Dad?"

Tania stepped forward, her feet coming up against the end of the bed. She moved to the side and padded softly along toward the head.

There was another cough—unpleasant and painful sounding.

"Dad?"

The figure jolted and an arm reached out. A

moment later the bedside light snapped on. Tania winced, narrowing her eyes against the sudden light. Her father lay staring up at her.

"Oh, Daddy!" she whispered, kneeling at the bedside. "What's wrong with you?" His face was gray and sweaty, his jowls unshaved, his hair disordered from the pillow. She took his hand. It was hot and damp.

"Anita?" he breathed.

She didn't correct him. For sixteen years she had been his daughter Anita—Tania had only existed for him for a few short weeks.

"Yes," she said gently, pressing the back of his hand to her cheek. "What's all this, now?" She forced a lightness into her voice that she didn't feel. "And I thought you were getting better, you silly man."

He smiled—but it was such a strange smile that it frightened her.

"I'm better *now*," he said, his fingers tightening on her hand. He lifted his head but let it fall back again with a sigh. "It's so *real*," he said, gazing at the ceiling for a moment then looking yearningly into her face. "So real. Almost like you're really here."

She didn't know what to say. The smells of the room, the feel of his hand in hers, the sound of his voice: all these were proof to her that she was not dreaming—but how had she come here? How could she *possibly* be here?

Last memory. Getting into a cool bed in an upstairs room in The Blessèd Queen. A room warmed by mellow firelight that flickered in a small stone hearth.

Blowing the candle out. Pulling the covers over her ears. Hearing the creak of Connor's bed from the next room. The snap and crack of the burning logs. Elias Fulk's feet on the stairs going down. Then the deep silence of a Faerie night.

And then . . . ?

A high, dulcet voice singing. Opening her eyes to find herself standing upright in a well of pitch darkness.

He thinks he's dreaming me. Is he? I can't really be here—the ways between Faerie and the Mortal Realm have been closed down. I can't be *here. And yet . . .*

And yet . . . The Dream Weaver had brought her to her sick father's bedside.

Her father coughed again. He reached for a box of tissues on the bedside table. Wadded-up, used tissues were scattered around on the bed, on the table, and on the carpet.

Tania pulled out a tissue and gave it to him. He coughed and wiped his mouth, balling the tissue in his fist.

"I was told you were getting better," Tania said coaxingly. "What are you playing at, Dad, getting worse? That's not how it's supposed to work."

"The doctor has seen me," he replied breathlessly. "I'm on about twenty different kinds of antibiotics, and your mother is watching me like a hawk."

"I should hope she is!" Tania glanced at the bedside clock. The red digital display showed 1:35. "Where is Mum?"

"She's sleeping in your room," her father replied, trying to rise on his elbows. "That way I don't keep her awake all night with my coughing and spluttering—which means she's much better able to fuss over me all day the way she likes to!"

"She needs to," said Tania, pressing him gently back. "You'd never look after yourself if it was left up to you. Honestly, Dad, you must be the world's worst patient. If it was up to me, I'd whisk you off to hospital and get you properly sorted."

"Don't worry, she's already threatened me with that. If I'm not better in a day or two, she's getting the doctor back in." He paused, his breathing loud and ragged in his throat.

Tania was about to say something when he looked at her. "I wish you were really here, Anita," he said.

She felt tears welling. *Oh god, Daddy—so do I! You've no idea!*

"Let's pretend I really am," she said with a smile. "I've got some good news. And you really, really have to believe this, Dad!"

"Go on," he said. "I'll give it a try."

"The illness in Faerie—it has absolutely nothing to do with you."

He gazed blankly at her.

"Dad? Did you get that? You had nothing to do with the baby dying."

He let out a long breath. "Are you certain of that?"

"Yes."

A single tear slid from the corner of his eye. "Are

other people sick?" he asked.

She bit her lip, fighting back her own tears. How much could she tell him? What *should* she tell him? "Yes, they are, Dad—but we think we've found a way to cure the disease. We're working on it right now."

His hand squeezed hers. "And then you can come home. . . ."

No, Daddy. I can't ever come home. The ways between the worlds have been closed down forever. Oh god, it hurts so much.

"We'll see," Tania murmured, her throat constricted with the agony of deceiving her father. "Maybe the King will find a way. . . ."

"Your name is Tania!" her father said suddenly, his eyes widening. "You're not my Anita—you're called Tania!" He pulled his hand away, his face full of fear and alarm. "What are you doing here? You can't be here."

"No, Dad—it's me," Tania said urgently. "It's really me."

But a new coughing fit took him. He sat up, pressing tissues to his mouth as he coughed, his shoulders heaving and shaking, the whole bed trembling with the violence of the attack.

Tania got up, trying to put her arms around him, trying to find a way to help, to comfort him. But when she reached for him, her arms went right through him.

"No!" She leaned over him, her hands passing through his body, passing through the pillows and the bedclothes. *"No!"*

She felt dizzy. Disoriented. The bedroom waltzed around her. She heard the door fly open. Her mother stood there, her back to the hall light—a silhouette in a blue dressing gown.

"Clive?" She ran across the room.

"Mum!"

Tania felt a coldness in her heart as her mother moved through her.

"Mum! I'm here!" Tania shouted in desperation. "Please! You have to see me! You have to be able to hear me! Mum! I'm right here!"

Her mother was leaning over her father, rubbing his back as the coughing subsided. Then he drew the tissues away from his mouth, and Tania saw there was blood on them, ugly and black in the dim light.

"Okay, Clive." Her mother's voice was steady and soothing, but it was the voice of panic kept under tight control. "We're done with this now. Try to keep calm and quiet if you can. I'm going to call for an ambulance. We'll soon have you feeling better. Just lie back if it's more comfortable. I won't be a moment."

She rearranged his pillows and helped him to lie back on them. His face was ashen, running with sweat. There was blood on his lips and fear in his eyes as he looked for a moment into Tania's face.

Her mother turned and walked quickly back to the door. Tania followed her, snatching at empty air. "Mum!" Her voice rang in her ears. *"Mum!"*

Tania lunged forward, desperate to make some kind of contact with her mother. But the floor seemed to turn to smoke under her feet, and she fell forward into a vault of blackness.

She heard a sweet voice singing far, far away. . .

"You rise at the opening of our eyes
We dance at your first earthward glance
Friends convene; none of them will ever leave
We will be young forever and a day

"Morning Star, we touch hands in the pale mist
Morning Star, the night is done . . ."

Tania awoke with the lurching sensation of falling. She gasped, fighting the bedcovers. She threw them aside and sat bolt upright.

She was so disoriented that she thought she was in her own bed in Camden. She scrambled out and felt cold wooden boards under her bare feet. Reality swamped her like floodwater.

She was in Weir.

Her Mortal parents were lost to her again—and after so short a glimpse. Grief weighed down on her.

She could still hear the echo of the Dream Weaver's song in her head.

It had not been an idle dream. It may not have been real in the way that the wooden boards under her feet were real—but it had been *true*! She was certain of that.

Anger was building in her. She had been given so little time in the Mortal World when she went to fetch Connor. She had to get to Beachy Head and step with him and Rathina into Faerie before the barriers came down between the realms. There had been no time to visit her parents, and for them to know she was in London but that they could not meet would have been too cruel for everyone. But she needed to find out how her dad was. So she had asked Connor to call. A casual catch-up call from a family friend. *Hi, how are things with you guys?*

That was all he had to do. And he had told her everything was fine.

He had lied to her.

She dragged a blanket from the bed and wrapped it around her shoulders. The fire had contracted to a haze of burning embers licked by tiny white flames. She took a candle to the fire and lit it.

She left her room and walked the narrow corridor to Connor's room. She lifted the latch and stepped inside.

It was a room similar to her own, small and dark and lit by the subdued flames of burning logs in the fireplace. She walked across the cool floor, holding the candle low over the bed.

Connor was on his side asleep. She almost wanted to hit him. She almost wanted to beat him with her fists as he lay there oblivious to her pain and rage.

She gripped his shoulder and shook him.

"You liar!" she spat, bringing the candle light close to his face. "Why did you lie to me?"

He awoke with a shudder, blinking dazedly into the candle flame. "What . . . ?"

"My dad isn't better at all," Tania snarled. "He's worse. He's really sick. You must have known that. Mum must have told you."

Connor sat up, pushing the candle away from his face. Hot wax splashed on his wrist and he grimaced in pain, rubbing at it with his other hand.

"Get a grip, Tania." His voice was irritated. "What are you talking about?"

She stood up, keeping her voice level. "The Dream Weaver sent me another dream," she said. "I was back home in Camden. Dad was really sick—coughing up blood."

He looked incredulously at her. "You had a nightmare and it's *my* fault?" he said. "How does that work?"

"Don't mess with me," snapped Tania. "Tell me the truth. What did my mum say when you phoned her?"

Connor let out a sigh. "She told me your dad was no better. He'd been to the doctor and he was on antibiotics—but so far they hadn't kicked in and he was getting worse." He held up his hands. "I just assumed they were still figuring out the best drugs to try him on. That's how it works. You prescribe the obvious antibiotics first then try others if they don't do the trick."

"He was coughing up blood, Connor!"

He paused, his brows knitting. "They should get him to hospital. It sounds like full-blown pneumonia."

"Mum was calling for an ambulance when . . . when

the dream—the *whatever it was*—ended. You should have told me he was no better! I trusted you to tell me!"

"Oh, really, is that what happened?" Connor asked sharply. "Because the way I remember it, you were desperate to be told your dad was all right so you could skip meeting up with your folks without feeling bad about it."

Tania stared at him. "That is so not true!"

"Then I'm sorry," he said, his voice conciliatory now. "I did it for the best, Tania. I wanted to save you agonizing about what to do. You'd already told me you didn't have time to visit them—I figured it would be easier for you if you thought your dad was okay." He raised his eyebrows. "I thought he *would* be okay." He lifted his hand and took hers. "I did it for you, Tania."

She swallowed, her anger draining. "It wasn't up to you to decide whether I could handle it or not," she said quietly, aware of the heat of his hand holding hers. "You should have told me the truth."

"I'm sorry. I won't do it again." His thumb stroked the back of her hand. "Always the truth from now on between us, okay?" He held the finger and thumb of his free hand a fraction apart. "Except for little white lies now and then," he said with a crooked smile. "Just to keep things interesting."

She looked at him. "You think this is funny?" she asked. "My dad's on his way to hospital and you're making jokes?" She pulled free of him and walked to the window. The night was like a black sheet pressed to the outside of the glass, showing the reflection of her face and the room behind her. She pulled the blanket close around her shoulders, wishing she had given herself time to get dressed.

"He'll be fine," Connor insisted, getting off the bed and twining a blanket around his waist. "Trust me—I'm a doctor. Almost a doctor, anyhow. But I know what I'm talking about, Tania. I really do. He'll be just fine." He frowned. "Now don't get mad—but are you absolutely sure the dream was . . . you know . . . *real*?"

"I heard the Dream Weaver's voice," Tania said, staring at his bare-chested reflection in the glass. "She was singing. It was almost . . ." She shook her head. There was something about the song that had been maddeningly familiar . . . as though she had heard it before, a long time ago.

"And you . . . you *trust* her, yeah?"

"Why should she send me dreams that aren't true?"

"Maybe she's working with that Nargo guy," Connor suggested. "We have only her word for what's really going on here."

That was a nasty thought. Tania could feel the ground slipping away under her feet as she considered the possibility of the Dream Weaver being false.

"I do trust her," she said after a pause. "There's something about her that . . . oh, I don't know . . . *something*." There! It was gone again. That sensation of familiarity—of instinctive confidence in the woman's ethereal presence.

"Fair enough," Connor said, coming beside her at the window. "If you're sure, then I've got no problems with her, either." He looked into her face. "So? What's the plan?"

"Same as before," Tania replied. "This doesn't make any difference to what we have to do." Her spirits lifted. "Over the sea to Alba and Erin and Tirnanog and fingers crossed we can actually do what's needed."

His eyes were piercing. "You're totally amazing, Tania, do you know that?" he said.

"Am I?" she returned his gaze, glad that all the recent aggression seemed to have faded, but suspicious of his glib words.

He nodded. "It can't be easy being you."

"Excuse me?"

"You're sixteen, Tania. You should be goofing off with your pals in Camden Market," he said. "You should be out buying shoes and racking up the bill on your cell. You shouldn't have to be doing all this crazy stuff." His fingertips brushed the hair from her cheek. "It's not fair."

"Fair?" she murmured. "What's fair got to do with it? And you're no better off than me. Stuck in a world that drives you nuts."

"Yeah, but at least I know who I am," he said, moving closer. "You've got two different people inside of you. A goofy, gangly kid called Anita, and"—his voice lowered—"and a beautiful fairy-tale princess called Tania."

"Some people might think that's a dream come true. . . ."

"Some people might wonder which fairy tale we're in," he whispered. "I'm hoping for *Sleeping Beauty*."

He leaned in, his mouth moving toward hers.

He's going to kiss me.

She was startled by this, but for some reason she did not immediately move away.

It's only a kiss. . . . Why not . . . ?

A fist hammered on the door, and it was flung open in a wash of yellow lantern light. Elias Fulk stood in the doorway, his face urgent in the sudden brightness.

Tania pulled away from Connor, relieved by the interruption. She had nearly made a bad choice there.

"Rise now and make haste!" called the innkeeper. "Horsemen have arrived in Hymnal by black of night—horsemen from Caer Liel. Word has it that they come on Lord Aldritch's command and they seek three strangers traveling in outlandish garb—a man and two women. They mean to seize you and take you to the earl. Come quickly or all will be lost!"

Tania left Connor to scramble into his Mortal clothes. She followed Elias down to the room where they had first met. Clothes and provisions were waiting for them by the glowing fire; clearly the landlord had had the foresight to gather them before going to his bed. As Tania came running in, Rathina was already there, pulling on a dark green gown.

"Thus ends a peaceful night's slumber!" growled Rathina, her eyes shining in the firelight. "I would we had the time to teach these night owls a lesson in courtesy, sister!"

"Another time, maybe," said Tania.

Elias handed Tania a heavy brown woolen gown.

"Unfit for a princess," he muttered, "but it will have to suffice! Be swift, my lady! We have little time to spare."

"It'll do fine," she said, tossing the blanket aside and pulling the gown over her head. Her fingers fumbled as she frantically tied the laces at the bodice.

Connor was with them a few moments later, his face revealing the same panic that gripped them all.

The innkeeper gave each of them a warm hooded cloak and a leather satchel of food and drink. Then he led them quickly through the darkened inn and out into a small enclosed courtyard, snatching up a closed lantern as he went.

They followed close on his heels as he led them at a run across the courtyard and away through narrow back streets, the lantern open a crack so that a slender beam lit their way.

As they slipped between the huddled buildings, Tania clearly heard a man's voice calling out something and the echo of horses' hooves on cobbles.

"How did they know we were here?" Connor asked as they hurried along. "*We* didn't even know we were going to be here till last night!"

"Sorcery, forsooth!" hissed Rathina as they ran. "Someone is using the Dark Eye of Auger, have no doubt of it. How else could Aldritch's minions have tracked us so swiftly? It is a bad happenstance, indeed, if all our movements are known!"

"It was never said that Lord Aldritch was adept in the Mystic Arts," said Elias Fulk. "Indeed, he was always said to scorn their use."

"It seems his distaste has faded somewhat," said Rathina. "If the horsemen have ridden from Caer Liel, then be most sure they come at Lord Aldritch's command."

"What is the Dark Eye of Auger?" asked Connor.

Rathina touched a finger to the center of her forehead. "It is a conjuration of the Dark Arts, Master Connor," she said. "A way of seeing over great distances—of spying out the movements of an enemy."

"Like Titania can do?"

"No! *Nothing* like that!"

The Dark Arts.

Tania shuddered at the mention of this sinister side of Faerie magic. Gabriel Drake had dared to look into those arcane skills, and he had become lost, his arrogant curiosity and greed for power corrupting him completely, until Rathina had defeated him on the field of battle.

But it was not Drake's grim fate that filled Tania with concern; it was the knowledge that her own Edric had flirted with the Dark Arts. With good intent he had called on their baleful spells and incantations, but she knew all too well how swiftly a pure soul could be corrupted.

And Edric was now in the service of Lord Aldritch of Weir.

But she could not—would not—believe that Edric's heart could have been so warped or his loyalties so altered that he would use the Dark Arts against *her*—to help her enemies to track her down.

He would never do that to me. He couldn't! It isn't him—it's someone else. It has to be.

"So, does that mean someone knows everything we've done since we left the Palace?" asked Connor.

"It may be so," said Rathina.

"Listen, I'm new here, right, and I don't know anything—but if it's not the Dream Weaver, is it possible that Aldritch is working for Nargostrond? Could they be in cahoots?"

"I do not give that credence, lad," said Elias, panting. "Lord Aldritch would not betray Faerie thus—and he would not bring this plague down upon his own people."

"Then what the hell is going on?" Connor demanded. "Who are those guys back there, and what do they want us for?"

Tania turned angrily to him. "You think any of us know that?" she snapped. "I certainly don't. I have no idea. All I do know is that we can't let them find us here."

"They shall not, my lady," said Elias. "Not while I have breath in my body. Come. This way. The stair is steep and uneven. Beware."

A narrow stone stairway led down between tall black buildings. The steps were slippery with moss and the rope handhold stapled to the wall was greasy and frayed. At the far end Tania could just make out the canal. As they descended, the sounds of the rushing water bounced off the high stone walls.

"The tide is on the turn," said Elias, his face ruddy and running with sweat as they stepped out from cover onto a paved wharf lined with stone bollards. An assortment of small sailboats bobbed on the running water. "That is good. The river will bear you away." He walked quickly along the wharf till he came to a white hulled sloop with a single mast. "This is the *Blessèd Queen*," he said breathlessly. "She will serve you well, I believe, although she has never been out of sight of land."

He stood at the paved edge, breathing hard, helping them down one by one into the boat. "Do not set the sails till you are on the ocean," he warned. "A white sail can be seen from above." He turned, indicating the high hill of the village. "A keen eye from up yonder could ruin all. Go now and good speed be with you. I will cast off the mooring ropes. If the men come to me, I shall do what I can to throw them off your trail."

Tania looked anxiously up at him. "Don't put yourself or your family in danger," she said.

He smiled, wiping the sweat off his brow and throwing the rope down to Connor. "Have no fear for me, my lady," he said. "I have kept the inn here for fifteen hundred years and more; I have learned how to deal with bothersome folk."

Rathina and Connor leaned over the gunwales and pushed hard at the side of the wharf. The *Blessèd Queen* edged out into the canal. Black water widened between Tania and the innkeeper.

"Look after yourself," she called.

"And you, my lady," he called back, lifting his lantern so the slender beam of light shone out bright as a star toward them. "Sail to good fortune! Farewell!"

The current of the retreating tide was surprisingly

strong, and the boat was carried quickly along. The slim lantern beam winked out and Elias was swallowed in the night.

Connor got busy inspecting the furled sail and checking the rigging. Rathina was at the stern, the tiller under her arm as she watched the banks flow past.

"What can I do?" asked Tania.

"There is a wooden staff in the keel," Rathina said. "If we come too close to the banks, use it to fend us off. It is hard to steer with no sail, and I can do little till we are out of this millrace."

The pole was almost as high as Tania was tall. She found the rocking of the boat tricky, and she needed to hold on to something as she moved about. She settled herself on a small triangular seat at the prow, the pole upright in her hands.

The night was windless and still. She shivered although the cloak was warm about her shoulders. She glanced back at Hymnal on its humpbacked hill. It was black against the dark clouds. Few lights were showing and nothing moved. But somewhere up there the horsemen of Caer Liel were hunting for them.

Who led them here? Hollin the Healer, perhaps? He hates me enough to want me dead. What if he's the one using the Dark Eye of Auger?

It made sense to her that the man from Alba might be guiding Aldritch's soldiers. He didn't simply detest her. From the way he had behaved the last time they'd met, it was clear he had a genuine terror of her.

Half-thing, he called her. She-witch.

But something about the idea of Hollin using the Dark Arts nagged at her. *I thought his magic was all pretense—a lot of hooey, with magic pebbles and incantations.*

Could it be?

Connor's voice snapped her back into reality. "Tania!" he spat. "Get the staff ready."

They had come out of the mouth of the canal and were now in the main body of the River Styr, caught by crosscurrents that were turning the sloop around and pushing her toward the bank.

The river had changed since they'd last seen it on their way to Hymnal. It was high and wide now, its waters lapping at the grassy bank.

Tania twisted herself around, heaving the staff out over the prow, ready to fend the boat away from the looming bank. But at the last moment the eddies let go of the vessel and sent it seaward. They had escaped Hymnal undetected. A sense of relief and elation swept over her.

"Now let us hope for a good east wind!" called Rathina.

Connor was standing behind Tania, although she had been too busy hefting the staff to notice his approach. "Not much hope of that unless the weather changes," he said, looking up into the roof of cloud. "There's not a breath of air." He rested his hand for a moment on Tania's shoulder then made his way back to the mast.

Zara could have whistled us up a wind, she thought disconsolately. *Or Eden . . .*

Or Eden.

She thought of her oldest sister with her solemn face and melancholy eyes and with her fall of prematurely white hair. Tania closed her eyes, holding that image in her mind, picturing Eden's face.

"Eden?" she mouthed the name, less than a whisper. "If you can hear me, send us a wind. Please—send a wind."

She felt something. The tiniest thing. A tingle in her fingertips. No more than that. Imagination, perhaps. Wishful thinking.

She opened her eyes. The ebbing tide was drawing them toward the mouth of the river. She could see the curve of the bay. Flecks of white on water. An arc of gray surf where the waves were breaking on the sand. The hunched dunes of Weir.

Hymnal—a dark ridge against the sky.

She puckered her brows, staring at the hilltop town. It looked as though the hill spiked with rooftops was sliding away beneath the clouds.

She blinked and looked again. No! Of course—it was the clouds that were moving. Moving ponderously westward.

And then she felt a cold wind on her face and in her hair. She lifted her face to the sky and smiled.

"Thank you," she said.

"The wind's come up," said Connor, stooping to loosen the ties that held the reefed mainsail to the boom. “That’s what I call a piece of good luck.”

“That’s what I call prayers being answered,” said Tania.

“Ha!” exclaimed Rathina, her eyes bright. “You called upon Eden, then! ’Tis good she can aid us so. Master Connor, set the mainmast, if you have the craft. And the jib also. We must make the most of this mystic wind.”

Connor gave the two of them a bemused look. “Everything has to be magic with you people,” he said, shaking his head.

The two sisters laughed aloud at his disbelief.

As Connor released the last of the leather thongs and hauled on the halyard to raise the sail, Tania turned her eyes to the darkling west.

Now their journey had truly begun.

The *Blessèd Queen* plowed the ocean, curtained in a fine salt spray. The choppy waves were capped white and foamed with lacy veils of spume.

Tania still was not quite used to the jolting as the prow was shouldered upward by the waves and then dropped—up and drop, up and drop—but she was at least able to brace herself when she saw the frothing crests of larger waves approaching.

It was not yet dawn, but away behind them the fleeing mountains of Weir were lined with a frail silvery light. The east wind was still blowing strongly into their triangular sails, and above them the clouds were being torn to scurrying shreds. Patches of black appeared through the clouds, and in the far gulfs of heaven stars glittered frostily.

Tania watched Connor rig the sails, wanting to help but knowing he had no time to teach her. Being of no use was frustrating, especially as Connor and

Rathina clearly had their hands full.

Rathina was at the stern, the tiller under her arm, her black hair blowing all around her face. Judging from her narrow-eyed expression, keeping a steady course was hard work in such a wind.

Tania leaned out of Connor's way as he looped the bowline from the jib sail around and around a cleat set at the prow.

"The trick is to tack to about forty-five degrees from the wind," he told her as he secured the rope. "Normally you'd use the boom to change the angle of the mainsail to the wind and then tack from port to starboard to keep a straight course. But as we aren't aiming for a specific place, there's not much point in doing that right now." The sloop dropped suddenly into a deep trough between waves and he stumbled forward, turning quickly to sit down against Tania on the triangular prow seat. "Whoops! Sorry about that," he said, lifting his arm to wipe the spray off his face. "I haven't quite got my sea legs yet."

"It is fierce," she said. "I'm impressed that you can stand up at all. If I tried, I'd probably topple overboard in about ten seconds."

He smiled. "Don't worry," he said. "I took a lifeguard course a few years back." He gazed into her face. "I'd save you."

Tania tried to shift away from him, but the seat was too narrow for her to avoid the pressure of his body against hers. The moment when she had almost allowed him to kiss her back in the inn was gone. Elias

Fulk's interruption had saved her from making a terrible mistake.

"Listen, Connor . . ." she began hesitantly.

"I know, I know," he said quickly. "Back off, Connor. Give it a rest!"

"I'm sorry. It's just . . ."

"You're still in love with Edric, aren't you?"

"I am. Yes, I really am." She attempted a smile. "Friends, huh? That would mean so much to me."

He nodded. "Yeah. Friends. Friends is good." He gave a crooked grin. "Boyfriends come and go—friends are forever, right?"

"I'm not sure that's—"

"Look, I'm sorry if I've been a total jerk with the come-ons and all that," he interrupted. "It's just me being an idiot. Am I forgiven?" He stood up, one hand closing around the bowline as the boat lifted and fell.

"You're forgiven," said Tania. "Of course you are."

"Great."

He made his way down the boat. Tania watched him thoughtfully as he checked the rigging at the mast and then moved to the stern to speak with Rathina. *He's a good guy. . . . Look how he jumped in to help us when any other person would have run for the hills. And the thing is, the idea of getting together with him isn't exactly off-the-scale gross. But I can't. I really can't. If the circumstances were different . . .*

Her fingers came up to touch the teardrop-shaped pendant that Edric had given her. The stone was a bond between them—not just an emotional bond but a mystical one, too. By tracking the black onyx stone Edric had been able to follow her into the Mortal Realm.

A disturbing thought hit her.

Could it have been Edric who had used the Dark Arts to follow them to Hymnal? Was he still using the stone to trace her movements? Was it the pendant that had drawn the horsemen from Caer Liel to Hymnal at dead of night?

Was Edric capable of betraying her like that? The thought pressed hard against her heart.

From love everlasting to hunting her down for his cruel master?

Edric? Could you do that to me?

She got unsteadily to her feet, and suddenly the stone felt as if it was burning hot against her flesh. With a fierce, violent movement she tore the necklace from around her neck and threw it into the sea.

A fist squeezed her heart, forcing the breath from her lungs as the necklace sank beneath the dark green waves.

Edric was gone from her—and now she had cast away the only reminder she had of him.

Would the agony of lost love never fade?

She closed her eyes.

Please let it get better, she begged. *Please don't let it hurt this bad for always.*

The night was ebbing slowly away. The coast of Faerie was a black ribbon along the eastern horizon, and above it the sky was pearly white.

The sea was lively still, but the spite seemed to have gone out of it, and Tania had even dared now and then to stand and stretch her legs.

She noticed that Connor was squatting, hunched with his back to the mast. He was half turned away from her and he seemed to be holding his stomach.

Seasick, maybe?

Odd, though—he'd shown no sign of it earlier, and the sea was a lot less rough now. All the same . . .

She got up and made her way toward him, the heavy gown encumbering her legs as she clung to the rigging with both hands.

"Connor? Are you okay?"

He twisted around, giving her a startled look. "Yes, I'm fine."

"You looked like you might not be feeling too good."

He stood up, his hands pushed into his pockets. "No, I'm doing great. How about you?"

"Better now that it's calmed down a bit." She turned to Rathina, sitting in the stern with the tiller held firm under her arm. "How's it going?" she called.

"All's well," Rathina replied. "Eden's wind is a boon to us; steady from the east, it pushes us on a fine western course."

"Actually we're heading more west-northwest than absolutely due west," Connor said. "Not that it matters, really."

Tania looked at him. "What does west-northwest mean, exactly?"

He threw out a straight arm, his hand pointing ahead but slightly to the left of the prow. "That's due west," he said. He swung his arm so his hand aimed out over the prow. "That's west-northwest." Another shift to the right. "Northwest." Another. "North-northwest." He adjusted his arm a final time. "And that there is north."

"Oh, I see," said Tania. "I'm impressed—except how do you know that?"

"My dad taught me to navigate."

"Yes, I get how you know the terminology, but . . ."

"Tania!" called Rathina. "Would you take the tiller for a while and give me some respite?"

"Of course," said Tania, glad to help at last.

She picked her way cautiously to the stern of the boat, lifting her skirts to avoid tripping. She took Rathina's seat, tucking the wooden tiller under her arm and gripping it with both hands.

"Keep the tiller thus," Rathina instructed her, positioning the wooden arm slightly left of center. "That way we shall keep a true course."

"No problem." As she held the tiller, Tania was immediately aware of a low thrumming that resonated through her entire body. It was an exhilarating sensation, although it took her by surprise how physically hard it was to keep the tiller at the point Rathina had indicated. It fought to move to the right, and it took a good deal of strength and concentration to keep it under control.

"I'm in sore need of something to eat," said Rathina, walking easily down the boat. "Would you join me, Master Connor? I'd hear more of your seafaring."

"It hardly counts as seafaring," Connor said. "We just messed around in the river, or sometimes we went out to Foulness Point and Virley Channel."

"I do not know these names," said Rathina, kneeling to open one of Elias Fulk's food bags. "But tell me—how does sailing in the Mortal World differ from what we do here?"

"Surprisingly little," said Connor, sitting on the narrow side bench by the mast and taking bread from Rathina. "Except that the cleats and the gooseneck swivel and such would all be made of steel instead of crystal."

The wind hummed in Tania's ears, and she soon lost track of their conversation as they spoke of clews and luffs and outhauls and sheets.

It's good that they're getting on. Rathina needs someone to take her out of herself. And she deserves it, too. She's suffered enough, surely?

Connor said something that Tania didn't catch and Rathina laughed.

While they chatted, Tania stared out into the unfathomable west, hearing Titania's voice in her head.

Beyond the flaxen coasts and heathered glens of Alba, beyond the emerald hills of Erin of the enchanted waters, beyond even dragon-haunted Hy Brassail, far, far away to the land of Tirnanog, the Divine Harper spins his songs at the absolute end of the world.

And that's where they were heading—on a quest to save the Realm of Faerie.

Connor was right. It was crazy. Absolutely crazy!

"Spirits of love and harmony, *look*!"

Tania had been watching the wind undulating across the sails, mesmerized by the patterns of ripples and puckers on the stretched white canvas. Rathina's voice broke the spell.

Her sister was pointing behind where Tania sat in the stern, her eyes wide in awe. Connor was also on his feet.

Tania saw a glorious change in the light. From dawning gray it turned suddenly golden, bathing her two companions in a rich effulgence. She twisted in her seat, straining to look over her shoulder.

Deep in the eastern sky threads of yellow light were swarming forward over the coastline of Faerie, veiling the sun so that it shone like a ball of burning copper low on the horizon. The golden filaments arched over the land, knitting together in an impossibly complex pattern, forming a gleaming, lacy shell that stretched beyond sight both to the north and the south—like an onrushing tidal wave of gilded water.

But even as Tania watched awestruck, she felt a terrible weakness invade her body, as though all the strength and energy were being sucked out of her, as though her muscles were being liquefied and her limbs turned to jelly.

She heard Rathina give a cry behind her, but she had no vitality left to turn her head. Her eyes were fixed on the golden wave. It was curling in on itself now, coming down rapidly into the sea beyond the coast, shrouding the land in its glowing aura.

And then in a moment the golden shield became still, and the sun was visible over its shining carapace: The land of Faerie was hidden under its protection.

Images filled Tania's mind: of men slumping asleep in the fields, of women and children falling to the ground, of dogs and horses and sheep and birds succumbing to the healing slumber of the Gildensleep. And far away and remote, on the southernmost corner of Faerie, her family gathered together with bowed heads and trembling limbs as they worked as one to create and maintain the protective shield.

Tania gasped aloud as she felt the strength flooding back into her body. The worst was over. The power of the Royal Family had been enough. For the time being, at least Faerie was safe from the plague.

Now Tania turned to see how Rathina was. She was kneeling, with Connor beside her, his arms around her. Her head lolled on his shoulder, face white. But then Rathina lifted her head weakly and looked into Tania's face, dark eyes shining.

"It is done!" she said breathlessly, pulling away from Connor and getting to her feet. There were pride and joy in her face as she stared eastward. She lifted a fist into the air, shouting out loud, "Glorious it is to be of the House of Aurealis on such a morn! August Father King, exalted Mother Queen, illustrious and sublime sisters, hail to thee!" She spread her arms, her head tilted back. "Take all, rend me to the bone if need be—I shall not fail thee!"

Then, as if her words had brought a thunderbolt down on her, she fell backward, her arms still held wide.

Tania let out a yell of alarm, but Connor was there—throwing himself behind Rathina, catching her in his arms as she toppled over.

"Is she all right?" Tania called, half standing as she tried to see Rathina's face. But her sister's neck was stretched back over Connor's upper arm, and all Tania could see was the rapid rise and fall of Rathina's chest under the bodice of the green gown. Apart from that her body was dreadfully still.

"I think she's fainted!" Connor shouted back. Very carefully he lowered Rathina's limp form into the bottom of the boat, kneeling over her, his fingers at her throat to test her pulse. "She'll be fine. I guess it was the excitement."

Tania let go of the tiller and scrambled forward along the boat, almost falling as her gown wrapped itself around her legs. "Are you sure she's okay?" she asked.

"She's got a steady pulse," Connor said, his fingers still pressed to the side of her neck. "Slow but steady."

"I felt really horrible while the Gildensleep was

coming," Tania said. "Like all the life was draining out of me. Maybe it was worse for her. Maybe that's why she's passed out."

"Maybe," Connor agreed. "How do you feel now?"

"Fine."

Rathina's body was stiff, her arms and legs stretched out rigidly, her fists clenched. Her eyes opened, but they were glazed and somehow silvery and she stared straight into the sky as though her mind was absent.

Her lips moved but there was no sound.

"Rathina?" Connor urged, leaning close. "Are you with us?"

"Hard it is . . . this far from Faerie," came a soft, gentle voice from Rathina's lips. "But I must speak . . . I will speak one final time. . . ."

Tania knew that voice.

"Dream Weaver," she said, moving up Rathina's body to kneel at her shoulder, "how's my father? My *Mortal* father?"

"I do not know," breathed the shimmering voice. "You are the conduit between the worlds, Tania. I cannot pierce the veil alone."

"Can you take me to him again—please! Just for a few moments. Just so I can see how he is?"

"In the waking world, Tania?" crooned the voice. "Nay, that I cannot do. Indeed, it is hard enough for me to speak with you now that you are so far from the land. My powers are bound to Faerie, and once you are beyond sight of the Realm, my voice will be gone. But listen well to me while you can, Tania Aurealis," whispered the voice. "Listen and take good heed."

Tania had to lean closer now; the voice was getting fainter by the moment.

"It is good news that I bring to you," sighed the voice. "Once you are upon the open ocean and the Immortal Realm is lost to sight, the doom of the earls of Faerie will hold no sway."

Tania frowned, her ear almost to Rathina's mouth. "What does that mean?" she asked. "I don't understand."

"The portals, Tania," breathed the weakening voice. ". . . only . . . the ways between . . . only in Faerie . . . are . . . they . . ."

The voice was gone.

"No!" groaned Tania, staring into Rathina's eyes. The silver sheen had vanished; her sister's eyes were wide and dark. "No! I don't understand what you mean!"

Rathina's body convulsed and she sat up, her eyes alive again, her chest rising and falling rapidly as she breathed. Her fingers gripped Tania's wrist. "What matter was that?" she hissed. "It felt like that time beneath the waves."

"It was," Tania said.

Rathina's eyes narrowed. "I pray for a time when I shall meet that creature face to face," she growled. "Then shall I show her in full measure how it feels to be overborne and made powerless by another!" She frowned. "What words did she have for you?"

"I'm not really sure," said Tania. "She was trying to

tell me something. Good news, she said. But I didn't get it before she . . ."

"Before we lost the signal," Connor said. He shook his head. "It's like when you drive too far from a local radio station. It gets fainter and fainter and then—pop! It's gone." He scratched his head. "There is a kind of logic to this world sometimes," he said. "I'm just going to have to fit it all together piece by piece."

"What did the creature say?" asked Rathina.

"She said the doom of Faerie would hold no sway . . ." Tania began hesitantly.

"Not quite," said Connor. "What she actually said was that once we were out on the open sea, the doom of the earls of Faerie would hold no sway."

"Yes. That was it."

"And then she said something about the portals and the ways between," Connor added. "And then we lost her. I suppose we could always turn around and go back—you know, see if we can pick up the signal again."

"Against such a wind as this?" said Rathina as a squall hit the sails and the boat rocked, making them all reach for safe handholds. "Nay, it would be too arduous an endeavor. We have no time for such an enterprise."

"Wait!" Tania said sharply. "Just wait a minute!" She shut her eyes tight, trying to think. Trying to fit the Dream Weaver's words together to form a coherent whole.

She lifted her head. "Yes!" she said. "I've got it! I'm

sure I have!" She looked from one face to the other. "The doom of the earls was that the ways between the worlds would be shut down forever," she said eagerly, a new hope kindling in her even as she spoke. "I think the Dream Weaver was trying to tell me that once we're out of sight of Faerie, I'll be able to get back to London again—back to Mum and Dad." She looked into Connor's face. "You'll be able to get home!" She laughed for pure joy. "We can both get back!"

IX

"Yes!" Connor shouted, reaching impulsively toward Tania. "Yes! That's exactly what she meant!"

They hugged tightly. Tania knew how much this must mean to him—how heavily his exile had been weighing on his mind since they had walked beneath the waves.

"We can go home!" Connor's voice was loud in Tania's ear as his arms wrapped around her. "Oh my god! I can hardly believe it!" He drew back, his hands on her shoulders, his face elated. "But it makes sense; of course it does. The King and Queen and all those earls have plenty of power *inside* Faerie—but once you move out of range, they can't do a thing!"

"I think you're right!" Tania exclaimed. "But how can we be certain?"

"Try that side step thing of yours," Connor suggested.

"What, *here*?" Tania said, her voice full of laughter as another gust of wind sent the boat rocking. "Don't be daft. This is a Faerie boat—it would disappear if I moved into the Mortal World. I'd be splashing about in the sea!"

"No, you're right; that's not a great idea." Connor looked intensely at her. "But when can we try it? How far are we from Alba?"

"I don't know."

"Whist awhile!" came Rathina's calm voice, breaking sharply into their elation. "Ere we try to dance upon a rose thorn's tip, let the task upon which we are bound not be entirely forgotten." She looked soberly at them. "I am glad indeed that your exile here may not be permanent, Master Connor, and I am blithe beyond measure that you, my sweet sister, can seek out your Mortal parents—but long is the road before us, and several are the strange lands we must cross to get to journey's end."

"Oh yes, of course!" Tania burst out, pushing Connor's hands away and reaching out to grip Rathina's fingers. "But you can't blame us for being excited—we thought we'd never get back again, ever. This means so much to Connor—it's going to make such a difference to him to know he can get home."

Connor looked at her. "Has it really been that obvious?" he asked.

"You have been kind of grouchy," she said. "But I totally understood why."

"Well, paint me officially un-grouchy from now on." Connor laughed. "And as soon as we get to Alba—Tania can do her thing and pop us back into

Ireland—even if it's only for a few minutes, you know? Long enough to phone home!" He looked at Tania. "You'll be able to call your mum and make sure your dad is doing okay."

"Yes, *yes*!" cried Tania. "And even if I can never move between the worlds in Faerie ever again, so long as I can do it in Alba, everything will be fine. It'll be more complicated, and it'll be way more time-consuming, of course, but there are ferries and air-planes that go from Ireland to England all the time."

"You can commute." Connor laughed again. "Between Faerie and Earth and between Ireland and England. That'll be pretty cool!"

"And you can get on with your life," said Tania. She sucked in a deep breath and let it out explosively. "Oh, please! Let it be true! Just let it really be true."

Connor let out a gasp and dropped to his knees, his hands over his face. "I can go home," he said, his voice choking as the full realization finally hit him. Tania touched her fingertips to his bowed head, understanding what this moment must mean to him.

She straightened, gazing back the way they had come. The bright glow of the Gildensleep was a slender golden thread on the horizon. The sky above was filling with blue daylight—and ahead of them, just out of sight, lay the land of Alba and the chance to put hope to the test!

It was exactly as Titania has prophesied when they had spoken in the water-mirror in the darkness and misery of the previous night.

This really was a glad new day.

"Then let us sail swift to Alba!" cried Rathina, heading for the tiller. "We have drifted off our true course. Tania, get the Mortal to his feet! There is work to be done if we are to make safe landfall."

Tania sat in the stern of the sailboat eating an apple while the blustery wind blew through her hair. Connor was at the tiller now—all through the long day the three of them had taken turns to guide the *Blessèd Queen* ever onward.

Rathina was at the prow, staring out over the sea.

The sky was cloudless but hazy above, and the sea was a wide green wheel, featureless, endless, enigmatic. And they at the hub. Quite alone.

"I've never been out of sight of land before," Tania said, turning her head to slowly take in the view of the horizon. "Not in a boat, I mean. In an airplane, yes—but that's different, isn't it? You look down from an airplane and it's kind of not quite real. Like CGI effects in a movie. But being on a little boat like this, out in the middle of nowhere . . ." She gave a shiver. "It's a weird feeling." She glanced at Connor. "Don't you think?"

He blinked and looked at her. "Sorry?" he said. "I was miles away. What were you saying?"

"Oh, nothing," Tania said, leaning an arm over the side and trailing her hand in the water, feeling the drag of their speed slapping against her fingers. "Nothing in particular."

The wind blew still from the east, but a lot of its

power was gone—it had lessened the farther west they sailed, and now, with the day fading and the sun low on the empty western horizon, it had grown gusty and difficult to gauge.

"What were you thinking about, then?" Tania asked him.

"The secret of immortality," he said, his eyes narrowed against the glare of the yellowing sun.

"Connor, there is no secret," she told him. "It's not like splitting the atom or discovering a cure for cancer. Immortality just *is*. This is not a world where you can solve everything scientifically—I thought you'd be getting the hang of that by now."

"I think you're wrong," Connor said mildly. He smiled as though to encourage her to follow his reasoning. "Just because no one here *knows* how it works, that doesn't mean it can't be figured out." His eyes shone. "Imagine it, Tania. The secret of immortality." He held a hand out, palm upward. "Right there—right there in our hand. Imagine the reception we'd get back home. The Estabrook-Palmer Cure for Death." Tania looked at him without speaking, but it did not pass her by that his name came first—and that she was Palmer and not Aurealis.

"We'd get the Nobel Prize for medicine for sure," he continued. "We'd be world famous. Benefactors of humanity. They'd go crazy for us!"

She laughed gently. "You're crackers," she said charitably. "But go for it, if it gives you any pleasure. Knock yourself out!"

The boat rocked suddenly. Tania turned and saw that Rathina had risen to her feet. She was standing tall in the prow, staring hard into the east, a look of alarm and concern on her face.

"Rathina? What is it?" Tania called. She followed the line of her sister's eyes but could see nothing—nothing but the smooth, dappled jade green face of the sea.

"Danger!" Rathina called. "Danger blown on the wind!"

"I can't see anything," Connor called, twisting his head to scan the horizon. "What kind of danger?"

"Someone is calling on the Dark Arts," Rathina said. "We are being followed!"

"Are you sure?" Tania was on her feet now, balancing herself with a hand on Connor's shoulder. "There's nothing there, Rathina."

"It is coming nonetheless," said Rathina, moving down the vessel. "It is upon the water." She looked at Tania. "Do not doubt me, sister. I know the taint of the Dark Arts in the air. We are pursued."

"How?" Tania asked. "How could anyone have got out of Faerie? Everyone should be asleep."

"Ask me not how, Tania," Rathina replied. "Simply believe what I tell you. A darkness dogs our trail, and it will go ill for us if we do not outrun it."

"We can probably put on a knot or two if we pay more attention to the wind," Connor said. "Rathina, will you take the tiller? I'll work the boom. If there is something nasty behind us, let's make sure we stay well away from it."

Tania knew to get out of the way as Connor loosened the ropes that held the boom. He began to feed them out, letting the long wooden pole swing, feeling for the wind in the mainsail. Tania clung to the mast as the boat picked up speed. She stared uneasily into the east.

Nothing. Not a sign of pursuit. Not a speck, not a dot, not a shadow on the sea.

But she knew better than to question Rathina's instincts. Somewhere out there something ruinous was stalking them.

As the daylight faded, Tania felt sure she could discern the faintest possible hint of a golden hem to the eastern sky: the Gildensleep, lost beyond the horizon but coloring the darkling sky nonetheless.

They had made good speed into the evening, although it had been hard work for Connor in particular, pulling on the ropes, swinging the heavy boom across the boat so that the mainsail caught every last breath of wind.

Tania turned her eyes westward again, peering out across the sea, searching for the first sight of land. Her head ached from the strain, but she wasn't prepared to let that stop her. At least she could do this one thing. At least she could . . .

She gasped. "I see something!" She stood on the

wooden prow seat, leaning forward, narrowing her eyes. The sun was below the horizon, and the waning light made the sky glow lustrous as a pearl, but there, where the sea met the sky, she felt certain she saw a sliver of solid darkness that had not been there before.

"About time!" said Connor, panting. "Can you make it out yet?"

"Not really," Tania called to him. "It's just a kind of dark streak. But I'm pretty sure it's land."

"The land of Alba!" called Rathina from the stern. "Fate winds a curious thread, to be sure. And we the first of Faerie to traverse this stretch of water for ten thousand years!"

As they sailed on, huge bright Faerie stars began to appear. They appeared in ones and twos at first, twinkling in the eastern sky, but then they ignited in a silvery wash that swept across the heavens until the whole sky was ablaze.

But their light illuminated nothing, and the remoteness of the jeweled sky seemed to make the sea even more black and daunting. Tania strained her eyes. Something was approaching them: something huge and dark, rolling in ponderously over the waves.

"Fog!" she shouted. "We're heading into some really thick fog!"

The stars and the sea and the distant land were suddenly obliterated as the thick black fog swept across their path, engulfing the small boat in its damp and blinding embrace.

"Do you see any lights on the land?" Connor called to Tania. "Any sign of towns or whatever?"

"No, I can't see anything now," Tania replied, looking back down the length of the boat. Even Connor's form was misty, and in this clinging fog one darkness seemed much like another.

But as they sailed on through the fog, she fancied she could hear a new sound. Waves breaking on a faraway shore, perhaps? No. Not that.

She listened intently.

It was a creaking sound—a familiar sound she recognized but could not put a name to. Muffled groaning. A leathery straining noise. Waves slapping hollow on . . .

A ship!

That was it!

Creaking timbers. Canvas sails taut in the wind. The smack of sea on a hull.

A huge looming darkness came up fast on her left.

"Watch out!" she shouted. "There's a ship!"

A host of red lights broke out above them in the fog. They were lanterns of red glass, swinging wildly, lining the sides of a great dark galleon, their shutters thrown back to reveal black timbers and sails and a mass of black-clad men leaning over the gunnels. There were shouts and whoops and the sound of ropes snaking down. A stone hook crashed onto the planks of the *Blessèd Queen* a couple of inches from Tania's foot. She jumped aside as more came pounding down, cracking the timbers, sending up splinters.

"Take them alive, my lads," called a harsh voice from out of the sky. "Do them no harm for the present. Let us learn who dares to sail these waters without Lord Balor's leave!"

Tania spun around, instinctively reaching for the staff that lay in the bottom of the boat: a weapon against the invaders.

A black shape moved toward her, and she saw the gleam of a curved crystal knife. She swung the staff hard, hitting the knife arm just above the elbow.

There was a sharp crack and a roar of pain. Tania drew back then thrust the pole forward again. The man doubled up as the butt of the staff rammed into his stomach. She used all her weight to follow through, and the man was pushed up against the gunnels. The side of the boat took him behind the knees, and he was flipped over with a shout. A fountain of white water rose as he plunged into the sea.

Tania could see Connor by the mast struggling in the grip of three men. And in the stern Rathina was warding others away with savage sweeps of the tiller arm. But more were coming, swarming down the ropes, tipping the small vessel wildly as they leaped aboard.

A curved sword was thrust toward Tania, sparkling like the crystal swords of Faerie. She hefted the staff, parrying the blade away. A black shape came hurtling down toward her.

"Tania!" Too late she heard Connor shout a warning.

There was a blinding pain in the side of her head, and the world exploded in an agony of red fire.

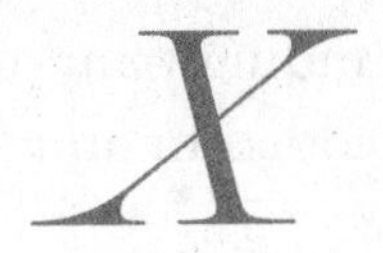

A furnace blazed in Tania's head, searing her brain.

Her face felt as though someone had hurled a volley of needles against her raw skin. There was salt water in her mouth. She realized she was lying on a hard surface. Her head pounded, heavy as lead.

Hands gripped her upper arms, dragging her to her feet. Brine ran down her face and neck. Hard fingers closed like a vice on her chin, wrenching her head up.

Gasping, she forced her eyes open. For a few moments all she could see was swimming black and red. Shadows and fire. Forming half-shapes that melted away again and reformed in meaningless blotches.

"A pretty mare, to be sure," said a voice as the world eddied around her. "She's no peasant girl, I'll warrant. Some grieving father will pay a fine ransom for her return." The fingers dug deeper into her flesh. "Hoy! Waken now, mare!"

The pain helped bring Tania to her senses. The

floating shapes settled and she found herself staring into a face stained red by the light of many lanterns. A man's face. Long and hollow-cheeked and deep-eyed with a black goatee and a fierce hooked nose, all framed by dark curling hair.

An instinct of fury made her snatch at the man's wrist and drag his hand away from her face. She glared at him, pulling herself free of the men who had brought her to her feet, aware of the clammy darkness of the fog swirling around her.

She swayed, dizzy, hurting.

"A spitfire or I'm much mistaken," said the man with a cruel smile. "Good. All the better. The fish that turns belly-up is poor sport." He peered into her face. "Are your brains addled or can you speak?"

She swallowed, her throat tight and leather dry. "I can speak," she croaked. She coughed again, drawing herself upright. "Why did you attack us?" she demanded. "Where are my friends?"

Ignore the pain. Ignore the way your head feels. This has to be dealt with.

The man stepped aside, and finally Tania was able to make sense of what was happening. She was on the deck of a large galleon. Beyond its high rails the fog blotted out the world. Black sails billowed like thunderclouds. Men stood around her, many holding up lanterns from which poured red light. They were dressed in simple clothes: leather or woolen tunics, leggings of animal skin or dark cloth. Some had bare feet; others wore high boots. Most had crystal swords thrust into their belts; others had daggers and bludgeons.

The man who had first spoken to her wore a long black coat tied at the waist with a red sash. There was a white ruff at his neck and lace at his wrists. Crystal buckles glinted on his boots.

Now Tania could see that Rathina was standing a few feet away, her arms twisted behind her back, held by a huge man. Close at her side Connor was on his knees, held down by two other men; one of them pressed a sword blade to Connor's neck.

Rathina's face was full of defiance. "Sister," she called, "are you well?"

"Sisters, is it?" said the bearded man. He looked sharply at Tania. "You will speak sense to me, mare, or I'll have the young dog's head from his shoulders." He gestured casually toward Connor. "Am I understood in this?"

Connor lifted his head, and Tania saw the fear and helplessness in his eyes.

"I understand," Tania said, forcing the anger out of her voice. She turned to Rathina. "I'm okay," she said. "Don't worry about me. What about you?"

"A few buffets, forsooth, but I bend like the willow and am not easily broken."

"Connor?"

He nodded but didn't speak. A sharp crystal blade grazed his throat.

The bearded man's eyes narrowed. "Whence come you, mare?" he asked. "I know not your accent, and there are alien words in your speech."

"My name is Tania, not *mare*." She brought a note of Faerie royalty into her voice, hoping it might give the man something to think about. "And before I tell you anything else, I'd like to know who you are and by whose authority you have attacked us."

"I am Theodore Welsh," said the man, and there now seemed to be an intrigued note in his voice. "Commodore in service to Lord Balor." He said this last name as though he expected Tania to recognize it. "And now give a full account of yourself and your companions and your purpose upon Lord Balor's waters or you will rue it." His face tightened. "And speak no riddles, neither, woman. I have heard nonsense enough from the lad and threats aplenty from your ebon-haired sister."

"A sword in my hand is all I ask of you, Theodore Welsh," Rathina snarled. "And then bring your men upon me in whatsoever numbers you choose. I'll spit 'em like sucklings!"

"Be still, woman!" shouted Welsh. "Or I'll send you home without a tongue in your head. And belike your father will thank me for it as a great kindness upon his house!"

Tania lifted her head and looked directly into Welsh's eyes, summoning all that she had learned of Faerie dignity and propriety. They had not even reached the shores of Alba and already their quest was in the balance. She needed to gain time to think. "I am Princess Tania Aurealis of the Immortal Realm of Faerie," she said, speaking loudly enough so that

Welsh's men could hear her. "My sister is Princess Rathina Aurealis, and our companion is Connor Estabrook, a good friend whose death the House of Aurealis would take hard, Master Welsh." She paused for a moment to let this information sink in. "We are on the business of King Oberon and Queen Titania of Faerie. You would do well to return us to our boat and let us go peacefully on our way."

There was incredulous silence for a moment and then laughter rang through the ship. Theodore Welsh grinned at her.

"A pretty fancy, maid," he scoffed. "But when I was a babe, my nanny told me that the Faerie folk were winged and very tiny indeed—and that they wore clothes made from leaves and petals."

"Then your nanny was mistaken, I'd say," replied Tania, trying to ignore the mockery of the sailors that surrounded them.

"Come, tell a more worthy tale," said Welsh. "Whence come you?" He looked her up and down. "Ha! I'd vow your father knows none of your errantry. What was it that brought you here? A wager? A game of truth or dare? A mishappenstance? Ill fortune and a capricious wind?"

"My sister is telling you the truth," called Rathina. "Are you so witless that you do not recognize royalty?"

Theodore Welsh drew his sword and took a step toward her, his face thunderous, the blade pointing at her throat. "By the howling of the Shee, if you speak one more word, woman, I'll give you a blow you'll not recover from!"

"Rathina—hush!" Tania said urgently.

Her sister glowered but said nothing more.

Welsh lowered his sword, turning slowly to look hard into Tania's face. The laughter of the sailors had stopped, and they were watchful now.

"Set her feet to the fire, commodore," called a rough voice. "That'll squeeze the truth out of her."

Welsh smiled as though the suggestion appealed to him. "I'll not be lied to nor mocked, maid," he said, his voice grinding as he brought his face close to hers. "Tell me the truth or I'll have you dance Lord Balor's hornpipe."

"I don't know what that means," Tania said quietly, holding his gaze.

"It's a merriment you'll not likely survive," he said. "A spar-strung rope looped tight about your neck and burning coals beneath your dangling feet. Then I'll have the truth from you, wench."

"You idiot! She *is* telling you the truth!" shouted Connor.

"Kill him!" Welsh called abruptly.

The sword was taken from Connor's neck and the sword arm lifted high. Connor shrank away from the coming blow, his eyes screwed shut.

"No!" Tania shouted. "I'll prove it to you! I'll prove we're from Faerie." An idea had come to her—but it would only work if she could get closer to Connor and Rathina.

"Hold!" Welsh held up his arm. The sailor became still, his sword ready to swing down at a word. The commodore stared at Tania. "If you can give me clear assurance that you come from out of the mythic east, then your worth to me will increase a hundred-fold," he said, his expression curious now but his voice still doubtful. "Lord Balor has sought for years beyond count for some proof that Immortal beings dwell beyond the eastern horizon where no one dare go." His gaze pierced her. "Do you tell me you are Immortal?"

Tania wasn't sure how to answer that. As half-Faerie, she had never really understood whether she was Immortal or not—and with the breaking of the covenant made between the King and the Divine Harper she could not be sure that anyone in Faerie still had that gift.

"How could I possibly prove that to you?" she replied cautiously.

"A sword through your heart might work the trick," said Welsh. "Dead, you be Mortal—alive, then 'tis likely otherwise!"

"No, that would only prove I'm not invulnerable," Tania said coolly. "I never said I was. Even a person with the gift of Immortality could be killed with a sword."

"A fair answer," said Welsh. "So—show me your proofs, and if all is as you say, then you will be most welcome guests in the fortress of Dorcha Tur. And if not—then the dungeons will keep you till your better sense prevails."

"Fine," said Tania. "But I'll need to be with Rathina and Connor. We have to be in physical contact with one another if the thing is going to work."

Theodore Welsh stepped back. "Heed me, maid," he said as she walked past him and across the deck toward Rathina and Connor. "Your boat is sunk, and I have men at my command who can shoot an arrow into a garfish at fifty yards. If you have thoughts of leaping overboard, dismiss them from your mind unless you wish to be food for crabs and urchins."

"That's not what I intend to do," Tania said. "Just let me hold hands with them, and I'll show you something that I'll bet you've never seen before."

"Release them, but keep a wary eye," Welsh called to his men.

Rathina stepped forward, rubbing her wrists now that she was free of the big man's grip. Connor was allowed to stand up, but there was still a drawn sword close by.

"What's the plan?" Connor asked under his breath.

Tania reached out her two hands to them. "Just hold on tight and you'll see," she said.

"Ahh!" Understanding dawned in Rathina's eyes. "Yes, sweet sister! Proof, indeed!"

Tania turned, standing between Connor and Rathina, holding them both by the hand. A faint smile crept up one side of Connor's face. Tania could sense that he'd caught on to her plan as well.

"Ready?" Tania said. "Move with me on three. One. Two. Three."

She sidestepped. But even as her foot was moving, she heard Connor's voice.

"Good-bye, commodore! Good-bye, you sucker!"

Someone gave a shout, and she felt Connor's hand wrenched out of hers.

Then the ship was gone and there was only dark air beneath her feet.

Part Two:

Beyond the Shores of Faerie

Tania knifed down into water that was so cold it tore the breath out of her lungs. She floundered, her head under the surface, her dress billowing up around her. She could still feel Rathina's hand in hers, the nails digging into her skin.

She kicked out, her lungs already hurting. Her face burst up into dark air. She sucked in a lungful of air and sank again, swallowing water. Panicking, she lost her grip on her sister. She struggled upward again. She was aware of her dress tenting up. It helped keep her afloat, but it made it hard to swim, great wet swaths of cloth rising like the mantle of a jellyfish all around her. Tania knew the thick material would soon become waterlogged and heavy. But at least they were not also wearing their cloaks—that added weight might have sent them both to the bottom.

She heard splashing and coughing close by.

"Rathina?"

"Yes. Is Connor with you?"

"No!" Tania cried, staring desperately around. The fog was gone and the stars were pinpoints in a black void far above the fretful waves. His hand had been ripped out of hers just as she was passing between the worlds. He must still be on the black ship. "I lost him."

"Tania!" Rathina's voice was shocked.

"I couldn't help it." Tania coughed, spitting out water. "We have to go back for him. I have to get back!"

"No, that were madness!" Rathina gasped.

Now that the water was out of her eyes, Tania could see her sister only a few feet away, her dress doming up on the surging sea.

"We can't just leave him there," Tania said.

"If you returned, how would you scale the sides of the ship?" called Rathina. "How would you save him? And what if you entered Faerie where the ship now lies? 'Twould be the death of you, for sure!" She fought down her dress and swam closer.

Tania had not thought of that. What would happen to her if she materialized in Faerie in exactly the same space as some other object? The image of herself emerging halfway through the hull of the ship was a terrifying one.

Tania kicked hard and turned, looking for land across the rise and fall of the bitter, oily waves. "We should get ashore," she called. "Try to find him then . . ."

"Indeed we should," said Rathina, "and with

utmost dispatch, Tania—ere our strength fades. Spirits of grace but I'd fare better without the encumbrance of this dress!"

Tania knew exactly what she meant—and the sea was deathly cold. They would need all their strength and endurance to survive.

A fluke of icy water splashed in her face; Rathina was swimming toward the low-lying dark spit of land, her arms cutting through the water, her feet kicking froth. Tania leaned forward, squashing down the plump of her dress, working to swim with her.

Soon they were swimming side-by-side—and in the distance Tania could see a mass of lights. A town! A seaside town lit by electricity!

She swam on with renewed energy.

"I'd shed this dress," she heard Rathina say, panting, "but I'd not make my entrance . . . in the Mortal World . . . dressed in nought . . . but my shift. . . . "

Tania's dress was now dragging at her, too, slowing her down, trying to drown her.

But the light-strewn shore was coming closer with every stroke. The long waves were higher now, crested with white foam, pressing inward, lifting them and throwing them forward. They would make it before their strength gave out.

Tania felt something hard under her foot. A rock. She pressed down, hoping for a firm hold, but her foot slipped away and her head went under for a moment. She came up spluttering and spitting brine.

Now the swell and roll of the sea began to work

against them. There were white breakers all around, and Tania's ears were filled with the smash of waves crashing onto a shoreline of great shining black rocks.

We'll never get ashore. We're going to die here.

She heard Rathina shouting in fury as she fought against a beating wave. Black water leaped skyward, resembling a snow-capped mountain. For a few moments her sister vanished into the turbulent night.

"Rathina!"

But as the wave broke and churned, Tania felt herself caught in its undertow. Her knee struck rock. She gasped with the pain, and her mouth filled with water. Her dress pulled at her, trying to keep her head under the surface. Trying to drown her.

Feet slipping on rock.

Fingers on a hard slimy surface.

Torn away.

Battling to keep afloat.

The crash and batter of surf.

And then a sloping surface that came punching up into her stomach from the depths. Foam all around her. Coughing and choking. She managed to keep a grip on the rock. Managed to find a toehold.

The waves were smashing and sucking, her clothes clinging to her body. Panting for breath, blinded by foam, she crawled over the rock with the ocean hissing in her ears.

She was ashore, on her hands and knees.

Rathina!

She heard breathless laughter from close by. The wild laughter of someone who has stood between the jaws of death and leaped clear.

Tania got to her knees. Rathina was lying on her back not two yards away, with her arms spread out and her feet in the foam. Her face was veiled by black ribbons of hair, her chest rising and falling as she gasped.

Tania crawled over to her and knelt, pulling the thick strands of Rathina's hair off her face. Their eyes met, and Tania threw her arms around her sister and held her while the sea churned below them.

Tania clambered over the huge rocks. A concrete wall cut across the night—high but not too high to scale. And beyond the wall? She had no idea. A town, she assumed—the town whose lights she had seen from the sea.

Rathina was at her side, laboring over the knuckled boulders. Despite the burden of their saturated clothing they managed to climb the wall without too much trouble.

Tania stood on top of the wall, her arms around her body, shivering in the chilly night, the wet folds of her dress glued to her back and legs. Directly ahead of them was a curving white path that circled an area of bare earth. Beyond that she could see a patch of mowed grass and a soccer field. Beyond those a large white building blazing with lights—and behind the building a town.

A soccer field. How strange and how ordinary. How . . . *Mortal.*

"Do you know this place, Tania?" asked Rathina, her shoulders hunched to her ears as she peered into the distance.

"No—I've never been to Ireland." She frowned. "I'm assuming this *is* Ireland, of course." They were definitely back in the Mortal World but *where* in the Mortal World? She stepped down off the wall and held her arm out to her sister, her heart aching that she had to return to Faerie so quickly. "Take my hand; we have to get back and find out what happened to Connor."

Rathina stood at her side and they laced fingers.

Tania concentrated and took the forward side step—into a lightless world. They found themselves standing on a sandy beach, under the Faerie stars.

Tania could hear the waves roaring and crashing at her back. She could faintly see the swelling ocean, and she was aware of a rugged coastline stretching bleakly in either direction.

There were no buildings. No glimmer of earthly light. No trace of living beings.

There was a cold, biting wind.

"So, sister?" Rathina muttered. "Whither now?"

"Welsh mentioned a fortress. . . ." Tania racked her memory. "Dorcha Tur, he called it. They'll take Connor there."

"And how do we find this place?" asked Rathina.

Tania frowned at her: Rathina's voice was uncharacteristically flat and lifeless. "We walk till we come to a village . . . or a farmhouse . . . or *whatever*," she said. "Then we ask."

Rathina looked at her. " 'Tis madness to wander the night thus. And what if the folk we encounter are as hospitable as Master Welsh? With a sword in my hand I'll face up to any brigand or marauder, but we are weaponless on a strange shore and I would fain seek a place to spend a warm night before we essay an assault on a fortress." She paused. "I feel sore in need of rest, Tania. I am weary to the bone—more weary than I can well explain."

Tania nodded. "I know; I can feel it, too. I think part of it is the Gildensleep: It's draining us all the time. I could crash out right this moment if someone put a bed in front of me."

"Then why not . . . *crash out*?" Rathina suggested. "Take us back to the Mortal World, Tania. We have no foes there, nothing to fear. Let us seek a warm fire and a downy bed for the night. Do they not have inns? Do they not welcome wretched travelers?"

"Wretched travelers with credit cards, maybe," Tania said. She stared into the night till her eyes ached. "What about Connor?" she muttered.

"He is a resourceful and keen-witted lad," Rathina said reassuringly. "We'd be of little help to him tonight, weak as we are. We will fare better in the morning, and if he is not dead, I have faith that we will find him!"

Tania gave Rathina a horrified look. "*Dead?*"

"I do not say he *is* dead, and I do not think it,"

Rathina said calmly. "On the morrow we shall return to Alba and seek Dorcha Tur by the light of the sun. And we shall effect such a daring rescue that the heads of his guards will spin like tops while we leap away from them o'er the hills to Tirnanog!"

Tania smiled wearily. "Yes," she said. "You're right. Of course you are. We should go back. Money's going to be a problem—but I'm sure someone will take pity on us."

Tania took Rathina's cold hand once more and sidestepped them back into the Mortal World.

Here the sea sounded less fierce and somehow the stars seemed to be farther away—smaller, dimmer, less radiant. Less bewitching.

They headed out across the cropped grass toward the big white building. Tania hoped it might be a hotel. They would have a telephone. Surely she would be able to convince the people to let her phone home—reverse the charges, whatever. Then she could speak to her mother and find out how her dad was doing. And her mum could give the people her credit card number so the two of them could have a meal and a room for the night.

Yes. That was a plan. That was a good plan.

They had crossed the green and were skirting the soccer field prior to crossing the road to the hotel, when a man appeared in front of them, stepping out from the darkness.

"Well, now," he said with a broad white smile. "Is it two selkies I see, come dripping from the ocean?"

The smile widened. "It's lucky for you that I chose this place to kick my heels tonight, for you could've come ashore anywhere from Dun Laoghaire to Bray Head, and then I'd have had the devil of a job tracking you down!"

XII

Tania gazed at the man in astonishment. He was a little shorter than her, stocky, with long black hair hanging loose to his shoulders. He had compelling dark eyes under thick brows and a wide-flaring beaky nose. His smile stretched broadly, creasing his olive cheeks. He was dressed in a loose white shirt that shimmered like silk, and black trousers that ended with slightly grubby bare feet.

He stood watching them with his bright, deep eyes, hands resting on his hips.

"Do you know us?" Tania asked at last while Rathina looked on with suspicious eyes.

"I do not," said the man, speaking in a soft, lilting Irish accent. "But I was expecting you."

"What do you mean?" Tania asked.

"My name is Michael," the man replied. "I do not know you fine ladies, but I had a feeling, an inkling, that if I came to this place on this night, I would meet someone who would benefit from my help." He bowed slightly. "And if you'll follow me now, I'll take you somewhere to dry yourselves off and maybe get a bite to eat." He raised an eyebrow. "Now, does that sound promising, or shall I be on my way and leave you fine ladies to drip and to shiver?"

Rathina frowned at him. "Do you *not* know us, sirrah?" she demanded. "Are you in the pay of Lord Balor? Have you followed us between the worlds? If you mean to lead us to our doom, beware, for you'll not live to profit from it, I swear that to you on the sacred stars of Faerie!"

Michael seemed startled by Rathina's ferocity. "I don't know any Lord Balors—there's none living in Dalkey village that I've ever heard of, and if there were, they'd want nothing to do with a peripatetic poet like myself."

Rathina turned to Tania. "Is the fellow moonstruck or does he dissemble, do you think?"

Tania shook her head. "I don't know." She turned to him. He had not shown any surprise at the mention of Faerie nor at Rathina's mode of speech, which should have been puzzling in itself. But she sensed that he was not an enemy—that he meant them no harm. "Who are you?" she asked him again.

"Michael Corr Mahone, or Mikey the Heron, as some would have it," he replied. "And I'm telling you no lies; on my mother's grave I'm not."

"You are then *Mortal*?" asked Rathina.

"Very Mortal," said Michael in obvious surprise. "All I'm offering is a warm place to rest and maybe a song or two."

"You're a singer?" Tania asked. "A musician?"

Michael rested the flat of his hand against his heart. "For my sins I am," he said. "Currently resident at the Iron Stone Tavern, Coliemore Road, Dalkey." He pointed away. "Will you be coming or not?"

Tania looked at Rathina. "Do you sense the Dark Arts about him?"

"Not a jot," Rathina said.

"Then I think we will go with you," Tania said to him. The strange man had her perplexed, but every instinct in her said that she could trust him—that he was truly here to help them.

"Would you tell me your names?" he asked, his eyes twinkling now. "And the story of how you came to be here, all alone and soaked through to the skin like mermaids caught up in a trawl net?"

"My name is Tania—and this is my sister Rathina." Tania chewed her lip. "Although as to how we got here . . . that's a bit of a long story, and I don't think you'd believe us anyway."

"Oh, don't be so sure," said Michael, walking away and gesturing for them to follow. "I'm as gullible as an oyster on the halfshell. But you'd best talk fast; it's only a short walk to the Iron Stone and I've a friend waiting there I should have met up with half an hour ago."

Rathina looked hard at Tania. She shrugged and

the pair of them fell into step behind Michael as he strode across the road and headed into the town.

Michael led them at a fast pace past the white building and along a road lined with tall trees. There were houses among the trees—set back from the road, fronted by high brick walls with wrought-iron gates.

Tania felt an unpleasant tingling in her body as they passed these gates—a reminder that she was now in a world where she was surrounded by the poison of metal: the deadly bane of Isenmort. She would need to be wary. The simple action of closing her hand around a metal doorknob would be enough to send a whiplash of pain up her arm.

Of all the people of Faerie only Rathina was immune to the bite of Isenmort—that was her gift, her royal birthright, as unique to her as were Tania's ability to walk between the worlds and Hopie's healing powers and Cordelia's rapport with animals.

The road curved and split in two. Michael took the left-hand fork, guiding them along a road of Victorian redbrick shops with ornate stonework and brightly colored frontages lit by old-fashioned cast-iron streetlamps. The shops were closed, but curtained windows glowed in many upper floors. A few cars were parked at the roadside, and a couple strolled arm in arm down the sidewalk, probably coming from the nearby restaurant.

Tania got the impression that this was one of those drowsy seaside towns that was rudely awoken in the summer months by day-trippers and tourists. But she also got the powerful feeling that under the surface an ancient, knowing heart beat strong and slow. Perhaps this was one of those rare places where the boundary between Faerie and the Mortal World was only tissue-paper thin. That might go some way to explaining why a Mortal man was given the insight to approach two Faerie princesses sodden from the sea.

They crossed the road behind Michael, and Tania saw a large double-fronted pub painted white with black piping along the cornices and decorative stone-work panels. Golden light flooded from its wide windows.

"The Iron Stone Tavern," Michael announced, turning to look at Tania. "The locals say it fell from the moon, if you can believe that. But there's nothing to fear here, ladies. And on a night like this there'll not be a tourist in sight!"

That's weird, the tourist thing. Like he read my mind!

He opened the door. Warmth and light spilled into the street, carrying with them the hubbub of cheerful voices and laughter and the savory smell of cooking.

They came into a long dark room full of people sitting on upholstered benches around the walls or perched on wooden stools at stone-topped wrought-iron tables and at the long dark-wood bar. The walls were paneled in polished mahogany that glowed in the golden light. The shelves behind the long bar were filled with bottles and gleaming glasses. Voices rang out to greet their entrance:

"Michael, my boy, where have you been?"

"Sure, and hasn't Rose been waiting for you near on an hour? You'll get your eye in a sling and that's a fact!"

"Where's your fiddle, Michael? We're gagging for a tune!"

No one seemed bothered by the fact that Michael was accompanied by two sopping-wet girls.

An elderly man sat at the bar, with long swept-back white hair and a grizzled beard. He scrutinized Tania and Rathina with brilliant blue eyes.

"And who are your companions, Michael?" he asked in a voice like ancient music. His crinkled eyes looked knowingly at Tania, as if he already understood who she was.

"Two waifs and strays," Michael replied. "In need of warmth and food." He called across the bar. "Ivan, do you have two mutton pies and two hot drinks for the young ladies?"

"That I do!" called the barkeeper. "Go and sit yourselves by the fire to dry. I'll be along shortly."

"I need a phone," Tania said. "I have to make a call."

"There's a pay phone at the end of the bar," Michael told her.

"Oh. I've no money."

"No problem." Michael smiled and pulled a handful of coins from his pocket. "I'll spring for a call to your mother."

Rathina scooped the coins out of his hand. Tania

was glad of her sister's quick thinking—tipped into her own hand, the metal coins would have burned her like hot coals.

As Michael led them off to the end of the bar, the old man spoke up. "We'll meet again, perhaps. One fine day . . . Stay safe till then."

"Yes, okay," Tania said. She turned to Michael. "How did you know I wanted to phone my mother?" she asked as she followed Rathina.

"Who else would a young lady need to phone but her ma?" Michael replied. "You'll be wanting to let her know you're all right."

"Yes," said Tania. "That's exactly it."

Curious but friendly eyes glanced at them as they passed. Tania felt neither self-conscious nor uncomfortable under their scrutiny, though she knew that she and Rathina must have made a strange sight, squelching as they walked along, seawater dripping from their gowns and wet hair glued to their skulls.

"I'll wait over there," Michael said, pointing to a huge stone fireplace that dominated the far wall.

The phone was fixed to the wall alongside the bar. Tania lifted the plastic receiver while Rathina fed coins into the slot and then pressed out the numbers as Tania recited them.

A short wait and then her mother's voice. "This is Mary Palmer's phone. Sorry I can't take your call right now. Please leave your number and I'll get back to you as soon as possible."

For a moment Tania had no idea what to say. She

choked with emotion at the sound of her mother's voice, then: "Mum, it's me. I'm just phoning to say I'm okay. I can't get home right now, but I'm fine. I'll call again when I have a chance. And . . . and . . . you and Dad had nothing to do with the illness. You know what I'm talking about. It was something else. Not you." She began to speak more rapidly now, afraid that the message time would run out before she finished. "I love you. I hope Dad is okay. Tell him I love him so much." She finished breathlessly, "I'll call again when I can."

Rathina was watching her. "Did she not wish to speak with you?"

"She was out. I left a message."

"How? With whom?"

"It doesn't matter." She put the phone down, careful not to touch the metal cradle. "I'll try again later."

At least she had been able to make *some* kind of contact with her parents. Perhaps her mother was at the hospital with her father. Perhaps that was why the cell phone was turned off.

They made their way to the fireplace. Stone seats jutted out on either side. Red and yellow flames danced over logs of sweet-smelling wood. To one side of the fireplace lay a wooden platform like a small stage, upon which rested a violin, a bent-necked stringed instrument that Tania recognized as a lute, and a shallow, wooden-framed hand drum.

Michael and a young woman sat together by the fire. The woman was dressed in a long dark skirt and a blouse of white silk and had long black hair plaited and tied with small cornflower blue ribbons. She turned as they approached, gazing at them with deep, thoughtful eyes.

"Hello there," she said, smiling darkly. "He found you, then."

"I did, that," said Michael. "Rose, this is Tania and Rathina. Tania and Rathina, this is my beloved gypsy runaway, Rose Maguire."

Room was made for Tania and Rathina up close to the fire. Tania soon saw the steam rising from her damp dress, and the heat of the leaping fire began to seep into her limbs.

No questions were asked, and Tania was glad of that. The landlord brought trays laden with fresh buttered bread and plates heaped high with slices of crusty pie from which the aroma of mutton and rich gravy arose. And there were tall frothing cups, too, brimming with hot chocolate laced with whipped cream.

Tania had not realized how famished she was until she tasted the tender mutton in her mouth. The cheerful sounds of the pub formed a backdrop to their meal. She thought of Connor, wondering fearfully where he was, hoping he was not being harmed. Rose and Michael sat hand-in-hand, gazing into the fire. Tania felt a pang as she remembered similar times with Edric.

"And now for song," said Michael once Tania and Rathina had finished. He stepped onto the stage. Eyes turned toward him as he picked up the fiddle and plucked the strings to check the tuning.

Rose stood at his side, the bodhran drum like a shield on her arm, the double-headed beater in her other hand.

"Good evening to you, lovers of good evenings," Michael announced. He gestured toward Tania. "Will you give a warm welcome, please, on the lyrical lute—my new friend Tania."

Tania stared at him in surprise and consternation.

"No, I can't . . ." she said.

"Yes, you *can*." Rose smiled.

Rathina leaned across the fire. "Play with them, in memory of Zara," she said. "The lute was ever your finest instrument."

"But I hardly remember," Tania whispered.

"You will," Rathina reassured her. "Play!"

Uneasily Tania turned and picked up the lute, settling its round belly in her lap.

Keep it simple. Give it a few bars to work out the key—then see how it goes. And be ready to make a dash for the toilets if you screw up.

Michael began to bow the fiddle, spinning out a slow, mournful melody, accompanied by the deep rhythmic beat of Rose's drum.

> *"In a land as far as the farthest star, yet as near*
> *as candlelight*
> *Strange music plays through a twilight glade,*
> *between the daytime and the night*
> *A mound there stands with ramparts grand, to*
> *encompass the rowan ring*

Where the horsemen nine, beyond all time, pay
homage to the Faerie Queen . . ."

Tania's heart caught in her throat—was he really singing about her mother? How extraordinary! She held down the strings of the lute and plucked tentatively. The mellow notes sang out. She felt for the melody, finding it quickly, her fingers moving almost of their own accord. A stream of notes hung in the air, dancing among the sonorous lyric, cascading into the gaps between lines, chiming like silver bells. Rose's high, clear voice joined in harmony to the song.

"Dressed in the colors of autumn and summer,
they kneel at her woodland throne
Three clad in tunics as red as the blood, three in
the poison green
Three in a yellow as rich as ripe corn, and each
with a steed of sorcery born
Enchanted forever, in fealty unending, unable
to seek their release

"An apple tree grows on the Faerie Queen's hill
that bears the fruit so round
Could they but pluck from the spreading branch,
three by three, three by three
An apple as red as the blood, and an apple
adorned in the poisonous green
And another as yellow as ripening corn, then
they would cast off

The Faerie Queen's bonds, and great lords
again would they be.

"But this doom she has deemed, her knights to
enslave, their land beneath her sway
They must pluck not the fruit, not suffer another
by magic, nor stealth
To come nigh the tree, but they bring them to
death
And none can approach, save she whose step is
an airy dance
And she who can thwart the Faerie Queen's will
With her true love at her side.

"In a land as far as the farthest star, yet as near
as candle's gleam
Strange music plays in a twilight glade, twixt
the waking world and a dream
A mound there stands with ramparts grand,
their laughter's the wind in the trees
Where horsemen nine, beyond all time, pay hom-
age to the Faerie Queen . . ."

* * *

"Sleepers, awaken!"

Tania opened her eyes. She was resting against the stone surround of the fireplace. Rose was leaning over her and smiling.

"It is time to go now," she said.

Tania gasped, sitting up and rubbing her eyes,

stiff from having slept so awkwardly. "Oh, I'm sorry!" She looked around. The pub was deserted now and the lights were low. On the other side of the hearth Michael was gently shaking Rathina into wakefulness.

"How long was I asleep?" Tania asked. She could remember little of the evening beyond that first haunting song. She had put down her lute and stepped from the stage. Then there had been another song, slow and soothing. And then it was as if a warm dark veil had come down over her mind, peaceful and soothing.

"A couple of hours, that's all," said Rose. "You're dry now, and warm—and you must be on your way. Michael and I will guide you to the edge of town—but from there you'll need to go on alone."

Tania looked into her fathomless black eyes. "Who are you?" she asked. "You seem to know things about us but . . . how *can* you? Are you from Faerie? Were you sent here to help us?"

"Were we sent?" Rose murmured. "I can't answer that—I have a mind filled with long winding corridors and many closed doors." She frowned. "As have you, I think, Tania."

"Are you all ready and set?" Michael asked, looking bright-eyed from Rathina to Tania.

"We are," said Rathina.

They made their way between the empty tables and stools, Tania careful not to brush against the black cast iron. The landlord stood at the open door.

"Will you be back tomorrow evening?" he asked

Michael as he stepped out into the night.

"That's my plan, unless events overtake me," Michael called.

The door closed behind them and the bolt was thrown with a sharp clack.

Only a few windows showed lights now, and the long peace of the night hung over the town. Rathina walked alongside Michael, her hands clasped behind her back, her head bowed. Tania and Rose came along behind.

"You sing a merry air, Master Michael," Rathina said. "But the words of that song where you spoke of the Faerie Queen—there was little sense in them, you know. Our mother would never enslave men to do her bidding nor hold their land in thrall." She turned to look at him. "And I have traveled Faerie all o'er, yet I have never seen an apple tree that bears fruit of yellow, green, and red."

"Well, songs are not always what they seem, Rathina," he said, smiling. "And maybe that one was about a different Faerie Queen?"

"There is no other," Rathina said solemnly.

"Maybe so," Michael replied. "If we had more time together, you could teach me the truth of things, and I could write some new verses. Maybe if we meet again I could learn at your knee?"

"A worthy aim, forsooth," said Rathina. "But tell me, where do you take us and what do you know of our quest?"

"I don't know anything at all," said Michael. "But

I'm taking you to Ballinclea Heights, if the name means something to you, which I doubt." He gazed into the sky, his eyes narrowing. "Something urges me on to that place—I have the strong sense that you need to be there."

"You speak in riddles, Master Michael," said Rathina.

"I know." Michael sighed. "I wish I understood more."

"I have something for you," Rose said to Tania. She pulled the something from a pocket or fold of her skirt. "Take it—you'll find it useful."

Rose dropped a leaf into her palm. A single diamond-shaped leaf, smooth and shiny.

"Thank you," Tania said, puzzled.

"It's called *doras oscail*," said Rose. "It has a virtue so that no door can remain closed against it." Her black eyes gleamed cannily. "I think it'll be useful where you're heading."

"Yes, thank you." Tania said. It was becoming clearer and clearer to her that these were not normal Mortals she and Rathina had met by chance. All Faerie drowsed under the Gildensleep, so surely they could not have come out of the east. But if not of Faerie—then where?

She looked keenly into Rose's face and a thought struck her. "Are you the Dream Weaver?" she asked.

"No, I think not." There was something in Rose's voice that stopped Tania asking more. She closed her fingers carefully over the leaf.

They came to a road that flanked a great flat-topped hill skirted with trees and shrubs and rising in folds of reddish earth and white rock high into the sky.

Michael pointed up the pathless hill. “That’s your way,” he said. “Good luck to the both of you—and I hope you find your friend.”

He turned, his arm around Rose’s shoulders, and the two of them moved quickly away and vanished into the trees.

“Thank you!” Tania called.

“Well, now,” mused Rathina, her fists on her hips. “What do you make of that coil, sweet sister?”

“I have no idea,” Tania said. “But I think we can trust them.” She held out her arm. “Take my hand,” she said. “I’ve got a feeling we’re near Dorcha Tur.”

Hand-in-hand they stepped forward. The world rippled and wavered.

The hill was much higher now, rearing to twice its previous height. A great black castle shimmered into being on the top.

They had come to the fortress of Dorcha Tur.

"I like not the smell of this place, sister; it reeks of malevolence."

They were in a stone corridor somewhere within the thick walls of the fortress. Wall-hung torches flared with a ruddy light, staining the low roof black with soot. So far they had not encountered any of the inhabitants, but a sense of menace followed them like an invisible mist.

The leathery little leaf had done all that Rose had promised. Their way in through the rear walls had been via a narrow postern door to one side of the formidable main gates. The door had no handle or lock on the outside. But the moment that Tania had touched the leaf to the heavy wooden panels, it had swung silently outward.

"A curious thing indeed for a Mortal woman to give you," Rathina had said, eyeing the leaf dubiously. "If the two minstrels are indeed of Mortal stock."

"My thoughts exactly," Tania had replied.

The open door had revealed a low, cramped black tunnel that burrowed in under the wall. Coming out of the tunnel, they had slipped past a gatehouse, lantern-lit and murmurous with low voices. Hugging a flanking wall, they found stone steps that led to a second door.

The *doras oscail* worked its magic again, and now they were within the castle keep and flitting soft-footed along a stonewalled corridor lined with heavy wooden doors. They came across black arches every now and then revealing winding stone stairways leading up and down. They encountered no one, although Tania had the strong sense that the castle housed many people.

"Sister, stop," Rathina said, her hand on Tania's arm. "The fortress is huge—we could waste a night and a day searching and not find our quarry." She frowned. "Are we certain that this is the castle of which the man Welsh spoke? Is Master Connor even here?"

Tania looked at her. "Someone or something sent Michael and Rose to meet us," she said. "There are only two reasons for that: either to help us or to cause us problems. Which do you think it is?"

"I could sense no falsehoods in them," Rathina replied. "I think they wished us well."

"Then we have to believe that this is Lord Balor's castle and that Connor is being held here. The only question now is—*where*."

"Had we weapons, we might snatch one of the denizens of this ugly furuncle and seek an answer from them at sword point." Rathina sighed heavily. "Or if Eden were with us, she'd use her Arts to sniff the boy out—and we'd be away with him in a ball of fire ere Lord Balor climbed into his britches!"

"Maybe Eden *can* help us," Tania said. "Come with me. I've got an idea." She ran quickly to the nearest door and pressed her ear to the panels. Gesturing for her sister to be quiet, she listened intently.

There was no sound from within. She touched the leaf to the door and it swung into darkness. Rathina lifted a torch from its wall sconce and they entered the room. It was small and bleak, with a narrow, deep window and six bare bed frames. A dormitory of some kind, Tania thought—but disused, judging from the broken crockery on the floor and the musty smell and the thick dust that lay over all.

She closed the door behind them. "Help me," she said to Rathina. "Hold my hand. I'm going to try to make contact with Eden."

She closed her eyes and took Rathina's hand and conjured Eden's face in her mind. A long face, solemn-eyed, careworn, framed with flowing white hair.

Yellow lights flickered behind Tania's closed eyelids.

"Eden?" A name hardly breathed.

The image that Tania had of her sister went white. From far away it seemed, a shred of darkness rushed forward. Suddenly it filled the white frame and it was Eden's face, haggard with effort and care, shadowed deep beneath the eyes. The blue eyes locked on to Tania.

"Sister." The voice was soft but clear. *"What is it? Quickly, now. I cannot hold this for long. My strength is stretched thin."*

"We need weapons," Tania said, her lips moving but her voice only sounding in her head. *"And we've lost Connor. Can you help us find him?"*

"I will try." Eden's hand rose and she moved an outstretched finger toward Tania. There was a sharp clattering at Tania's feet, and she felt an icy pain in her head—and then she saw behind her eyes an image of Connor strapped by leather bonds to a tilted wooden board in a deep, dark chamber in the bowels of the castle.

"Thank you, thank you." Tania gasped, wincing from the pain in her head. *"How is the Gildensleep working? Are you . . . ?"*

But the image of Eden fizzed out like a spent candle flame and there was only darkness behind Tania's eyes.

"By the spirits of justice and fate," said Rathina, pulling her hand from Tania's and staring down at the boards between them. "This is all I would have wished and more."

Two swords lay on the floor. One was a Faerie sword, its blade a keen-edged length of pure shining crystal; the other was of Isenmort—Rathina's own sword, the sword that she had picked up on the battlefield of Salisoc Heath, and whose bitter blade she had plunged through the body of her true love, the treacherous Gabriel Drake.

"And I was shown where Connor is being held," said Tania. "I can see the way there clear as anything."

Rathina stooped and picked up the swords, handing the crystal blade to Tania and stepping back to practice thrusts and parries on shadows. "Then let's to him, sweet sister," said Rathina, her voice animated now for the first time since they'd come ashore. "And let's teach manners to a lord whose minions waylay innocent folk upon the high seas."

It was the strangest sensation. Eden seemed to have planted in Tania's brain a route through the maze of the castle's corridors and winding stair towers so that she instinctively knew which turn to take, which stairs to descend—and also where to find a shadowy corner to hide when people were near.

The mystic intuition led them to a curious room in the bowels of the castle. Its ceiling was low and domed, and a raised octagonal platform made of mortared stones occupied most of the space. Set at regular intervals into the chest-high platform were deep, slanting holes or slots. The room itself was unlit, but jutting spokes of torchlight fingered up from the holes, hazing the air and giving the room an eerie, otherworldly feel.

"What manner of place is this?" murmured Rathina. "My skin crawls to be here. There is some great evil close by."

"Shh!" hissed Tania. She could hear a voice booming from beneath them. She leaned over one of the slots and found herself staring down into a great, wide, torchlit chamber. Rathina moved to the next spy-hole and leaned forward.

The lower end of the peephole flared out so that most of the chamber was visible. The stone floor was maybe twenty feet below, and it took Tania only a moment to realize into what kind of room she was staring.

It was a torture chamber.

Hideous instruments and devices and machines filled the cavernous room—contraptions whose use Tania didn't even dare think about. But some items she recognized: a rack, a table loaded with sharp implements, a stone griddle held by blackened ropes above a brazier of burning coals.

And in the center of the room, bound onto a tilted table of scarred and punctured wood, was Connor, surrounded by smoking braziers, stripped to the waist, his face and body running with sweat. Tania's heart pounded at the sight of him, the blood suddenly cold in her veins. She clutched at the stonework lip of the peephole.

Tania lifted her head and saw Rathina staring wide-eyed at her.

"Did I not say this place reeked of malevolence?" Rathina hissed.

Tania nodded silently and looked down again. Connor *seemed* unhurt, so far as she could tell, save for a stain of dried blood at the corner of his mouth. But he looked exhausted and terrified. His eyes, Tania realized, were fixed on something just out of her range of vision.

And the something had a voice: the same booming voice she'd heard earlier. "An immortal creature such as yourself can have no idea of the burden of death," it said. "In youth the grave seems impossibly distant. But the years pass, ever more fleet, and always the specter of oblivion looms larger."

The speaker came into view, and Tania caught her breath. He was a tall, broad-shouldered man clad in dark leathers, his hair grizzled, curling on his shoulders, his face smooth-shaven but fissured like a crag. A long brown leather cloak dragged across the floor behind him, and his boots rang on the stone.

It was not the man that held Tania's gaze but the creature that walked with clicking claws at his side. It was a huge white lizard, its legs splayed, body low to the ground like a crocodile's. But it did not have the gnarled hide of a crocodile; its shining skin was smooth, scaled and ribbed like a fish. Its long, broad tail whipped slowly back and forth as it paced, its head wedge-shaped with protruding yellow eyes and with a yellow forked tongue that flicked in and out between fanged jaws.

A studded collar was bound around the creature's thick neck, and from the collar extended a chain that was caught and held in the man's right fist. And now came the final shock: The man seemed to be wearing a *metal* gauntlet. Tania felt certain that the glove, chain, and collar were all made of Isenmort!

Metal? How? There is *no metal in this world!*

Connor's despairing voice interrupted Tania's thoughts. "For the last time, I'm not Immortal," he groaned. "Yes, I sailed with Tania and Rathina from Faerie—but I'm not one of them. I'm an ordinary human being from a completely different world."

"Enough of this," said the man. "Do you think me a fool? Do you seek to gull me with talk of other worlds? There is no other world than this."

"You're wrong," Connor said. The man glared and the lizard growled with a noise like fingernails scraping down slate. "Lord Balor, I'm not disrespecting you," Connor pleaded. "I understand it's hard to believe—I wouldn't have believed it myself a few days ago—but I'm telling you the truth. I'm not Immortal and I don't know the secret of Immortality." He looked fearfully around the room. "You've shown me what these things can do to me—I get it! But I can't tell you stuff I don't know."

"You would stand amazed at the things I can glean from an unwilling guest," Lord Balor said, now slowly circling the wooden board, the creature pacing always at his side. He stopped in front of Connor, lifting the hand that held the chain—the hand in the iron gauntlet. "Do you know what this is, boy?" he croaked. "This is iron: the substance you Immortal folk know as Isenmort, I believe. I know of your fear of Isenmort. I know that the Immortal folk dread its touch as deeply as do the people of Alba." He moved closer, the iron hand raised above Connor, the fingers spread. "Only I, of all men and women born in this world, can endure the touch of iron! Only I have that power!"

No. You're wrong, thought Tania, glancing at her sister. *Rathina has the same gift.* But how had Lord Balor obtained it?

She saw that the iron chain was attached to the wrist of the gauntlet by a metal loop. The lizard lifted its head and growled.

"Would you know how I came by this adornment, boy?" asked Lord Balor. "It was sixty years ago now that one of my captains found an open boat upon the sea—a boat that came from the dark islands of the south, from the sinister land of Lyonesse." Tania felt herself start at the mention of the Sorcerer King's homeland. "There was a magician aboard, a warlock sent to spy on Faerie and to learn the whereabouts of their captive King. But his ship was blown off course and he found himself instead a prisoner in this room, half starved and near to death. He was unwilling to reveal his secrets—at first." He glanced around at the ugly devices that surrounded him.

"In the end he was eager to tell all to me," he continued. "So eager that he wished he had more secrets to reveal. He told me of Isenmort—of an alchemical substance not native to this Realm and how it was a great bane to all the living things of this world, even to the Immortals of the east. I wanted this bane for myself, and he helped me with conjurations and incantations. I paid a heavy price. I paid with my own flesh, my hand torn by dark magic from my arm, my blood boiling in my veins! The warlock of Lyonesse conjured *Isenmort* from the air and with fell flames seared this iron hand onto my bleeding wrist. It is with this hand and this chain and with the collar of *Isenmort* that I am able to bind the Great Salamander to my will." He lifted the iron hand high. "I, Balor of Dorcha Tur, am the only man in all the world who is able to bear iron and to wield iron, because this iron is welded forever to the stump of my right hand." His eyes blazed. "And now—you will tell me the truth or I shall set the iron to your flesh and you shall be burned to the bone!"

Connor turned his head away and gasped, writhing as the iron hand came down spread-fingered onto his chest.

The Great Salamander's tongue flicked. Lord Balor pressed down on Connor's breastbone. Tania held her breath.

Then Lord Balor drew his hand back, his voice uncertain. "It does not burn you!" he said. "How can this be?"

"I told you," Connor said, panting. "I don't come from this world. Now do you believe me?" His voice rose to a shout. "I come from London, England! The *real* world. I shouldn't even *be* on this planet!"

Balor stared at him for a long time. "Perhaps you are speaking the truth, boy," he said at last. "But if I cannot glean from you the secret of Immortality, then you are useless to me." The iron hand reached for Connor's throat.

Tania was about to shout—to make herself known

in the hope of preventing Balor from hurting Connor. But even as she drew in her breath, Connor cried out.

"The others are Immortal!" he shouted, straining his head away from Balor's hand. "The two girls. They're both Immortal. If you kill me, you'll never find out anything else about them." He was gasping now, his chest heaving. "Let me go and I'll find them for you. I promise. I'll bring them to you." His eyes were circular with hope and fear. "Believe me, I want to know the secret of Immortality as much as you do."

"Treacherous dog!" Rathina hissed, her hand grasping Tania's, her violent grip crushing her fingers.

But Tania did not think so. "No! He's playing for time," she whispered, pulling her hand from Rathina's. "He's faking it; I'm sure he is."

Lord Balor was leaning over the tilted board, his face close to Connor's, his iron hand gripping Connor's hair.

"Tell me this," he growled. "How did the two women evade my men? Commodore Welsh said they became invisible. Is that another of the powers of the Immortal folk? To become invisible at will?"

"No. No, not really," Connor said. "It's not quite like that. Tania has the power to . . . to move out of this world and . . . and back again. That's how they did it. That's how she brought me here in the first place."

"Why did you travel with them, boy?" Balor's voice

was a throaty growl. He stood erect and began to pace the floor, the Great Salamander moving sinuously at his side. "What was their purpose with you?"

"I don't know what they wanted me for," said Connor, a new confidence creeping now into his voice. "They didn't confide in me, but I think they trust me. Tania knows I can't get home without her—she'd never expect me to turn on her. Let me go and I promise I'll find a way to bring them to you. But I want something in exchange." Connor swallowed hard. "When you find the secret of Immortality, let me share it with you. That's all I ask. I can even help you worm it out of them. And then you can force Tania to take me home." His eyes shone with a cold light. "That way we both get what we want."

"Ha!" Balor's voice was a derisory explosion. The iron hand came slapping across Connor's face, wrenching his head sideways. Tania winced as he cried out in pain.

"I'll need no help," mocked Balor. "I know how to find their secret once I have them in my grasp." He stared fiercely at Connor's agonized face. "And I do not need to release you, boy. I need only wait for them to come slinking out of the night in search of you. Even with all their tricks of the senses, they'll not escape Dorcha Tur once they pass within its walls. My guards are warned and wary." He lifted his iron hand and balled it into a tight fist. "It is only a matter of time before I have them in my clutches."

Tania heard the sound of heavy footfalls. She

sprang upright, turning to the closed door. Rathina was at her side in an instant, her Isenmort sword at the ready.

As Tania watched, her heart hammering, she saw the door latch lifting.

Tania caught Rathina's wrist and dragged her into the deep shadows behind the raised stone octagon. They crouched there together, hardly daring to breathe, listening as the door was pushed open.

"They are not here," declared a guttural voice.

"How can we know that for sure?" asked another. "Commodore Welsh says they have the power of invisibility."

"Aye," mocked the first voice, "and I am King of all the Faeries! The women tricked him, that's all!"

The second voice became low. "Then you do not believe in the powers of the Immortal folk from across the sea?"

"Speak such thoughts only in whispers," murmured the first. "But I believe the testimony of my own eyes, Dalbach. I would speak this to no other, but Lord Balor is fuddled in his wits if he truly thinks there are Immortal beings beyond the eastern horizon."

The second voice sounded uneasy now. "You say our lord is mad, then?"

"I say he fears death above all things," said the first. "He has walked this world one hundred and fifteen years, and he knows the span of his life is drawing to its close. All things has he mastered, man and beast, land and sea—but this one thing eludes him: how to master death itself!"

"But if there be no Faerie folk, whence came the iron? Answer me that, friend Laragh."

"I cannot," said Laragh. "But we need look not to the distant east for unnatural happenstances—is there not enchantment enough beyond the River Blackwater? Go seek out the Witch Queen of Erin before you give mind to the Faerie stories of the east. Come, there are many more chambers and arteries to search this night ere we can take to our beds!"

Tania heard the sound of boots clattering on the stones, then the thud and click of the door closing.

"Well, now," said Rathina, grinning in the light from the spy-hole. "So, we are but chimera? Flibbertigibbets of the mind, forsooth. It will work in our favor that they do not think us real."

"Yes, it will," said Tania. "We need to find a way to get Connor away from that crazy lord down there." Tania had been vaguely aware of the low rumble of Balor's voice running under the conversation between the two soldiers, but now as she leaned in to look through one of the spy-holes again, the deadly lower chamber was silent. Connor seemed to be alone, his head tipped exhaustedly to one side, his features contorted in fear and discomfort.

Tania longed to call down to him, to let him know they were close by. But she didn't dare; Balor might still be within earshot.

Tania closed her eyes. *"Eden? I can see him—but I don't know how to reach him. Help me, please?"*

There was no response. Either Eden's power was spent or the eye of her mind was concentrated elsewhere. Either way Tania and Rathina were alone.

"We search for stairways leading down," Tania decided. "Okay?"

"And we should avoid all contact with these people," added Rathina. "We fight only if we must."

Tania nodded. It wasn't only the overwhelming odds that worried her; it was the thought of having to bring her blade down on living people. She had fought without qualms the undead soldiers of Lyonesse and she had lifted her blade against their monstrous King—but she had never had to use a sword against ordinary men.

They slipped silently out of the viewing gallery, swords in hand, ears straining for the slightest sound as they crept along the corridor. The castle was on alert. Tania was reconciled to fighting if they had to—but she clung to the hope that they might make their rescue and escape without bloodshed.

A corkscrew stair took them deeper. The air was dank and stale in these lower regions, the torches fewer and farther apart. White mildew patched the stones, and there was a foul smell.

Footsteps!

Tania pressed Rathina into an alcove. A troop of armed men stamped past, their boots ringing and echoing.

They moved out of cover, gliding silently along a leftward spur of the corridor. It ended in a single heavy door, bolted and barred and secured with a great stone lock.

"I think this is it," Tania whispered, glancing back along the dark slot of the corridor. "I think it must be."

"A fine place for a snare," Rathina murmured, pointing her sword back along the way they had come. "A single way in—and we two caught like butterflies in the killing jar if our enemies come upon us."

"I can't help that," said Tania. She drew the almond-shaped leaf from a fold of her bodice and touched it to the door. The bars lifted. The bolts drew themselves back. There was the dry scrape of stone on stone—and the door swung ponderously inward.

Tania ran into the high, circular chamber. Connor was there—his round eyes amazed as he stared at her. There was a raw, red welt on his cheek where the iron hand had struck him.

"Thank god!" he choked, relief flooding his face. "I thought . . . I . . ."

"It's okay," Tania said, moving quickly between the ghastly instruments of torture. His fingers strained for her against the leather thong. She took his hand in hers. It was cold and clammy. "I'm so sorry," she said. "I lost hold of you. I couldn't get back."

"There's a guy here—a crazy guy," said Connor, gasping. "He knows you're coming for me."

"Yes, I know."

Rathina was at Connor's side now. She began to saw at his bonds with her sword. Tania sliced through the leather thongs at Connor's wrist, supporting him as he slumped forward.

"Have they used you ill, Master Connor?" Rathina asked, bringing her shoulder up under his arm. "Can you walk?"

"They smacked me in the mouth on the ship to try to get me to tell them where you'd gone," Connor said breathlessly. "But apart from threatening me with some of the nasty stuff in here, they haven't hurt me too much." He hunkered down, taking deep breaths and rubbing his legs. "So stiff!" he said. "Give me a moment to get the blood flowing again."

Rathina picked up his shirt and cloak from where they lay discarded on the floor. He nodded his thanks and began to dress himself, grimacing as he bent his numbed limbs. Rathina glanced apprehensively toward the open door. "I'd be out of this place as swift as may be," she said. " 'Tis a bag to catch a woodcock!"

"Rathina's right," said Tania. "It's too dangerous in here. Do you know where Balor went?"

"No." Connor stared at her, buttoning his shirt. "He's got an iron hand, Tania, and he's got this huge lizard-thing he keeps on a chain. A metal chain!"

"Yes, I know." She pointed upward. In the high dome of the ceiling the peepholes showed as dark, gaping mouths. "There's a room up there for people to watch what goes on in here."

"Oh, nice. . . ." Connor shook his head. "It's totally medieval here," he said. "And not civilized medieval like Faerie—it's like blood-and-guts medieval."

Rathina ran to the door, leaning into the dark corridor, listening.

"I hear no one," she said. "But 'tis most strange. Why are there no guards? Why is Master Connor left alone? Are we lured here to our destruction?"

"Let's worry about that later," said Tania. "Connor? You okay now?"

"Yes. But I could use a shower."

"I don't think they have plumbing here," Tania said wryly.

"No. Neither do I."

They raced from the chamber, Tania pausing for a moment outside to close the door and shoot the bolts and lower the bars. Until the door was opened, no one would realize Connor was gone.

They ran along the corridors, Tania leading, Connor next, and Rathina bringing up the rear. At every corner and intersection Tania paused, listening. Several times they had close calls as small bands of men traversed a corridor ahead of them or were heard approaching.

"Do you know the way out of this warren?" Rathina

asked in a low voice while they waited at a junction for footsteps to fade.

"From the ground level we went down three sets of stairs to get to the torture chamber," said Tania. "If I've calculated it right, we should be back on ground level now. We just need to find an exit."

"And then get through the gates before we're caught," said Connor, his voice anxious. "Have you seen the size of those gates? There's no chance we could get them open without someone seeing us. And they have horses stabled here. Even if we get clear, they'll run us down in no time flat." He looked hopefully at Tania. "Unless you can get us out of here with your between-the-worlds trick?"

"I'm not doing that unless there's absolutely no other choice," Tania told him. "This hill is much higher here than it is in Ireland—I noticed that when we first climbed it. We'd appear in midair. The fall could break our necks."

"It's got to be the gates, then," said Connor.

They had come to a wide vestibule from which several corridors led. Tall arched doors stood on a stone threshold, and there were narrow window slits to either side.

"Hush!" said Rathina, lifting her hand. She tilted up her chin and sniffed the air. "I smell horses!" she said. " 'Tis a good smell. It reminds me of my own Maddalena. There are stables close or I'm no judge." She smiled. "Shall we ride? Such speed would aid us."

"Fine," said Connor. "But that still leaves the gates!"

"I can deal with the gates," said Tania. "We just have to get to them in one piece, that's all."

"To the stables, then," said Rathina.

Tania touched the leaf to the arched doors and they swung open. Connor stared at the doorway then looked questioningly at Tania.

"Long story," she said. "I'll explain later."

With Rathina now in the lead they came into a wide cobbled bailey over which mountainous stone walls reared. There were windows, but they were thin and dark. Rathina pointed silently, and they headed for a long range of buildings set up against the wall.

Tania pressed the leaf to a great square door. It swung out, releasing the scent of hay and oiled leather and the musk of horses.

The long stable room was unlit, and it was a few moments before Tania could make out the stalls.

"Can you smell their sweet breath?" murmured Rathina, walking forward over rustling straw. "A crime it is to trammel such creatures in so grim a citadel."

Tania saw her step up to a dark horse and gently fondle its head. "There, there, my lad," she crooned. "We'll do thee no harm. Fear not." She looked back at Connor and Tania. "I do not have my sister Cordelia's way with beasts, but I know horses. Master Connor, will you seek saddles and bridles? Tania, remain at the door. See that no one intrudes while we get ready."

Tania stared nervously out into the bleak night, her sword ready in her hand. She heard soft sounds behind her—the clatter of a hoof on stone, the snort of heavy breath, the slap and creak of leather, and the chink of crystal trappings.

The clack of hooves came up close behind her. Rathina was leading two horses, Connor a third. "Mount up, sister."

Tania climbed awkwardly into the saddle. She could feel the animal breathing beneath her. She twisted the reins through the fingers of her left hand, her sword steady in the right.

Is this crazy? Are we really going to be able to run the gates like this?

But what was the alternative? Even if they managed to escape Dorcha Tur by using that same postern door, they would be on foot in a land alive with Lord Balor's hunters. As wild and as reckless as this seemed, if they made it through the gates on horseback, they would at least have some hope of outrunning capture.

Rathina pressed her heels into her horse's flanks. Tania followed with Connor alongside her.

The din of hooves on stone rang between the high walls. But still no one came.

The night held its breath. The stars trembled in the sky. The walls pressed in on them like the jaws of a trap. Tania could hardly hear the percussion of the hooves above the drumming of the blood in her temples.

They turned a corner and saw the gatehouse ahead of them. All was in darkness. Tania had a sensation between her shoulder blades like a slow fire burning in her spine.

Clack, clack of hooves on stone. Jingle of harness. Groan of leather.

The gatehouse came nearer. Even the guardroom set into the outer wall was in darkness.

Where are the guards? What is *this?*

A light flared, sudden, harsh in the gloom, red as fresh blood.

A man ran from the guardroom carrying a lantern like those from the ship. Another followed. Then another. A door cracked open behind them and more soldiers came pouring out, lantern-lit, their swords gleaming rosy as they swarmed the three riders.

"Do not kill them!" roared Lord Balor's voice from high on the walls. "They are useless to me dead!"

Tania's horse reared, the breath blowing from his nostrils, his eyes rolling. Rathina let out a shout of anger and defiance.

More soldiers appeared on the walls, strings tight on yew bows, arrows aiming into the snare of the courtyard.

"The leaf!" Rathina shouted. "Swiftly, sister!"

A hand grasped for Tania's reins. She swung her sword, and the man jumped back. But she was surrounded, her horse agitated, turning this way and that, whickering and stamping.

She pulled the leaf from her bodice and impaled it on the tip of the sword. Then she drew back her right arm, and using all the power of her back and shoulders, she hurled the sword toward the closed gates.

It ran like white lightning through the night,

striking the door and quivering in the wood, singing shrilly. Voices rose all around Tania and hands reached for her again now that she was unarmed.

But the moment the crystal sword pierced the wood, the heavy beams lifted and the massive bolts withdrew and the great doors heaved themselves open into the courtyard.

"Ride!" Rathina screamed. "Ride!"

The soldiers were in an uproar now, snatching at Tania as she kicked her horse into action, trying to rip her from the saddle. But Rathina was among them, her sword whirling, the iron blade sending the men reeling backward with shouts and screams.

The air became shrill with arrows, glancing off the walls and striking up from the cobbles. Tania kicked out, leaning low over her horse's neck as she urged it forward. She felt the impact as the horse struck men aside. She felt fingers trying to close on her ankles, hands groping for her on all sides.

"Stop them!" Loud as the tumult was, Lord Balor's voice was louder still. "Do not kill them! He who takes a life shall pay with his own!"

Tania found herself in the deep darkness under the arched gateway, the noise of hooves ringing in her ears. She saw Rathina just ahead, riding furiously—and Connor was at her side, his head thrust forward between his horse's ears as he beat his way through the milling soldiers.

And then they were beyond the rear walls. More arrows rained down, skipping on the stones or embedding themselves in the ground.

Down the steep flanks of the hill the three horses went careering. It was all Tania could do to cling on as they galloped out onto the flats, turf kicking up high in their wake, trees all about them, the wind howling.

"Ride on!" Rathina's voice was an exultant shriek. "We must ride on till the dawn!"

Far into the night they rode, urging on their tiring horses over open moorland and through woods of hazel and oak and star-burnished holly.

Rathina set the pace, and Tania was content to take her lead. She allowed the animals to slow to a trot for short periods of rest before pushing them into a canter again, the rhythmic triple sets of hoofbeats becoming as much a part of the night for Tania as the jingle of harness and the rasp of her own breath. Connor rode beside her, keeping close, his tired eyes narrowed against the wind.

At first Tania had heard pursuing hoofbeats and the distant voices of shouting men. But as the night wore away and Rathina drove them relentlessly on, those sounds faded and were lost.

For short periods over open ground the three horses were brought to a gallop, and then Tania's whole body surged with the power of the animal as it sped on under her, and the night wind seemed to fill her brain like a dark cyclone.

It was early the next morning before Rathina called for a pause in their flight. They had come into a vast, rock-walled ravine filled with birch trees, the canopy of leaf-laden branches forming a screen against the fast-rising sun. A stream trickled over stones in the cleft. It seemed to Tania curiously similar to many lovely places she had seen in Faerie.

Rathina insisted they take the saddles and bridles off the horses, using only a running line to stop them from straying as they filled their bellies with grass and stooped their long necks to drink from the stream.

Then at last Rathina allowed them to catch their breath. Tania threw herself to the ground, exhausted by the long ride. Connor dropped into the lush grass, lying on his back, his arms across his face. Rathina sat cross-legged, her sword resting on her knees, a tired smile touching her lips.

Now there was time for Tania and Rathina to tell Connor all that had happened since they had been parted.

"We don't have a clue who those two musicians were or why they were helping us," Tania concluded. "But they led us to you, and the leaf that Rose gave us worked every time."

"They are good folk; that is certain," added Rathina. "And for now we must be content with that."

"There's not a whole lot for me to tell you," said

Connor. "The ship docked, and I was thrown across a horse and taken to the castle. I must have passed out, because the next thing I knew I was tied to that board and being shouted at by Lord Balor." He looked at them. "I guess you heard me telling him that I'd sell you out," he added. "It was the only thing I could think of to stop him from throttling me on the spot."

"Don't worry," Tania said. "In your position I'd have done exactly the same. Anything to gain a bit of time. But why did he leave you alone in there, do you think?"

"I don't know," said Connor. "I assumed he'd finished interrogating me. I'd told him everything he wanted to know."

"And more besides," murmured Rathina, eyeing Connor thoughtfully. "It was a convincing display of cowardice and treachery, Master Connor."

Connor looked at Rathina, a slight smile on his face. "I'm betting you were worried I was really going to sell you out," he said.

"I am unsure as to the exact meaning of your words," Rathina said, "but I did doubt you; that I will admit. Such lies do not trip quite so readily off the tongue among those I usually count as friends. You playact very well, Master Connor—I was all but persuaded of your villainy." She frowned. "But Lord Balor shares that same illusion as do you," she continued. "The belief that Faerie Immortality is a thing that can be enticed forth and caught in the hand, like a bird whistled down from the branch." She shook her head.

"Why do Mortals pursue such foolishness? To seek the secret of Immortality? You'd as like pluck stars from the skies to use as lanterns. 'Tis madness. Pure and simple."

"I agree with you," said Connor. "I had plenty of time to think while I was tied to that board and waiting to get my throat cut." His smile became bleak. "I realized something that had been pretty much staring me in the face ever since I came here." He looked from Tania to Rathina. "This isn't Earth," he said. "This probably isn't even in the same universe as Earth. This is some other place completely. I've been so busy trying to get my head around ways to make sense of all the stuff that goes on here that I never stopped to think that it's a total waste of time." He laughed breathlessly. "Physics and science and everything else that make our world tick don't mean a thing here." His smile widened and he held up his hands as if in surrender. "So, that's it. I give in. The place is crazy, period. I get it now."

"I'm glad about that," said Tania. "But look, this isn't your world. You came here to help us, and you *have* helped us. But we're in Alba for a reason, Connor, and we can't waste any more time."

"I know that," said Connor. "I didn't get caught on purpose."

Tania took a breath. "I know," she said. "I'm sorry. But the thing is, you don't need to stay here anymore. I can walk you back into Ireland right now." She looked urgently at him. "You should go, Connor.

Seriously. Right now. Before we get you into even more trouble."

Connor's smile faded. He sat for a long while looking into her face, saying nothing.

"My sister gives you wise counsel, Connor," said Rathina. "This quest is for the benefit and succor of Faerie alone. It is none of yours. You should not risk yourself further for us. Go, with the grateful thanks of all good folk. Go home, Connor."

Connor stood up, his face unreadable. Tania watched him closely as he made his way down to the thread of rushing water. He pushed his hands into his pockets, head bowed, staring down as the clear water bubbled and played over the smooth white pebbles. The fingers of his right hand moved in his pocket as though running over something.

Why is this hard for him? What's he thinking? It's a no-brainer, surely?

At last he turned, his face serious and determined. "Sorry," he said. "Thanks for the offer but no can do. I started this thing and I want to finish it."

Tania opened her mouth to protest, but he didn't give her the chance to speak.

"How do you think I'm going to feel if I bail on the two of you?" he asked. "I know I'm not *Faerie*—I don't have any special powers like you—but I can help; I know I can. I *want* to help. And unless you tie me up and drag me back to Earth against my will and just dump me there, I'm *going* to help." He looked at Rathina and then at Tania. "I'm coming with you," he finished. "Discussion closed."

Rathina stood up, her hand extended. He took it and she gripped the hand tight between the two of hers. "You do us honor," she said. "I will make it my duty to see that no harm comes to you."

"Thank you." He turned to Tania, his eyebrows raised.

She stood up and gave him a quick hug, thinking of Edric and how he had once been the man promising to stand always at her side. "You're totally loopy!" she said into Connor's ear.

"So what else is new?" he replied, smiling broadly, his hands curling for a moment around her waist. She stepped quickly away—out from between his hands—but there was nothing in his expression to worry her.

"As to our quest," Rathina broke in briskly. "We are in an alien land, and no doubt pursued by bitter enemies. What next, sister? Do you have any clear idea of the road that lies before us, for upon my oath, I do not."

"We have to find Caiseal an Fenodree," said Tania. "Mother said that the people there would help us."

"Find it how?" asked Connor. "I don't suppose she gave you directions?"

Tania shook her head. "All I know is that Caiseal an Fenodree is here in Alba," she said. "To get to Tirnanog we have to travel west through Alba, then through Erin and Hy Brassail. Mother said I should ask the way to the Caiseal, but I'm not sure how good an idea that is now. Lord Balor wasn't even born when

Titania left Alba—she wasn't to know that this whole area would be under his control."

"A good point," mused Rathina. "Dare we make ourselves known to the people of this land?"

"I vote we forget the Queen's people," Connor suggested. "We should head west—find Erin on our own. What do you say? Who's up for it?"

"I'm not sure," said Tania. "We'd have no idea what we were getting ourselves into. Those two guys we heard talking—they sounded like they were scared of what goes on in Erin."

"Aye, true enough," said Rathina. "They spoke of a Witch Queen. I'd know more of *her* before we venture into the west."

"I agree," said Tania. "Sorry, Connor. We don't know a thing about Erin or Hy Brassail. The Queen's people could be our only hope."

Connor's brows knitted, irritation crossing his face. "If we don't dare even ask for directions to that castle you're talking about, how will we ever find it? It could be miles away. It could be at the other end of the country! It might not even *exist* anymore. A lot of stuff can happen in five hundred years."

"Connor makes a good argument," murmured Rathina. "Who can we trust in this unknown land? Whose word will guide us true?"

"Maybe no one's word," said Tania. "Maybe we need to try and contact Eden again?" She looked at her sister. "Rathina, will you help me?"

"I will."

Tania sat, drawing Rathina down to sit facing her. They interlocked the fingers of both hands. Tania closed her eyes. The sun was high and bright by now and the world behind her eyelids glowed with a red light.

"Eden?" She tried to picture her oldest sister again the way she had in Dorcha Tur. But the image would not come, would not hold in her mind. *"Eden . . . ?"*

She could hear Rathina's breath—strangely loud and labored. Rathina's fingers tightened on hers—and then her grip became weak and Tania had the horrible sensation that Rathina was being pulled away from her.

Her fingers snatched at nothing.

She could hear Rathina's voice, calling frantically from far away. Connor's voice as well—shouting in alarm.

A coldness filled her chest. Her limbs became heavy. She couldn't open her eyes. Her head swam, and her whole body tingled and stung as though her veins were swarming with wasps.

The ground gave way under her, and she fell into a dizzying white void.

The pain was unbearable. It clawed in her abdomen, doubling her up, forcing her knees into her belly. She wrapped her arms around herself, hugging the pain while agonized tears ran from her eyes. The light now was golden—but it was cruel gold, bitter and spiteful, hot needles piercing her head, searing her thoughts.

Then the pain eased. She was able to breathe again, and the light in her brain was white and soft. Shaking, she pulled herself up. She swayed, exhausted in the aftermath of the pain.

She opened her eyes—but nothing changed. The light was still white, diffuse, opaque all around her. She was in a world of bright mist.

A gray shape formed, moving toward her.

"Eden . . . ?"

"Nay, sister—she cannot come."

"Sancha . . . ?"

The misty shape came closer and was Tania's solemn-eyed sister, clad as ever in a simple black gown, her long chestnut hair tied back, her face slender and pale.

"You look tired. . . ."

"As are we all, Tania. The Gildensleep drains us."

"I'm lost, Sancha. I don't know which way to go. I thought Eden might—"

"Eden cannot squander her power on you, Tania." The voice was critical but not unkind. *"All Faerie depends on her."*

"And on me! On me, too, Sancha!"

"Indeed. That is why I am here. What do you need? If it is in my power, I shall give it. But Tania, you cannot call on us again. You bleed the power from us."

"Yes. Yes, I understand. . . . I have to know the way to Caiseal an Fenodree. I need to get there . . . I need—"

The words were ripped from her mouth as a great wind took her body and flung it up and far away. Tania found herself speeding along as fast as a falcon, meadows and woods and hills and downs rushing away beneath her.

From high above she saw a narrow valley filled with birch trees. She saw three horses and three people by a thread of silvery water. Two women and a man. One of the women was her—sprawled lifelessly on the ground while the others knelt over her.

She saw the valley curve to the north. There was open country, lush and well tended. There were farms and small villages. A range of rounded hills. A deep, dark forest. A lake as blue as the sky. An island shrouded in mist. The pinnacles of tall steeples and towers. A castle.

A voice in her ear, faint and far away.

". . . Caiseal an Fenodree . . . remember, Tania . . . remember . . . "

"She's waking up!"

A dark blur. Pale faces. Worried eyes.

Tania blinked. Two heads framed by the night sky.

It was hard to form words, hard to move her lips. "You've got stars in your hair. . . ." she murmured.

"Does she dream still awhile?"

"No. She's just a bit out of it, aren't you, Tania? Do you want to try sitting up now—or are you okay where you are?"

"Up," Tania mumbled, reaching out with her arms. "Up, please."

She was helped into a sitting position. She felt like someone woken in the middle of the night by having a bright light shone in her face.

"What happened?" she asked.

"You keeled over," said Connor. "One moment you were sitting there with Rathina, the next you were out cold like you'd fainted. Only we couldn't bring you around."

"How . . . long . . . ?"

"All day and half the night," Connor said. "Do you remember what happened? I just figured you overloaded your brain trying to make contact with Eden. Is that what it was?"

"Did you speak with our sister?" asked Rathina.

"Yes. Well, no. Not with Eden—with Sancha."

Clarity began to return to Tania's mind like clouds clearing from a summer sky. "I know the way to Caiseal an Fenodree!" she said. "I can take us there!" She tried to get up, but her legs wouldn't support her.

"Rest yourself now, Tania," said Rathina. "You have tried your strength to its limits. The night is already half done. Let us see what the dawn brings."

She stretched out her hand over Tania's forehead, moving it down to cover her eyes. Tania lay back in the grass and was swallowed by darkness.

Galleon clouds sailed high across the blue sky, huge and stately, shining like silk as they passed in convoy across the sun. The wind was fresh and clean from the north, and Alba lay open before them, a land of forested hills and heathered glens and wide, flower-scented meadows.

Tania had awoken at dawn, stronger and refreshed by her long sleep. The pain and the weakness were gone—perhaps only temporarily—but the relief filled her with hope and purpose.

And she knew the way to the white palace in the lake—the palace where her Faerie Mother had been born and raised.

Tania had been concerned at first over the time wasted while she was unconscious. Plenty of time for Lord Balor's hunters to track them down, but whether by luck or some greater design, they saw no sign of pursuit as they climbed into the saddles and rode out of the ravine.

They avoided farmlands and any sign of human habitation, keeping to the open land, moving steadily northward.

Rathina was clearly intrigued by the land they were traveling through. "'Tis strangely like Faerie," she murmured, "and yet the air has a different scent and the colors are mayhap a little less rich. Curious, indeed."

It was late afternoon now, and the sun was standing on the western horizon. They had been traveling through dense forest and the trees seemed to have no end. The sun threw blinding arrows of slanting light through the branches, so that the forest was alternately filled with deep shadow and a glaring radiance.

"Are you sure this is right?" Connor asked, peering into the green gloom ahead of them. "This looks like it could go on forever. Wouldn't it make more sense to head west after all?"

"The palace is this way," Tania said. "You have to trust me, Connor."

"But what if Sancha was just a hallucination?"

Tania frowned at him. "You think I can't tell the difference?"

"I don't know—can you?"

Rathina came trotting to catch up to them. Her face was anxious as she drew level.

"Problem?" asked Tania.

"A feeling," said Rathina. "Some danger. Near to us but . . ." She paused, her eyes narrowing. "But . . . veiled," she finished. "I do not understand it, but we should be wary."

"Is it Balor, do you think?" asked Tania. "Might he have picked up our trail?"

"Possibly," said Rathina. "How far to Caiseal an Fenodree, do you think?"

"I'm not sure."

"This is crazy!" Connor said under his breath.

"Dark evening, day is ending
Through the night our path is wending
As we softly tread the gloaming way
O harbinger of twilight dusk
Share your evensong with us . . . "

Rathina's voice was like a gentle wind through the leaves, singing to herself as they rode on under the trees in the last failing light of day.

Tania was beginning to have doubts. Surely they should have come to the palace by now? And she was strongly aware of Connor riding at her side: He wasn't saying anything, but she could feel his disapproval.

Maybe he was right. Maybe this was a waste of time.

"Do you feel anything?" Tania called back to Rathina.

"It rises and fades," Rathina replied. "At times chilling me to the bone—at others nothing but hints and rumors. But there is *something*, of that I am sure."

"What's that?" Connor was leaning forward in the saddle, staring through the trees.

Tania followed the line of his gaze. Yes—there was

something, a glittering in the distance—as though scatterings of Faerie stars had fallen to Earth and were shining like diamonds.

They emerged from the trees and found themselves gazing out across a wide dark lake stippled with points of light.

"We were seeing the stars reflected in the water!" said Connor breathlessly.

Maybe three hundred yards away, out in the middle of the night-black, star-flecked lake, there lay on the water a ball of pure white mist.

"This is it," Tania said in relief. "We've found it!"

"Great," Connor said dispassionately. "What's the plan? Yell for a boat or swim across?"

"I would not advocate overmuch shouting," said Rathina, turning in her saddle and staring back the way they had come. "Danger presses hard upon us. There is a cruel claw in my mind's eye, and it reaches toward us. Tania, we dare not remain here long!"

Tania gazed out over the lake, remembering her mother's advice. *Use these words to ensure that you are greeted as friends. Speak the words 'caraid clainne.' Remember them, Tania . . .*

"Tania!" Rathina's voice was an urgent hiss. "The danger is upon us!" Tania stood up in the stirrups and called out softly.

"Caraid clainne!"

Tania's voice fell flat, engulfed by the still night. She called again, louder this time, "Caraid clainne!"

"What is wrong?" hissed Rathina, her iron sword ringing as she drew it. She swung her horse around to face the forest. "Tania! Why does it not work?"

"I don't know."

"Are you saying it right?" urged Connor, panic showing in his face.

"I think so." She leaned perilously far over her horse's head, shouting again, "Caraid clainne!"

The mist hung on the water. The stars sparkled on the lake. The trees gathered like a silent army at their backs.

Nothing happened.

A wind blew through the clustering trees—or perhaps the rustling and creaking were not the wind at all—perhaps they were horsemen. . . .

"Tania?" Rathina's voice was a low growl as she peered into the trees. "We must act!"

Tania noticed a movement on the water. The reflected stars were shifting position, gliding over the inky surface, creating new patterns on the lake, circling, forming whirls and eddies of light points on the smooth black water.

"Something's happening!" she said. "Look, it's working!"

Gradually the shifting stars began to move more rapidly, coming together into racing arrowheads of silver that skimmed the lake—that drew together, scintillating and twinkling until the entire width of the lake was empty and a path of starlight led from the bank at their feet across the lake and into the heart of the mist.

"Is that real?" said Connor, his wide eyes brimming with the silvery light. "I mean—will it hold us, do you think?"

A smile touched the corner of Tania's mouth. "Let's see."

She pressed her heels into her horse's flanks and gave a flick of the reins. Without any display of unease or fear, the horse stepped carefully down the bank and onto the path of stars.

Water splashed as the horse walked out onto the lake. Tania could hear a sound like voices—long, high notes that hung in the air around her—as though the stars were singing.

The path across the lake was only wide enough for a single horse. Connor followed Tania and Rathina came last.

Tania turned in the saddle to make sure that her companions were all right, and she saw that the path of stars was unraveling at their heels, the flecks and motes of light skipping away over the black water to find their original places and to reflect the sky once more.

The mist expanded as Tania rode forward. She glanced back again. The eaves of the forest were dark and sinister. And then the mist was all about her, and there was nothing left to see.

She was aware of her horse's head dipping as it clambered up a sudden slope. The ground evened out, and she could smell flowers.

"Crazy," muttered Connor. "This whole thing—totally crazy!"

The mist rolled away, and they were on a path of gray pebbles and the palace of Caiseal an Fenodree filled their vision.

It was a grand edifice of pale gray stone set in gardens of trimmed hedges and well-tended flower beds. The palace itself was buttressed by round towers traversed by battlements and topped by slender conical roofs that rose to pure white points. Light shone out from many windows in the high flanking walls, and torches sent flames up from the ornate saw-toothed balustrades.

But it looked old to Tania—old in a way that the ancient castles and palaces of Faerie never looked. The gray walls were stained by the centuries, the slate roofs patched with lichen, the towers fingered by ivy.

It looked Mortal. It looked . . . *real.*

Connor and Rathina rode up on either side of her, and the three of them brought their horses to a standstill on the beachy path. The mist was gone now, and they could clearly see the lake and the distant forest. The purpose of the mist seemed to be to mask the castle only from the outside; once within, the enchantment was no longer necessary.

"So"—Rathina's voice was little more than a breath—"we come at last to the Mortal cradle of our Mother's infancy. Will they remember her, do you think? I'm told Mortals are fickle and forgetful."

"I'm not sure that's true," said Tania.

"I guess we should knock or ring the bell or something," Connor said. "Let's hope they like unexpected guests from overseas."

"Unexpected *relatives* from overseas . . ." murmured Tania. "Rathina and I could be their long-lost great-great-great-great-grandaunts or something."

"Now that's going to take some explaining. . . ." He looked keenly at her. "Here's a question," he said. "What are you going to tell them about us? Who are you going to say we are?"

"We should play it by ear, I think," Tania said. "Kind of ease them into the idea gently if we can. All we really need from them are directions out of here."

"So, up front we're just three travelers?" Connor asked.

"Something like that." Tania nodded. "Yes—we'll tell them that until we know what they're like. Neither of you say anything else unless I do, okay?"

"Fine with me," said Connor.

Rathina raised an eyebrow. "It should at least be . . . interesting," she said. "But I will tell no lies, sister—remember that." She dismounted and led her horse forward, her sword back in her belt. Tania and Connor followed suit, their feet crunching on the pebbles as they approached the palace's large square door.

They had hardly crossed half the distance when the door was thrown open from within. A group of people emerged, some carrying candelabrum. The two foremost figures were dressed in fine clothing that reminded Tania of oil paintings she had seen of noble folk in the times of the Stuart Kings.

They were a man and a woman in their middle years. The man was clad in tunic and knee britches of dark blue with a large white collar and long white cuffs. Black hair cascaded in curls over his shoulders, framing a narrow, bony face with a high forehead and heavy-lidded eyes. He was smiling as he walked toward them and his arms were spread in greeting.

The woman was wearing a gown of aquamarine picked out with golden ribbons and bows and also with a wide, white lace collar and a foam of lace at her wrists. Her red hair was drawn back and tied at the nape of her neck, leaving only a cascade of ringlets to frame her face with its high cheekbones and wide full-lipped mouth. Even at a distance Tania could see that the woman's eyes were seagreen and full of intelligence.

The other folk formed a half circle around them, dressed in plain browns and grays, holding the multi-armed, wooden candelabrum high, their expressions seeming cautious but intrigued.

"Welcome, wayfarers," called the man, looking them up and down. Tania got the impression that he found their disheveled appearance amusing.

You try looking good after what we've been through!

"Yes, welcome indeed," echoed the woman. "Welcome to the gentle haven of Fendrey Holm. I am Lady Derval and this is Lord Cillian Fendrey, my most revered and beloved husband."

Fendrey? Yes, Fenodree could easily have been shortened like that over time.

"I'm very glad to meet you," Tania replied. "I'm Tania Aurealis, and this is my sister Rathina." She assumed the royal surname would mean nothing here, and besides, she and Rathina looked nothing like princesses right now. "And this is our friend Connor Estabrook."

"Thrice the guests, thrice the welcome!" said Lord Cillian. "You come at an auspicious time. Tonight is the Festival of Danu Danann—of the children of Danu, the great annual celebration of our people. Many are gathered from far and wide—feasting in the grand banqueting hall. Come within, I pray. There is easily room enough for three more travelers at table!"

"You are very trusting, my lord," said Rathina. "Some might greet strangers more warily."

"We have no need to fear you, mistress," said the

lord. "None that wish us harm may cross the lake. It is a magic that has existed for time out of mind, although in these less wondrous days, none that live could conjure such a marvelous defense."

He said it is magic, thought Tania. *They never use that word in Faerie.*

"But it serves us well," added the lady, "and it ensures that all who come to our door are folk of good intent. Please—we have stables and grooms who will tend your horses—come into our home and thus honor us with your presence."

"I hope your defenses are mighty, lady," Rathina said gravely. "I fear a deadly foe pursues us. We have fallen foul of a brigand by the name of Lord Balor." Her eyes narrowed. "I trust he is no friend of yours?"

"Indeed he is not!" said Lord Cillian, exchanging a grim look with his wife. "A worse rogue does not draw breath from Skerry Head to the White Stones of Braw! But you need have no fear of him or his followers: The magic of the lake will not let him pass. In Fendrey Holm you need fear no peril." He beckoned them forward. "Come. Come."

Three of the servants took the reins of their horses and led them away.

"This is more like it!" Tania heard Connor murmur as they came to the doorway. Beyond it was a wide entrance hall brilliant with candlelight. A floor of ochre and white marble stretched away under a high ceiling of ornate plasterwork spanned by spreading fingers of delicate, tawny brown timber.

Tania paused on the threshold. She looked closely at Lady Derval. The red hair, the high cheekbones, the green eyes—yes, it was easy to see how this smiling woman could be of the same stock as Queen Titania.

Tania stepped into the long hallway, and the door swung closed to shut out the night.

"How came you to fall foul of the brigand Balor?" asked Lady Derval as they paced the hall toward a tall pair of doors that stood closed at the far end.

"He captured Connor," Tania said warily. "We managed to free him—but I think they're still chasing us. How much land does he control around here?"

"Through fear and slaughter his influence has spread wide," said the lady. "But still some folk resist his cruel dominion—and await the day when the prophecy will be fulfilled."

"Prophecy?"

"Do you know he holds the Great Salamander in thrall to him by the use of cold iron?" asked the lady. Tania nodded, shuddering as she remembered the sight of that strange lizard beast. "Ah—I see from your eyes that you have encountered the creature. He captured it, so they say, in the land of Hy Brassail, where such behemoths abound. It is said that a day will come when a champion will arise to sever Balor's iron hand from his arm—and on that day the Great Salamander will reveal a fantastical secret that will shake the skies!"

They were approaching the tall doors now. Tania

could hear a hubbub of voices from beyond. Two liveried servants stepped forward and reached for the crystal door handles.

"No!" Rathina's voice was a wild scream. She flung herself forward, her sword springing from her waistband. "Get back!" She swung the sword in a wide arc, sending the servants jumping back.

"What is this, madam?" called Lord Cillian, his face filled with alarm. "Why do you draw a blade in this place?" Then he saw the sword and he let out a cry. "By the singing of the Shee—she bears a sword of iron!"

There were cries of consternation from the servants.

"Mercy upon us!" wailed Lady Derval. "They are agents of Balor! How can this be?"

"No, we're not!" shouted Tania, running toward her terrified sister. "Rathina, what are you doing?" She halted, standing as close as she dared to the scything blade. "What's wrong?"

"Treachery and peril!" Rathina shouted, her eyes blazing. "I feel it now! I feel it as fierce as the noonday sun when clouds are blown away! We are betrayed. The evil I sensed did not follow us, sister. It lies ahead! It lurks beyond these doors—and it will be the ruin of us all."

The double doors were pushed open from within and the noise of revelry billowed out as a black-clad figure stepped into the doorway.

Tania's heart stopped. It seemed that all the air

was gone from the room. She stared as the young man smiled and bowed his head, his dark blond hair falling forward over his eyes.

"So, you're here at last," said the man.

It was Edric.

Part Three:

The Dark Arts

Tania stared at Edric. Unable to draw breath. Stunned beyond thought.

"Captain Chanticleer of Weir!" Rathina spat, spinning to aim the iron sword at Edric. "I should have known it was the stink of Dark Arts that fouled the air!"

Edric turned to her. "Greetings, my lady Rathina," he said smoothly. "Wouldst thou kill me? That were scant courtesy from a long-awaited guest. I fear our hosts would take it amiss."

Rathina hissed, her expression venomous. "It was you I sensed out on the ocean—the peril that haunted us. You from the start!"

"I am not your enemy, my lady," Edric said, his voice firm and clear. "Put down your sword; none here wish you harm."

"Yeah, right!" came Connor's voice. "You chased us all the way from Weir just to say hi, I suppose?"

Edric's eyes turned to him. "Still with us, Connor?"

he said. "I'd have thought you long gone, your tail between your legs and whimpering for home."

Connor's voice was clipped but steady. "Yup, still here," he replied lightly, but there was a cold glint in his eyes.

It took Tania every shred of self-control to find the strength to hold Edric's eyes and to speak to him. Even then such a void of misery ached inside her that she could hardly bear to look at him.

"What are you doing here?" Her voice was strained. "How did you avoid getting caught by the Gildensleep?"

The noise from the banqueting room had lessened, and Tania was aware that many eyes were fixed on them—not least the lord and lady, staring from one to the other in silent consternation.

"Such questions will be answered to your satisfaction, Tania," Edric said. "But for now may we not defer to the kindness of our good hosts and join the banquet? We will have ample time to speak together over the course of the evening."

"Stop it!" Tania shouted, her whole body contracting in a spasm of hurt and denial. "Stop talking like that!" She could feel her face burning. "Why are you talking to me like that?"

It was more than she could stand. He had never used that Faerie formality with her before—they had always spoken to one another in normal English. It had been one of the bonds that held them together—the way they could step away from all the stiff procedure and ceremony of Faerie and just be themselves.

Themselves? And what did that mean?

Herself: a half-Faerie, half-Mortal split to the heart by the contradictions of her two lives. And Edric? Who was he now? Not the boy she had met in school, that was certain. Evan Thomas was long gone and in his place was this Captain of Weir—who still looked like the person she loved but who stood aloof from her and spoke like a polite stranger.

A flash of concern came into his face and he stepped toward her, his hands lifting as though to embrace her.

"Stand back!" growled Rathina, the blade hovering at his breastbone.

"Don't be so stupid!" Edric said fiercely. "Do you think I'd hurt her? *Ever*?"

His eyes were intent on Tania's. "I *will* explain," he whispered. "Trust me—please."

She took a long shuddering breath. "Put the sword away, Rathina," she said.

Reluctantly, her eyes glowing like embers, Rathina let the point of the sword droop. "Harm her and you die," she said to Edric. "There will be no further warning." She slid the sword into her waistband. "Well, now," she said, hands on hips. "Who shall untangle the knots of this sinister imbroglio?"

"I do not understand," Lord Cillian broke in, stepping forward. "Captain Chanticleer—you led us to believe that these good people were friends of yours. Indeed, those were your very words when you and your companion came here: that you were expecting three great friends to arrive imminently from the far northern fiefdoms of Alba!"

So, Edric has not told them where we really come from. . . .

Lord Cillian's forehead contracted in a frown. "And here you are in conflict! Have you played me false, sir?"

"I have not, my lord," said Edric. "Hot blood, high hearts, and misunderstood motives are at the root of our discord."

Connor turned to the lord. "I thought you said only good people could get across the lake," he demanded. "If that's true how did *he* get here?" He glared at Edric. "What did you do—use some of that Dark Arts stuff to sneak your way through?"

"Stop it!" snapped Tania, feeling protective of Edric under Connor's attack. She turned her eyes to him. "Who are you here with, Edric? Lord Cillian mentioned a companion."

Edric hesitated and Tania could see the unease in his eyes.

"Who is it?" she asked again.

"Hollin," Edric said, avoiding her gaze. "But he's under my command, and he won't be a problem, I promise."

Hollin the Healer! The very thought of that man made Tania feel sick to her stomach. The last time she had encountered him he had tried to have her thrown to her death from a high window of Veraglad Palace.

Only the intervention of the earl marshall had saved her life, and still Hollin had spat his fury at her: *"The half-thing must be destroyed ere it taint us all!"*

Tania was the half-thing that needed destroying. But it wasn't his hatred that chilled her heart; it was the fact that his loathing and his invective were fueled by a deep terror of her. Hollin truly believed that she was an evil thing that needed to be annihilated.

And he was *here*? And Edric was asking her to believe that he had control over the fanatical healer?

"He will be no *problem,* forsooth?" cried Rathina. "Nay, not with his head severed from his neck he will not!"

"No violence, on your mercy!" cried Lord Cillian.

Then a new voice sounded, and Hollin stepped suddenly into view from the banqueting hall and stood at Edric's side.

Tania stared at him. A large man of middle years, tall and broad-shouldered, he was dressed as she remembered: in a plain yellow habit with a rope belt. A thin white circlet banded his tawny hair, a sapphire stone shining in the center of his forehead. But in his green eyes there was none of the madness that she had seen when last she had confronted him.

"If my death is the only proof of my repentance, then kill me now, my lady," said the healer, taking a step forward then dropping to one knee, his head bowed. "For know you I come on my lord's bidding and mean no evil to you nor to your companions."

"This is bull!" Connor snapped, looking at Tania.

"We can't trust him—he tried to kill you!"

Rathina's hand was on her sword hilt again. "Say the word, sister," she growled. "One clean sweep and the world will be cleansed of this canker."

But as much as Tania feared and mistrusted the man, she was not prepared to have him killed like that.

"Why are you here?" she asked, lifting her gaze from Hollin and looking at Edric. "Why have you followed us?"

For a long moment Edric looked into her eyes without speaking, then: "To save you," he said. "I'm here to *save* you, Tania."

The banqueting hall of Fendrey Holm was ablaze with the light of a thousand candles and vibrant with voices. Musicians set on a low dais in one corner of the room vied to be heard over the hubbub, the measured tones of harpsichord, viol, and lute forming counterpoint to the sweet singing of a trio of boys in white robes.

Three long tables were set near the tapestry-covered walls, leaving a wide-open space for dancing. Even in her distracted and uneasy state Tania couldn't help but be amazed at the extravagant display. The tables were decked out with crystal candelabrum, their flittering light glinting down onto the elegant white tableware and onto knives, forks, and spoons of exquisitely carved and decorated crystal, as blue as a summer sky. Down the center of the room there ran an enclosed stream of clear water with banks of stones and moss picked out with reeds and water lilies—and in the water swam shoals of small shining goldfish.

The food was sumptuous and plentiful, filling the long hall with a multitude of rich aromas, both savory and sweet. Servants in white moved discreetly among the guests, removing empty dishes and replacing them with fresh courses: from oysters and mussels and crayfish in bowls of crushed ice to roasted chicken and beef on the bone and other steaming meats to creamy yellow bread and platters of salmon and trout and perch. And there were bowls of salad and of flowers, the perfumes of primrose and marigold mixing with the aromas of sage and rosemary and chives.

For those who had had enough of savory food, there were great flagons filled with strawberries and tureens of baked damsons and plums and gooseberries sprinkled with sugar and nutmeg and cinnamon, served with ewers of fresh white cream.

People would come and go from the tables, making their way to the center of the room to join in the stately and lively dances. Tania was almost giddy from the whirl of brightly colored dresses and tunics.

But she felt alone and detached—as though she was watching it all from some cold and secluded place, her nose pressed against the glass. Even having Rathina on her right and Connor to her left did not anchor her, and her mind drifted in a sick haze.

She'd been given little choice but to join the banquet. What else could she do? Let Rathina loose on Hollin, spill his blood on the tiled floor? And as for

Edric—Tania's emotions were so tangled by this meeting with him that she was beyond thought. She and Connor and Rathina had been led to seats at the table and food had been placed in front of them.

The Festival of Danu Danann had continued.

Tania ate virtually nothing—two small mouthfuls and her stomach had contracted like knotted rope. She had one aim in mind—one purpose in enduring all this—and that was to find a way to speak quietly with Lord Cillian or Lady Derval and tell her true reason for being here—and then to ask them for help in getting to Erin. Once she had that information, they would retrieve their horses and ride away from here—from Edric and the healer, from all of this deadly confusion.

She looked around the huge room. There was Edric seated at the middle table—only occasionally visible to her through the rainbow swirl of dancers—speaking with Hollin and with the lord and lady. Looking so . . . so casual—so *natural*. Why wasn't his stomach in knots? Why wasn't he ill with the pain of lost love the way she was?

Love never dies in Faerie?

Big joke!

"You're not eating."

Tania turned to look at Connor seated at her side. "I'm not hungry."

"You will be," he said. "It's best to get something in your stomach while you have the chance. You might be glad of it in a few days' time."

She smiled without humor. "Nice impersonation of my *mother,* Connor."

"Which one? Queen Titania or Mary Palmer?"

She winced at this.

"Sorry," he said quickly, his face remorseful. "That was harsh. I take it back, okay?"

She nodded.

Demons and angels fought for control in her mind. *What would you give to go back a few months and make some different choices? Remember the first time Gabriel Drake appeared to you—in the hospital after the boat crash? Knowing what you know now would you still follow him? Would you still take his hand and let yourself be pulled into Faerie?*

"Tania? Will you dance with me?"

A hand on her shoulder jolted her out of her thoughts. She twisted in her chair, staring up into Edric's face, noting that the formality had gone from his speech.

"You want us to *dance*?" She didn't even try to keep the incredulity out of her voice.

He held out a hand. "Please." His eyes pleaded even more than his voice. "They're playing a saraband."

They had danced the saraband together on the eve of the Hand-Fasting Ceremony of Cordelia and Bryn.

In the Royal Palace of Faerie two young lovers twirling deliriously together—twenty million years ago on the other side of the world! Tania thought.

She could feel Connor's eyes on her, and at her other side Rathina was watching her attentively over the rim of a crystal goblet.

"Are you sure that's such a good idea?" Tania asked, keeping her voice neutral now. Playing it ice-cold. But she felt light-headed all the same—as if the festivities were getting into her brain.

"Yes. I'm quite sure." He drew back her chair and took her hand. She found herself standing and walking to the far end of the table, hand-in-hand with Edric. She glanced at him, tall and handsome at her side.

"Where's the necklace I gave you?" he murmured.

"I . . . lost it. . . ."

"That's a shame."

She blinked, trying to focus her mind. "I threw it away."

"It doesn't matter." He smiled. "Don't worry about it."

"Are you messing with my mind?" she asked, the candlelight dazzling her.

"What do you mean?"

"I was planning on saying no to dancing with you."

"I'm glad you said yes." He led her to the outer edge of the dance floor, the joyful dancers swinging past them like figures on a magical carousel.

"I *didn't* . . . say . . . yes. . . ." Dreamy now and vague . . .

His lips came close to her ear. "Don't overthink it—enjoy," he said. They were among the dancers, hands clasped, whirling to the triple meter of the music, her eyes on his face and his eyes looking deep into her as though nothing else existed but the dance and the flashing candles and silvery light of his enchanting gaze.

"Are you happy, Tania?"

"Yes. Yes, of course."

She was alone with Edric on a wide veranda of white marble. Beyond the carved balustrade the land stepped down in terraces of fir and holly to the water's edge. There was the smell of pine, fresh and intoxicating. The still, black water reflected the sky so that both above and below, the world was sewn with twinkling diamonds. Faint music played from far away, floating on the air.

"I'm glad," Edric murmured as they leaned on the cool, white rail, their arms touching, her head tilted slightly to rest on his shoulder.

It was curious—she couldn't quite remember how they had got here. She remembered dancing and laughter and music, the thrill of being in Edric's arms, the wonder of his shining eyes. But then it all became a blur. A nice blur—warm and soft and comforting.

Although . . .

"Edric . . . where are we . . . ?"

"Does it matter?" he whispered, and she could feel his lips touching her hair. "We're together again; that's all that matters."

"Again?" As she spoke, a cautionary voice called out from the peaceful daze of her mind. A voice telling her that this was not real, that their love and their happiness were broken and ruined.

She pulled away from him and looked into his silvery eyes. "This is all wrong," she said, the words melting and falling apart in her mouth, the white bliss stirring in her mind, becoming threaded with gray. . . . "This isn't . . . true. . . . None of it is!"

Edric's hands came up to cradle her cheeks. There was sadness in his face now and loss in his voice. "I should have known . . ." He groaned, the silver light flickering and fading in his eyes. "I should have known this wouldn't work."

And then the sheen was gone from his eyes and they were brown again. Tania's head was suddenly clear.

She pulled away from him. "What did you do to me?" she spat. "What *was* that?"

Edric moved toward her. "I wanted you to be happy; that was all. Nothing bad . . . I promise . . . nothing bad. . . ."

It all clicked into place. The dizziness, the euphoria, the sense of peace: they had all been a trick, a mind game that Edric had played on her.

She lashed out, her hand striking hard across his cheek, snapping his head sideways. "How *dare* you!" she cried. "How dare you do that to me!"

He was trembling now, a red stain burning on the side of his face. "I couldn't bear how unhappy you were," he said. "I wanted to do something good for you . . . something to make you feel better."

She was livid, almost too angry to speak. "You

wanted to make me feel better by . . ." She choked, unable to think of the words to express the depth of her revulsion. "You used the Dark Arts on me, Edric? How could you *do* that?"

"Because I love you and I can't stand our being like this!" he cried. "It's too hard, Tania; it's killing me." He leaned heavily on the balustrade, as though his legs were failing under him.

Tania took long, slow breaths, trying to calm herself down.

"The worst thing you could have done . . ." she began hesitantly. "Absolutely the *very* worst thing you could ever do to me is to try and control my mind like that." She looked into his defeated face. "That's what Gabriel Drake did, Edric! Don't you get that? He got inside my head with the Dark Arts and he manipulated me and he tried to *kill* me with it!" She swallowed, her throat parched and aching. But she needed to finish. "No matter what motives you had, no matter what you were trying to do—you have no right to violate my mind like that." She stared at him. "Do you not get that? Do you not get how horrible that is?"

He nodded slowly, his head hanging. "I'm sorry," he murmured.

"You promised me you'd stop using the Dark Arts, Edric," she said harshly. "So, what happened to that?"

"I needed to use them to find you," he said quietly. "There was no other way."

She narrowed her eyes in suspicion. "Why did you *need* to find me?"

He lifted his head, and she could see tears in his eyes. "Because I can save you, Tania," he said. "I can save you, and then we can be together again."

She frowned. "You said that before—that thing about saving me. Save me from what?"

He stood up straight, running his arm across his face, breathing hard. "From yourself, Tania!"

XIX

Wide marble steps led down from the veranda toward the lake, winding steeply under the tall dark trees.

Edric and Tania sat side-by-side, close but not touching, on a low step near the motionless, starry black sheet of the water. The smell of the trees was all around them, and the steps were velvet with fallen pine needles.

Edric was speaking, his voice soft as he spun out his story. "Something is wrong in Faerie," he said. "It's like something . . . something *fundamental* to Faerie has . . . has changed." He looked at her. "You don't remember how the Immortal Realm was in the old days—before the Great Twilight, before you went missing, before the Queen was lost." A longing tone entered his voice. "It was wonderful, Tania, truly wonderful. Day after glorious day, night after star-bright night. And then . . . then things began to go wrong, to go bad. And it all started after you made that first side step into the Mortal Realm."

An unpleasant thought stabbed at her. "You think the bad things started all because of me?" she said breathlessly. "Is that what you're trying to tell me?"

He looked sideways at her, as though ashamed. "I don't think you're *doing* bad things," he said. "I think maybe bad things are happening because of who you are. And a lot of other people think the same—Lord Aldritch for one." He held up a hand to stop her speaking. "Wait! Listen. Hear me out on this. You know you're not . . . not *whole*. Ever since you found out about the Faerie half of yourself, you've been freaking out about it. 'Should I stay with Mum and Dad in London? Should I live in Faerie with my *other* family?' It's been eating you alive."

She stared at him, furious. "Well, what do you expect? I can't just shrug and carry on like nothing's changed. *Everything* has changed! I'm not just me anymore—I'm two different people. You try it, Edric. You imagine how that feels!"

He reached out and caught her hand. "Exactly!" he said, his eyes shining. "That's exactly my point."

She tried to pull away, but he held her hand firmly in his. "I know how to put it all right for you," he said, leaning toward her. "And once everything is right inside you—I think everything will come right in Faerie, too. Not immediately, maybe, and not easily. But I know for sure that while your soul is split between Faerie and the Mortal World, things are never going to be right. You're like . . . I don't know . . . like the eye of a hurricane and all of Faerie is whirling around you in total chaos." His other hand caught her now. "I can make you whole, Tania. I really can."

She stood up, wrenching herself free and stepping down to that final marble slab against which the dark water lapped. She wrapped her arms around herself, staring out over the lake.

Was it possible? She had always somehow thought of herself as the *savior* of Faerie: the princess who had found the lost Queen and destroyed the Sorcerer King. Had she been wrong about that? Was Hollin right to fear her? Was she really a terrible danger to the Immortal Realm?

She felt Edric at her back. "I know why you're scared of the Dark Arts, Tania," he said. "But you needn't be. If a person approaches them with a good heart, they can't damage him—I'm certain of that. I'm not Gabriel Drake, Tania. I won't hurt you. I love you. I will always love you. I know how to make everything better. That's why I asked Lord Aldritch to allow me to follow you." His voice was insistent, but Tania didn't get the sense that he was lying to her. "I know a spell—an incantation—something from deep within the Dark Arts, something that will make you whole again. And then . . . and then we can be together." His warm hands curled around her upper arms.

"Sounds great," she said flatly. "Go for it, Edric. . . . I really can't wait."

"You don't believe me —"

"What makes you say *that*?" She glanced at him over her shoulder, her voice sharp. "Why is Hollin here?"

"Aldritch would only let me go if I agreed to Hollin coming with me," Edric said. "He knows this land—he was born here." Tania gazed out over the lake.

"And you tracked me using that necklace you gave me, right?"

"At first," Edric admitted. "But you don't need to wear black onyx for me to find you, Tania—not now. You're in my blood—and I'm in yours. We're never going to be free of each other. You do realize that, don't you? In Faerie love is forever."

"Apparently . . ." she said heavily. "So? What's this amazing cure for being *me* that you've come up with?"

"Which would you rather be: Princess Tania or Anita Palmer?"

She turned, staring up into his face. "What do you mean?"

"I know an incantation. It's hard, but I can perform it—I'm certain I can—and it will make you whole again, Tania. All you have to do is decide who you want to be—and the Dark Arts can do the rest. I speak the ritual words, I light the blue flame, I scribe the profound circle—and it's done!" His face was eager now. "No more double life, Tania, no more tearing yourself to pieces over who you really are. You will be either one hundred percent a Faerie princess—or you'll be one hundred percent Anita Palmer. Forever." He smiled. "And whichever you decide, I'll be with you. I'll be by your side if you choose Faerie—or I'll renounce this world forever and go with you to London if you prefer."

She gazed at him, dumbfounded.

"You can do that . . . ?" she whispered.

"I can!"

Her heart leaped. No more doubt, no more pain—just herself, whole and complete and at peace. Oh! What wouldn't she give for that?

For a rapturous moment she actually believed she was capable of making that choice. But only for a moment.

Tears ran down her cheeks. She caught hold of Edric and clung on to him, pressing her head to his chest, hearing the rapid beat of his heart against her temple, digging her fingers into his back. He stroked her hair and she could feel him trembling.

"My dad is worse," she mumbled into his tunic front.

"I don't understand. What do you mean?"

She looked up into his face. "My dad—in London—he's really ill, Edric. How could I choose to be a Faerie princess and never know what happened to him? It's impossible." She wiped the tears out of her eyes. "And what will happen here if I give it all up and become ordinary Anita Palmer of Camden Town again?"

He opened his mouth, but she pressed her fingers to his lips, silencing him. "I know you think I'm the cause of everything that's wrong here—and maybe I am. But even if that is the case, it's far too late now for me to just up and walk away. If I started all this chaos, then I've got to end it." She shook her head. "I can't *be* just the one person, Edric—don't you see? I can't abandon my parents and I can't give up on Faerie. I'm sorry but I *can't*!"

"Listen to me," he said, his arms strong around her. "You must think this through properly. When I cast the incantation—when you become a single, complete person—you'll forget all about your other self. It'll fade away like . . . like a dream. That's the beauty of it. That's the whole point."

"It doesn't matter," Tania said. "That isn't important to me. I need to be *both* of me right now, Edric—I really do."

"But what if you fulfill your quest, what if you make things right again in Faerie, what then?"

"Oh, I don't know. I don't *know*!"

A voice came ringing down through the trees. "Tania! Are you there?"

She stepped out of Edric's arms and called back. "Yes! Rathina, I'm here!"

"By the spirits, you've led me a merry dance, sister!" There was the patter of feet on the marble stair. "Connor and I never saw the going of you, Tania! It is thoughtless of you to wander off alone when . . ." Rathina came into view under the low branches, her eyes like gimlets on Edric. "Or *not* alone, it would seem," she growled, disapproval strong in her voice. "What is this, sir? A secret tryst with my sister? Fie upon you for such uncourtly behavior!"

Edric bowed low, then turned quickly to Tania. "Think carefully about what I said," he murmured. "Sleep on it and give me a better answer in the morning." He passed Rathina and went bounding away up the stairs.

"Well, sister," Rathina remarked, her eyebrow arched. "And what sweet nothings have been passing between you and the handsome captain of Weir?"

Tania swallowed hard. "Let's find Connor," she said. "We need to talk."

The Festival of Danu Danann was drawing to a close. Many of the revelers had already retired for the night, and Tania, Connor, and Rathina were climbing a long stairway with Lord and Lady Fendrey. Servants carried candles to light their way.

"I'm sorry we've been such a bother," Tania said.

" 'Tis nothing; do not even think of it," Lady Derval said, although Tania could tell from the unease in her eyes that the strangers at the feast had been something of a trial for her.

"We have arranged for you to sleep in the west tower," said Lord Cillian. "There is a fine suite of rooms under the roof—a lofty bower far from any fear of being disturbed."

And far away from Edric and Hollin, I would imagine, thought Tania.

The stair spiraled upward and ended in a short hall with a door at the far end. A servant opened the door, and the lord and lady ushered Tania and the others into a room already glowing with candlelight.

"Rest easy and be refreshed," said Lady Derval, gesturing for the servants to leave. "Sleep well, honored guests. Sweet dreams attend you."

All good-nights were said, and Rathina, Tania, and Connor found themselves alone at last. Connor explored the comfortably furnished room, opening doors and finding three bedrooms beyond.

Tania walked to the tall open window and looked down over the lake and out across the distant, night-shrouded forest.

"So, what words passed between you and the captain of Weir?" asked Rathina.

Tania turned. It was time to tell them of Edric's offer.

"You don't actually believe him, do you?" Connor demanded when she had finished. "For heaven's sake—first he tries to brainwash you with that nasty mojo of his, then when that's a bust, he comes up with a story of how everything will be just fine and dandy if you let him put some other kind of magic spell on you." He snorted with derision. "He's got to be kidding!"

"At the very least Master Chanticleer deludes himself if he thinks he can subjugate the Dark Arts without mischief coming to him and those about him," Rathina said with a sigh. "Is not the fate of Lord Drake proof enough of that?" Tania saw the hurt in her sister's eyes as she spoke of the unworthy man she was doomed to love for all eternity.

Tania had sat in an armchair to tell her tale, her legs curled up under her. "Edric says he's a better person than Drake," she responded, feeling for Rathina in her never-ending anguish.

"Does he? By the spirits," murmured Rathina, "that were a pretty conceit. My lord Drake was a kind and noble soul until. . . ." Her voice trailed off, but it was obvious what she had been going to say.

Until the Dark Arts ruined him.

Tania looked sympathetically at her sister. "Edric is certain he can control the Dark Arts."

"He would!" scoffed Connor. "And he's not going to find out he's wrong till it's too late. And to turn up with Hollin of all people!" He paced the floor. "Listen. I'll tell you what's really going on here. My guess is Aldritch sent them after us, and their orders are to get us back to Weir any way they can. Aldritch has already made it clear that he's not on Oberon's team anymore—for all we know, he's planning a rebellion. And if he is, what better bargaining chips than two of Oberon's daughters locked up in his castle?" He glared at Tania. "That's what this is all about! And if we've got any sense at all, we'll get out of here right now and put as many miles between them and us as quickly as possible."

Tania turned to Rathina, who was sitting cross-legged on the carpet with her iron sword across her lap. "What do you think, Rathina?" she asked.

"I think slipping away from here at dead of night will not be a simple task," she said. "We know not where our horses are stabled nor where we might find provisions for our road. And how are we to cross the lake? Will the stars form a bridge once more—for if not it will be a long swim. And what of Lord Balor and his hunters? 'Tis too much to expect they have left off the chase. We may find ourselves entrapped and carried back to Dorcha Tur."

Tania nodded. "And we came here for a purpose, don't forget," she said. "We came here to find out all we could about Erin. I'd hoped to have a quiet word with Lord Cillian and Lady Derval during the evening, but I never really got the chance, not with their servants all over the place. But we *need* to speak to them, guys, and we can't do that till morning." She sighed and unfolded her legs. "Here's the plan," she said. "We go to bed and get a good night's sleep. Then in the morning I'll make it really clear to Edric that I'm not prepared to let him use the Dark Arts on me." She frowned. "In fact, I want to make it clear that I don't want him using the Dark Arts again, ever."

"And if he won't listen?" asked Connor.

"I'm hoping he will," Tania said. "Then we'll talk to the lord and lady and see if they can tell us anything about Erin."

"And then away—like arrows from the bow!" said Rathina.

"Exactly," Tania said, getting up and heading for the closed door of a bedroom. She turned the handle, looking back at them. "Don't worry. Remember what the lord and lady told us: No one who means harm can come to the island. Hollin might be as bad as ever, but he's not going to cause us any problems while we're here. The old magic won't let him!"

Tania awoke. Something had pulled her out of a deep, dreamless sleep. A sound—subdued but sharp, like the click of a lock. The creak of a floorboard in the darkness.

Was there someone in the room?

She lay absolutely still, not even breathing, her eyes wide as she tried to fathom the gloom of her bedchamber, faintly illuminated with a powdery light where the stars shone in through the open window.

She thought she saw a shadow slink across the room. Her heart thundered in her ears, deafening her. Slowly she sent a hand gliding between the sheets. Across the bedside table her fingers tracked, feeling for something solid.

The shadow moved again—silent as smoke—and now it was at the foot of her bed. She fancied she saw a narrow glint in the starlight. The blade of a crystal knife.

Whoever it was circled the bed and leaned over her.

At last her hand found the stem of a candelabra. Her fingers closed around it and she made a sudden movement: swinging her arm, smashing the heavy crystal candelabra into something solid.

There was the shudder of impact and a grunt of pain. Then fingers snatched at her wrist and she heard hissing breath. The pain made her drop the candelabra. The sliver of crystal came plunging at her face. She wrenched her head sideways and something thumped down hard on the pillow.

She lashed out with her free hand, feeling cloth under her fingers, hearing a ripping sound as the knife was pulled from the pillow and raised for a second blow. She scrambled out of bed, trying to drag herself free, but the attacker kept hold of her wrist.

"Rathina!" she screamed. "Help me! *Rathina!*"

The hand yanked at her, and she lost her footing, falling heavily down by the side of the bed, still held fast. She snatched at the hand, trying to prize the fingers loose. A silhouetted head and shoulders reared over her. An arm rose—and again there was that glint of evil light as the knife was raised.

And another glint: a blue gleam in the center of the looming head. A jewel that caught the starlight for a moment.

Hollin!

Using all her strength, Tania twisted on the floor, turning onto her side, dragging Hollin down so that he fell grunting across her, his weight pinning her. She tried to heave him off, but she found she could hardly move.

"Now I have you, half-thing!" His voice was hideously close to her face, his breath sour.

She saw the knife arm rise and fall. She blocked it with her forearm, but the pain was intense, jarring her to the shoulder, weakening her.

And then there were confused noises, the sound of hammering feet across the floor, and finally some light as Connor came running in, clutching a candlestick and shouting. He caught hold of the back of Hollin's robe with both hands. Snarling with the effort, he dragged the man off Tania, and they both went tumbling.

Tania got to her feet, gasping, swaying, unsteady. Connor's candle lay guttering on the floor, and in its light she saw the two men struggling together with Hollin on top. But Hollin had dropped the knife—it lay on the floor close by. Tania snatched it up, and with a cry she threw herself at Hollin. If she had been able to, she would have thrust the knife deep in his body.

But even as he fought with Connor, he threw back an elbow, catching her in the face and sending her spinning. Pain exploded in her head and red lights burst across her field of vision.

"Hold, there!" Rathina's voice, cold and commanding. "Move but a hair of your head and I will pin you to the boards, wretched miscreant!"

Tania pulled herself up. Rathina stood straddling

Hollin, the point of her sword hovering just above his throat, a five-armed candelabra held high in her other hand. Connor scrambled free and got to his feet, panting hard. He stooped and picked up his candle, holding it close to Tania's face.

"Are you all right?" he said, gasping. "Did he hurt you?"

"I'm okay," Tania said, shaking her head with pain.

"He meant your death; that much is certain!" said Rathina. "Perhaps it is best to finish him here and now."

Hollin lay on his back, held down by the iron sword's blade, his eyes hooded, his chest rising and falling.

"Well, deceiver?" Rathina growled. "Was this your intent all along? To mask your true purpose and to slay my sister in her sleep?"

"The foul half-beast must die," snarled Hollin.

"And with such a dark deed in your heart, how came you to pass through the magic that protects this place?"

Hollin snorted. "The old magic of Alba is easily circumvented," he said. "The spell only denies entrance to those who mean harm to the lord and lady of Fendrey Holm."

"So you got through because it was only *me* you wanted to hurt!" said Tania.

"Indeed," snarled Hollin." And would that I had succeeded."

"Did Edric send you to do it?" demanded Connor.

"Did he?" He stared at Tania. "My god, I just bet he did—and you *believed* him!"

The sound of hurried footsteps came to the open door.

"Tania!" Edric ran into the room, carrying a many-armed candelabra, banishing the shadows with its light. He was half dressed, his face distraught. "Something woke me," he cried. "I knew you were in danger! Somehow I knew!" He stared at Hollin. "You!" he spat. "What are you doing here? What have you done?"

"Less than I'd hoped, boy," snarled Hollin. "And more than you could ever have accomplished."

Edric stared at Tania. "Has he harmed you?" He put down the candelabra and moved toward her, but she held up her hands to ward him off.

"No," snapped Connor. "Sorry, she's just fine. Hard luck."

"Oh, shut up, you fool!" shouted Edric. He glared down at Hollin. "Why did you do this?" he exploded. "Have you gone mad?"

"Do not speak to me as though you have authority over me, boy," said Hollin, his eyes burning. "You have none and never did!"

The breath hissed between Edric's teeth. "This was the plan all along?" he choked, his voice clogged by anger. "To use me as a cat's-paw to find the princess and then to murder her in her sleep? Is this why Aldritch agreed to this—is that why he asked for you to accompany me?"

"Why else, fool!" snapped Hollin, turning onto his

side and lifting himself on his hands while Rathina's sword prevented him from further movement. "Think you he trusted you to do the right thing when the moment came? Had the half-thing agreed to be cured by your Arts, then she was to be allowed to live. But she made it clear to you she would not be healed—and my orders in that event were to finish her before she could do more harm." His face grew ruddy and spittle showed white on his lips. "And had any of you the heart and stomach to do what was needed, she would be dead now and all Faerie saved! The doom of that Realm lies on your hands. All of Faerie shall be destroyed in plague and madness unless you cut out the very soul of this she-witch and burn it in the sacred flames!"

He lunged upward, shouting in agony as he beat aside Rathina's iron sword, throwing himself at Tania with fingers curled into claws.

"No!" shouted Edric. "Stop! Stop now!" He raised his arms, his eyes shining like silver moons. Black threads spun out from his spread fingertips. The blackness snaked through the air and wove a web around Hollin's body, stopping him dead, lifting him into the air, his arms and legs flailing. "Begone!" Edric howled, his voice deep and vicious.

"No! Do not! I shall—" Terror possessed Hollin's face, then he was gone. Vanished away in the beat of a heart. The wisps of blackness drifted for a moment. Then there was nothing.

Edric dropped to his knees, gasping for breath, his

eyes burning with the ferocious silver light.

Connor gasped. "What was *that*?"

"A hex of banishment," murmured Rathina, looking uneasily at Edric, her sword clasped between her two hands. "You have grown mighty in power, Master Chanticleer."

"Where have you sent him?" asked Tania.

"I don't know," said Edric, panting. "I just wanted him . . . gone."

"Kill him!" snarled Connor. "You can't trust a thing he says!" He glared at Rathina. "Kill him now before he can do any more harm." He reached for her sword, and she had to pull away to stop him from trying to wrest it out of her fingers.

"Connor, stop!" shouted Tania, horrified by his brutal suggestion. "Just *stop*, will you?"

Connor spun on her. "You're out of your mind if you trust him!" he said. "Do you want to be the next one zapped out of existence? Do you?"

Tania looked at Edric. The silvery sheen was fading from his eyes, and he looked both worn out and afraid . . . as though shocked by the extent of his own powers.

"Edric . . . ? Are you all right?"

"No." His voice was subdued. "No, I'm not." He gazed up at her with haunted eyes. "How can I be all right after what just happened?"

Tania only just stopped herself from falling to her knees and throwing comforting arms around him.

"It's a trick!" hissed Connor.

Edric looked at him. "Connor," he said with a sigh, "if I wanted you dead, you'd be dead, okay? If I wanted to hurt Tania, she'd already be hurt. You can believe me or not, but I'm telling the truth. I had no idea what Hollin intended to do."

"I believe you," Tania murmured. "But what's going to happen now?"

"I can still perform the Zauben enchantment, Tania, and make you whole. All you have to do is choose."

"I've already chosen," Tania said, her voice quiet but resolute. "I can't do it, Edric."

His eyes begged. "Can't you do it for me?" He held a hand out to her. "Tania—for *us*?"

She took his hand. "There's no us," she said. "Look what you just did, Edric. Hollin could be dead for all you know—or worse than dead—and straightaway you want to use the Dark Arts on me! You think you're in control, but you're not. You're being taken over. And one day there'll be nothing left of you at all." She felt numb. "I can't watch you turn into a monster, Edric. It's too cruel."

"Then I'll never use the Dark Arts again," he said vehemently, gripping her hand, twisting her fingers.

"You . . . can't . . ." she said. But something strange was happening. The world was warping around her. All the colors were running and flowing into one another. Rathina stumbled at her side. Two voices called out urgently. A white light invaded her mind. She felt feather light. Floating.

Lifted off her feet. She was drifting into a white sky. Beneath her she saw the realm of Faerie shrouded in gold. She felt her life being drawn out of her, pouring down like a golden rain. Strength needed to keep the shield of Gildensleep whole. Strength that she could not afford to lose.

Tania opened her eyes to candlelight. She was lying on the bed. Rathina was at her side, sitting gray-faced.

Edric and Connor were at the foot of the bed talking in subdued, angry voices.

"What happened?" Tania asked, wincing as her own voice rang in her head.

"We collapsed, sister," murmured Rathina, lifting her head and looking at Tania. "The Gildensleep drains us more at every turn. It does not bode well. I fear the sickness will only get worse."

Connor moved quickly to Tania's side, his hand resting on her forehead.

"You're hot," he said. "How are you feeling?"

"In a word?" she groaned.

"Yes—I can guess the word," Connor said with a slight smile. "Rathina only just came around, and she's just the same." He frowned. "I don't know what to do. You're not actually ill, neither of you. If we were back home, I'd prescribe some kind of pick-me-up or energy booster . . . or a couple of days' bed rest. But the way you're both being drained . . . I don't know how much more of it the pair of you can take."

"I told Connor that's why we should do what I

suggested," added Edric, arriving at the other side of the head of the bed. He looked at Tania. "I can help you. I can keep your energy levels up."

"So you say," retorted Connor. "With some more of that voodoo of yours."

Edric shook his head. "What you're doing is incredibly important," he said to Tania. "Let me help you. I can create a barrier—a way to stop you being sucked dry like this."

Tania sat up, fighting the discomfort. "No," she said. "My family needs my strength." She touched Rathina's arm. "Our strength."

"So do you," Edric insisted. "If this keeps happening, how are you going to get to Tirnanog?"

"And how do you know where we're going, anyway?" demanded Connor. "More black magic, I guess."

"No," Edric snapped. "Not black magic. I know the old legends of the Divine Harper and his powers. Why else would the King and Queen send Tania to Alba unless they wanted her to find Tirnanog and ask for the Divine Harper's help against the plague?"

"Yes," Tania murmured, cautiously getting off the bed, allowing Connor to steady her as she got to her feet. "That's where we're going—and we need to go now. We can't afford to waste any more time—not if these attacks are going to keep happening. How long was I unconscious?"

"A few minutes, that's all," said Connor.

"I want to come with you," said Edric. "If you won't accept my mystic help, then at least make use of my sword arm! You have no idea what dangers you're walking into." He stared into Tania's dubious face. "You can trust me—you surely know that by now. I would never betray you—any of you. Let me help!"

"In your dreams!" growled Connor. "I'd rather bring a snake along."

Tania looked helplessly at Rathina.

"Look not to me for advice, Tania," said Rathina. "I have a long history of bad choices. You and you alone must decide on this thing."

Tania looked deep into Edric's brown eyes. "You need to make a promise to me," she said slowly. "Never to use the Dark Arts, no matter what the circumstances."

"I promise," Edric said without hesitation.

"Even as a last resort," Tania added. "Even then you mustn't use it."

"Think well on it, Master Chanticleer," warned Rathina. "If great danger assails us and you are certain that only your Arts would suffice to save Tania's life—what would you do then?"

Edric stood looking into Tania's face.

"I would find another way to save her," he said at last, and a touch of Faerie formality came now into his voice. "I would not use them, not even if your life was made forfeit by my choice."

XXI

Servants were roused and sent to call Lord Cillian and Lady Derval from their beds while Tania and the others quit the tower and waited in the now-silent banqueting hall. Any visible signs of the Festival of Danu Danann were gone and all that lingered were the faint smells of roasted meat and flowers and candle wax. The long tables were bare now, their polished surfaces reflecting the light of the few candles that had been lit to banish the dark.

The lord and lady arrived, heavy-eyed from sleep and wrapped in fur-lined velvet cloaks.

"What matter is this?" asked the lord, staring at his guests. "Is there more conflict among you that you must rouse me to arbitrate?"

Tania stepped forward. "It's nothing like that," she said. "We have something to tell you." She frowned. "It's going to be a bit of a shock. You might want to sit down."

* * *

Lord Cillian and Lady Derval sat in stunned silence as Tania finished her tale. Lady Derval was the first to speak. "You are the child of the lost daughter of Lord Arvan and Lady Maeve," she said slowly. "The child of the seventh daughter who sailed alone into the east in search of the mythical land of Faerie?"

"I am," Tania said. "And so is Rathina."

Lady Derval looked closely at Tania. "Now that I am told, I see the familial resemblance in your face."

"And you do not come from the northern fiefdoms of Alba?" Lord Cillian asked. "None of you? You all come from . . . from the east?"

"We do," said Edric. "From Faerie."

"All save Connor," added Tania. *But I think you've got enough to deal with right now without my trying to explain where* he *comes from!*

"And the man named Hollin was an enemy here to kill you, and he has been . . . sent away?" asked Lord Cillian.

"He was a dangerous man," said Edric. "He has been dealt with." Tania looked at him, wondering where the healer had been sent—and whether she had truly seen the last of him.

"And you say Titania is a *Queen* in . . . in . . . Faerie?" asked the lord.

"She is *the* Queen," said Rathina. "Consort to King Oberon and mother to many daughters."

The lord and lady looked at each other.

"I thought the tales of the mythic eastern lands were but flights of fancy to prevent our people from venturing into dangerous waters," said Lord Cillian. "I thought the truth was that there were treacherous reefs and deadly leviathans beyond the horizon. I never thought Faerie *real*."

"It is, my lord," said Rathina. "And it is in great peril."

"So you must travel into the west to seek a cure for the plague that contaminates your Realm," said Lady Derval. "And you would have us give you guidance on your path?"

"We would," said Edric.

"But we know little more of the lands beyond the Blackwater than we do of your own Realm," said Lord Cillian. "It is said that the land of Erin is full of wild magic and that it is ruled over by a beautiful enchantress, a Green Lady who dwells in a palace made of flowers."

"We do not go there, so caprice runs free," added Lady Derval. "There is no communion between our lands. The waters of the River Blackwater are deep and wide, and insanity comes to any who drink of it . . . or so it is said."

"The Blackwater runs through a vast dark forest," continued Cillian. "The Gormenwood, it is named. It forms a barrier between the farmsteads and hamlets of Alba and the strange land of Erin."

"All the same, we have to get into Erin," said Tania. "Do your legends say whether the Green Lady is dangerous or not?"

"There are few stories beyond what we have

already told you," said Cillian. "And none that suggest she is cruel or malevolent. But if the tales are true, then Erin is a land running wild with enchantments beyond all understanding." He shook his head. "But you are not common folk—perhaps your own magics will prevail?"

Tania shot Edric a quick glance.

"We have few magics, sir," he said. "But perhaps the long estrangement between Alba and Erin has allowed imaginations to flourish unchecked."

"Aye, perhaps," said the lord. "But I'd not be the one to try the perils of the fallen bridge—if it exists."

"What's this fallen bridge?" asked Tania.

"It is said that in times long gone there was commerce between Alba and Erin, and a bridge that crossed the Blackwater," Lady Derval replied. "But there was a battle and the bridge fell. Legend says its ruins are guarded by a dark creature who will ferry travelers across the water . . . for a price. . . ."

"What price does this creature exact?" asked Rathina.

"The secrets of the soul," said Lady Derval with a shudder.

"Can you guide us to the fallen bridge?" asked Edric.

"There is a road, an ancient road, that leads into the Gormenwood," said Lord Cillian. "It is unused and long overgrown, but once it led to the bridge, I believe. But I'd not go with you under the eaves of that forest."

"You won't have to," said Tania. "Just tell us where it is—we'll do the rest."

"And let us hope Lord Balor is not hard on our trail," added Rathina, "or trapped twixt the Blackwater and the sinister power of Dorcha Tur we shall be."

"I think we can aid you there," said Lord Cillian. "There are deep tunnels that lead out under the lake and far into the countryside. We will ready your horses and give you such provisions as you can carry, and weapons, if you wish. I will appoint a captain to lead you to the westernmost exit. From there it will be less than a day's ride to the eaves of the Gormenwood."

"Most excellent, my lord!" said Rathina. "Then let us away ere the moon traverses a hand's breadth across the sky." She stood up, frowning suddenly as she looked around. "Where is Connor?" she asked.

"He was here a minute ago," said Tania, looking from person to person. "Where can he have got to?"

"Not far, for sure," said Rathina. "So—let us find him and be on our way. Erin calls us, and I would learn the secrets of a land where enchantments have gone wild!"

Tania found Connor in the long entrance hall that led from the main gate to the banqueting room. He was sitting quietly by himself in a corner, his legs drawn up, his chin on his folded arms.

"What's up?" she asked, crouching to look into his pensive face. "What are you doing out here on your own?"

"Just thinking," he said.

"About?"

"Stuff."

She let out a long breath. "You're not pouting because Edric is coming with us, are you?" she asked. "Because I'm not going to be impressed if you are."

"I'm not pouting," he said, looking closely at her. "But I think it's a bad idea."

"It's done," Tania said. "He's coming. Period."

Connor nodded. "I know."

She looked into his face, trying to guess his thoughts. "Listen," she said after a short pause. "That offer still holds, you know. I'll take you back home anytime you like. No one will think the worse of you. You've already done so much, Connor. You needn't feel ashamed of yourself if you want out."

"I don't want out," Connor said. He pulled himself to his feet and Tania rose with him. "And I'm not jealous of Edric. I'm worried about you, that's all."

"I'm fine."

"No, actually you're not," Connor said. "Okay, you're fine some of the time—but you could have another of those collapses any moment without warning. You and Rathina both. And then it's just me and Edric—and I know exactly what he thinks of me."

She frowned at him. "I don't know what you mean. You think he'd *do* something to you? Is that it?"

"It's not impossible," Connor said. "What if he gets mad and does that black-smoke whammy on me while no one's around to stop him?"

"Why would he?"

"Because he's half crazy with that Dark Arts thing," said Connor. "I know you've bought into that whole thing about him promising never to use it again. But if you ask me, he's addicted to it. And like any addict he'll tell you whatever you want to hear just to shut you up." His eyes burned into hers. "I'm telling you, Tania, when push comes to shove, he'll use those Dark Arts of his again—and that's a stone-cold certainty!"

A captain of Lord Cillian's guard led the four riders into a tunnel that opened in the deep cellars of the castle and delved under the lake. The atmosphere was tense as the lord and lady saw them off.

"We bid you farewell and good fortune," said Lord Cillian. "But as for that—I know not what kind of fortune can aid you against the enchantments of Erin."

"Fear not, my lord," said Rathina. "Good spirits watch over us."

"Thank you for your gifts," Edric said. "Our journey will be much easier thanks to your generosity." From their saddles swung leather panniers filled with food and with stone bottles of drink. Tania and Connor now had sharp crystal swords at their hips, given by the lord and lady. Edric had not needed Lord Cillian to gift him a weapon—he had brought his own sword from Weir.

"And thanks for your hospitality," said Tania. "I wish we could have spent more time with you."

"Return if you can when all is done," said the lady. "There is much more I would know of Queen Titania of Faerie and of her dauntless children."

The tunnel was wide, with a high curved roof clad in red bricks. It led westward, burrowing under the lake and leading them far from the island palace of Fendrey Holm. Stone braziers ran along the center of the hard-packed ground, throwing shadows in all directions as the horses clopped along.

They rode in heavy silence for a while, and it was Connor who first spoke, glancing up at the arched roof. "I wonder how many tons of lake water there are up there?" he muttered. "And I wonder how good at engineering tunnels these guys are? I can't see us surviving a roof fall."

"You think that's helpful?" said Edric, glaring at him.

They held each other's gaze. It was Connor who looked away first.

No one spoke again for some time, although now Tania found herself glancing uneasily upward and imagining the old brickwork collapsing under the weight of the water. *Thanks for putting that idea in my head, Connor!*

The echo of galloping hooves suddenly filled the tunnel behind them. They came to a halt as the rider approached, reining his horse in.

"News from Lord Cillian," called the rider. "A band

of Balor's men have been seen close to the lake. They may have tracked you from Dorcha Tur. My Lord says that Balor and the Great Salamander are not among them, but he bids you take care on the road west. Balor is full of sinister craft and will use the Great Salamander to hunt you down if he can. And my lord says, may the burnished eyes of the Deena Shee look down benevolently upon you!"

The rider turned his horse around and went galloping back to the palace of Fendrey Holm.

Tania quickened her horse so she came up alongside Lord Cillian's captain. "I don't know much about the Salamander," she said. "Will it be able to track us while we're down here?"

" 'Tis said the Great Salamander can see the wind," replied the captain, "and hear the flap of a butterfly's wings fifty leagues hence. 'Tis said he can scent the white flowers that grow upon the hills of the moon." His eyes glittered as he looked at her. "But 'tis also said that fear lends the imagination wings and that dragons lurk 'neath a child's truckle bed when the candle fails."

"Meaning no one really knows."

"Indeed, my lady."

"And what about Erin?"

"Ah!" And now his eyes were wary. "I suspect that it will not be long before you will know more of that uncanny realm than I, my lady." His voice lowered. "More, perhaps, than it is safe to know."

* * *

The tunnel became steep, and the floor was now scattered with stones and pebbles. Tania felt a cool fresh breeze on her face, pleasant after so long in the stifling depths.

They passed through a cave and found themselves in a land of low rolling hills and forests silent under the night sky. In the east there was a hint of gray light.

Lord Cillian's captain brought his horse to Tania's side. He rose in the stirrups and pointed. "There is no road through these lands, my lady," he said, "but if you follow the straight path westward, you will come to the Gormenwood before this day is done. Seek then for the ancient road through the forest—it has stone markers. You will know them when you see them. It is then but a short ride to the Blackwater, so it is said." He looked at her, and she could see the concern in his face. "Trust nothing in the land of Erin, my lady," he said gravely. "All there is delusion and deceit!"

He turned his horse and rode quickly back into the cave mouth, never once looking back.

Rathina rode up alongside Tania. "The day is almost upon us, sister," she said. "Shall we rest till the sun is up?"

"No," Tania said. "We ride now—and we ride fast!"

She flicked the reins and pressed her knees into her horse's flanks, urging him forward into the night. The others rode with her, and as they galloped through vale and copse, the sun rose at their backs and the sky was streaked with amber light.

Erin lay ahead. Now Tania really began to feel that they were drawing closer to Tirnanog and to their meeting with the Divine Harper.

XXII

It was early afternoon. They had paused in a forested valley where water trickled and spumed down white rocks. They ate, keeping to the shade of the trees—all but Tania glad for a brief time to be out of the saddle and sheltered from the sunshine.

Tania felt deadly tired, but she hated having to stop and rest. While she fretted to be moving again, she noticed that Connor was sitting by himself, his back turned.

Pouting? *Still?* She hoped not. They had enough to worry about.

She got up, swallowing the last of her meager meal. "We should be going."

"Sister? So soon?" Rathina looked up at her. "The horses are tired."

"We'll rest properly once it gets dark," Tania replied.

Edric nodded and got to his feet, gathering food

scraps and putting them back into the leather panniers.

They rode on to the end of the valley. The land opened before them, all grassy meadows and huddled groups of trees, stretching peacefully away toward a line of gently undulating hills.

"Are we still heading in the right direction?" asked Tania, peering into the west. "I thought we'd have hit the Gormenwood by now. Maybe it's on the other side of those hills?"

"I think we need to turn that way," Connor said, pointing a little to the left.

"Why?" Tania asked.

"It'll take us directly west," Connor said. "We want to go directly west, don't we? I've been keeping an eye on the sun—I think we're heading northwest right now."

"I too have been watching the sun, Connor," Rathina said, her voice puzzled. "And true west lies yonder." She stretched her arm out ahead of them.

"I'm not so sure," said Connor.

"Princess Rathina is right," said Edric. "We should head straight for the hills."

Connor glared at Edric. "Why am I not surprised that you'd vote against me?" he said. He looked at Tania. "I'm *sure* I'm right. But I guess it's up to you."

Why is he insisting on this? Is he just doing it to try and prove himself against Edric? I really don't need this right now!

"I'm sorry, Connor," she said. "I think Rathina and

Edric probably have a better feel for this kind of thing than you or I." She smiled encouragingly. "We'll go their way, if that's okay."

"Fine!" Connor snapped, kicking his heels into his horse's sides to spur it onward. "Whatever."

Tania frowned. If Connor kept this up, she was going to have to consider sidestepping him back into the Mortal World and leaving him there whether he liked it or not.

The sun was low and in their eyes when they first noticed a line of deep darkness in the west. Gradually it grew more dense, like a sinister wall across their path, made all the more dark and disturbing as the setting sun threw it into deep shade.

It was a forest unlike any other they had encountered. It stretched before them from horizon to horizon, and hardly any light filtered through the gloom that brooded under its heavy canopy.

" 'Tis the Gormenwood, have no doubt," murmured Rathina, leaning low over her saddlebow and staring into the densely packed trees. "Would that we'd come here when day was still strong—little chance we have of finding the old road through in this twilight murk."

"Lord Cillian said there were markers to show where the road entered the forest," said Edric, rising in the stirrups and staring left and right along the gloomy forest eaves. "But even if they could be seen in the dark, which way do they lie from here? Left or right?"

"Left, if anyone cares what I think," said Connor. "I said all along we should bear left."

There was a difficult silence.

"Okay," said Tania at length. "We'll go left—at least until it gets too dark to see what we're doing. Then we'll rest for the night and see if things are clearer in the morning."

"Those are the markers of which Lord Cillian spoke or I am a fool!" murmured Rathina.

"Yes," agreed Tania, staring at the bleak figures half hidden by bramble and briar. "I think you're right."

The night was upon them, and several times Edric or Rathina had suggested they should stop. But Tania wanted to continue for just a little while more . . . just a little while. . . .

And then, moments before she had planned on finally calling a halt, they had seen two black shapes up ahead, shrouded by the trees but starkly different to the impenetrable dimness of the rest of the forest.

They were two human forms carved from black stone: a man and a woman standing on ivy-mantled plinths about four yards apart, set so that the statues faced into the forest. Both figures seemed ancient, the stone riven with cracks and stained with gray lichen. And both the man and the woman stood with one arm outstretched in warning and the other crossed over their faces, as though warding something off whilst hiding their eyes from a dreadful sight.

"And what do you think they fear, sister?" asked Rathina, leaning close to Tania and speaking in a low voice. "What do they dread to see?"

"Erin, perhaps?" murmured Edric.

Tania walked her horse to the dark gulf that lay between the two figures. She leaned forward, staring into the heart of the darkness.

Then she straightened her back and turned to face the others. "I don't care what they're afraid of," she said. "We're going in. And we'll ride until we can't follow the road anymore."

"You want us to spend the night in there?" asked Connor.

"Yes." She looked into the three uneasy faces. "Balor is probably on our trail, right? So, what do you want us to do: make camp here out in the open where he could sneak up on us in the middle of the night or head into a forest that everyone in this country avoids?"

"There's wisdom in this," Rathina said, nodding. "If the people of Alba dread the Gormenwood, then the more so would they avoid it at night."

"I think you're out of your mind," said Connor. "Look how dark it is in there—we could lose ourselves in ten seconds flat. I vote we camp here and leave the forest alone till morning."

"No," Tania said decisively. "We're going in."

She heard Connor give a snort of annoyance. But she didn't care how offended he was. She was determined: they would go into the Gormenwood.

* * *

It was clear, even in such deep darkness as there was under the spreading trees, that the forest road had not been used for a very long time. The grass grew tall where the canopy of branches was thinnest, and elsewhere, ferns and sorrel, wild strawberry and columbine tangled across the path.

Tania knew that Connor was hanging back, making it clear that he didn't approve of their adventure, but she couldn't be bothered with his childishness right then—he'd get over it. She had assumed his bad temper would go away once he knew he could go home anytime he wanted. But if anything, he was in a worse mood now. Was it just his hatred of Edric that was making him act out like this, or was something else going on? And if so . . . what?

There was another thing puzzling Tania, too. She was finding the Gormenwood neither oppressive nor foreboding now that she was actually under the trees. From a distance she had not liked the look of it at all—but inside there was a peacefulness. It reminded her of being under the tent of her bedclothes as a child—safe from all harm, knowing that her parents were close by.

Her parents! Somewhere in another world, her Mortal father was sick in hospital, and far away in Faerie, the King battled to keep the Gildensleep alive. And maybe the fate of both of them lay with her.

"Does this forest seem dangerous to you?" Tania asked Rathina. "I mean—does it give you bad feelings?"

Rathina leaned close and whispered. "None that

can pierce the ill-boding oppression of having Master Chanticleer close to hand."

Tania looked at her, startled by this. "You can still sense the Dark Arts in him?" she whispered back, careful that Edric should not overhear.

"Aye, as thick and deadly as quicksand." She looked into Tania's eyes. "But I think you need not fear him, Tania. His oath holds true, I believe . . . for now—but still the Dark Arts cling to him."

"Is it definitely Edric you're sensing?" Tania asked softly. "It couldn't be Balor or the Salamander?"

Rathina frowned. "Mayhap you are right, sister," she murmured. "I had thought the danger to be from the Dark Arts, but now that you speak, I begin to wonder." She shivered. "If it is not Edric, then it is something else close by. Be wary. . . . We have not outrun our danger."

Tania glanced over her shoulder. Edric was only a few paces behind them, but his head was bent down, as if he was nodding in the saddle. Connor was a little farther back, and she could make nothing of him except a moving silhouette.

"Sister?" Rathina's voice was no more than a breath.

"Yes?"

"If the Dark Arts take Edric and he betrays us, we will have little time to act," Rathina whispered. There was sadness in her eyes. "Do you understand what I am saying to you? We will have to be swift and sure if we are to prevail."

Tania swallowed hard. "You mean . . . to stop him. . . ."

"Indeed. A sword to the heart is surest, Tania—if it comes to it."

Rathina's words chilled her through and through. "Oh *god*," Tania whispered. "I hope not."

Rathina reached out and gripped her hand, her voice trembling as if she understood perfectly the terrible pain that such an act would cause. "As do I, sweet sister." She sighed. "As do I."

We'll ride until we can't follow the road anymore.

Through the ever-deepening night, the gloomy path through the forest lay clear ahead of them.

Tania caught herself almost falling asleep on several occasions.

Just a little farther—then we'll stop.

Just a few yards more.

At last she saw ahead of them a patch of starry sky through the forest roof. There was the sound of water gurgling and splashing. And then the jagged hump of a wide, broken stone bridge, jutting out over a broad, dark river.

"The Blackwater, I deem," said Rathina. "Can you see anything of yonder bank?"

"No," Tania said. "Nothing, really. It might be more forest."

"How wide is it, do you think?" Edric asked, bringing his horse alongside the two sisters.

"I'm not sure, maybe fifty yards?" Tania ventured.

"At least that," said Connor, and now the four of them were side-by-side where the forest gave way to the rushing river. "Didn't someone mention a ferryman with a boat?"

Tania saw a lump of darkness rise from beside the ruins of the bridge and come moving slowly toward them, one hand grasping a long staff, the head deeply cowled.

The horses whinnied and backed away.

Tania felt a cold terror snatch at her heart as the dark figure stopped in front of them. The keeper of the Blackwater bridge.

"Well, now," said a voice. "Who comes hither to offer up the secrets of their souls and to pass through into the land of Erin?"

Part Four:

Of Witchcraft and Wonderment

XXIII

The speaker threw back the cowl to reveal the young face of a woman, round cheeked and smiling, her eyes clear blue, her brown hair curling down over her shoulders. Tania found it impossible to guess the woman's age—there was something almost childlike in the wide-eyed candor of her gaze, but there was wisdom there, too. This didn't look like a dark enemy in search of the secret of their souls.

"We want to cross the river," Tania said in surprise. From Lord Cillian's words she had expected something . . . less . . . *human*. "My name is Tania, and this is my sister Rathina." She motioned to the others. "Edric . . . and Connor."

The young woman nodded to each in turn, smiling still. "I am called Coriceil," she said, "although that is not my name. The ferryboat is ready if you can pay the toll."

"Excuse me," said Connor, leaning forward in the

saddle. "We were told this road hasn't been used for hundreds of years."

"That is true," replied Coriceil.

Connor frowned. "Have you been here all that time? Just . . . waiting?"

Coriceil laughed gently, one hand gesturing toward the river. "The ferryboat awaits those who are willing to pay," she said.

"And how is the payment exacted, lady?" asked Rathina.

Coriceil turned and walked back to the river's edge. "Will you come or stay?" she called. "The choice is yours."

"The river guardian gives little away," murmured Rathina. "It seems we must take a leap of faith."

"Either that or find another way to cross the river," said Edric.

"No, we cross here," said Tania. She slipped out of the saddle and led her horse down the gentle slope to the brimming river. The boat lay in the shadow of the broken bridge: a long wide vessel with a flat bottom and no obvious means of propulsion.

A leap of faith, Rathina had said—yes, that was exactly what was needed here. Coriceil stood to one side, watching her without any expression, neither of warning nor encouragement.

Tania paused before stepping down into the boat. "If angels existed, I think they'd look like you," she said. "Who are you?"

"I am the river guardian," said the young woman.

"The keeper of the secret temple, the dancer on the sea, the wanderer who has come home." She held out her hand to Tania. "You of all people need have no fear of me."

"I'm not afraid," Tania said, scrutinizing the woman's face, seeking for any sign of malice or deceit. But in the end what else could she do but put her trust in this enigmatic creature? All of Faerie depended on the quest—she had to move forward, despite her doubts and fears.

She took Coriceil's hand and stepped aboard the ferryboat. Her horse balked for a few moments at being led from firm ground, but Coriceil touched a hand to his neck and he quieted and walked aboard with a hollow clatter of hooves.

One by one the others followed, and once Connor's horse stepped aboard, the ferryboat slid out into the black river and the waters slowly widened between them and the land of Alba.

Coriceil took Tania's hand again, gazing deep into her eyes. Although the woman's hand was warm, Tania shivered at the touch. A painless but disturbing sensation traveled up her arm and into her chest, like ice threading through her veins.

"Ah, your wounds are deep, Tania," Coriceil said, her smile saddening. "Your soul is divided and you are at war with yourself." She sighed deeply.

Tell me something I don't already know.

"But do not fear," Coriceil continued. "You are strongest where you are split—and I see your many selves, plucked out of time, coming together to heal you when your need is greatest."

Coriceil released Tania's hand.

"No, wait!" said Tania. "What does that mean? I don't understand."

But Coriceil had already taken Rathina's hand. "Such sadness," said Coriceil, and her other hand also came to hold Rathina's. "Such grief and loss and remorse. You are dying of love, and I can see no end to it, no cure, no respite."

Rathina's face contracted in pain. "Never?" she whispered.

Coriceil looked into Rathina's face, holding her gaze. Tania felt sure something passed between them, although nothing was said aloud.

Rathina dropped her head, tears brimming in her eyes. "Thank you," she said. "There is some comfort in certainty, even a certainty as bitter as wormwood."

Now Coriceil moved to stand in front of Edric. He offered his hand and she took it. A flicker of pain or unease crossed her face. "You know that you cannot keep your promise," she said. "You know that you do not have the strength. And yet . . . and yet there is a towering love in your soul, a deep devotion that nearly tips the scales." She shook her head. "It will not be enough." She sighed. "It will not save you from what is to come. Another must save you; another must try. . . ."

Tania bit her lip. Edric's face was unreadable, as if his features had turned to stone. She thought she understood what Coriceil meant: that he would use the

Dark Arts again. She could not trust him to keep away from them. *Another must save you.*

Now Coriceil was standing in front of Connor. He seemed reluctant to give her his hand, and for what seemed like a long while, she stood with her hand open in front of him.

"Connor?" Tania said.

Connor's eyes flicked toward her, then he put his hand in Coriceil's.

There was silence, broken only by the slap of water on the hull of the ferryboat. They were in midstream now, and the darkness of Erin was drawing closer.

"You are a man of great secrets," Coriceil said coldly. "You bear with you a stolen treasure. Ah, and another secret, buried even deeper—a secret too dark to speak!" Her eyes shone with a sapphire light. "Give up your secrets willingly, stranger to this domain, or suffer the consequences."

Connor tugged his hand free, frowning, massaging his fingers as though the woman's touch had pained him. Coriceil gently shook her head and moved glidingly to the prow of the boat.

"It is done," she said. "All have paid. Erin awaits."

Great secrets? A stolen treasure? And a secret too dark to speak? Tania stared at Connor, but he had turned away, his hands in his pockets. She could not see his face.

The ferryboat bumped softly against the far bank of the Blackwater. Tania had guessed right: A thick forest pressed against the river on this side as well, the trees crowding against the bank, their branches overhanging the flowing water. Willows dipped their long, mournful branches into the inky glide, their leaves rustling softly. A dark slot among the trees suggested the continuation of the road.

Tania led her horse off first, followed by her sister and then by Connor, and finally Edric.

"Connor?" Tania said, trying to catch his eye. "Can we talk?"

He shook his head and moved a little way off, as if by putting distance between himself and the others, he hoped to avoid the questions that were growing in Tania's mind.

As the last hoof of the last horse left the boat, the vessel slipped silently away from the bank. Coriceil stood in the center of the wide deck, her cowl lifted again, her back to them as the ferryboat was lost in the shadows of the fallen bridge.

"A strange creature, indeed," said Rathina, turning from the river. "Some ancient river spirit given Mortal form, I deem her. Neither evil nor good but filled with power, nonetheless."

Tania walked to where Connor was standing. He was staring into the forest, his arms folded over his chest, his face stiff.

"What was she talking about, Connor?" Tania asked, her voice calm but firm. "What did you steal?"

"I didn't steal anything," Connor replied. He turned to her, his face suddenly angry. "It was all nonsense. She was just saying whatever came into her head. I've seen it on TV a dozen times. It's called cold reading; it's a magic trick, that's all."

Tania looked into his eyes. "What did you steal?" she asked again. She knew the other two were watching.

Connor tried to outstare her, but in the end his eyes flicked away from her face, and the anger was replaced by a look of shame. He thrust a hand into his pocket and brought out a round object that filled his palm.

"It's nothing," he blurted, looking from face to face. "It's just an old brass compass. I thought it would be useful, that's all."

"You brought it through from London?" Edric asked, stepping forward to look at the thing in Connor's hand. "No—it's old, too old for that." His voice became sharp. "Where did you get it?"

"I don't have to answer to you," Connor snarled. "Who do you think you are? I heard what she had to say about you," he said, pointing across the river. "We all heard it. You can't be trusted; you're too screwed up to keep your word. Let's talk about *that* for a minute, shall we?"

Rathina had also come closer now. She gazed at the brass compass, her eyes wide. "I saw such objects," she said. "In Helan Archaia—in the Hall of Archives in Caer Regnar Naal." Her eyes darted to Connor's face. "That is where you found this thing!" she cried. "You took it despite the edicts of the King that nothing should be removed from that place. You stole it and kept it hidden in your shame!"

"Okay, I didn't tell you about it," Connor admitted, his cheeks flushed. "I knew you'd make a big deal out of it. It's only a compass, okay? It's not a doomsday weapon or anything." His voice became a little more conciliatory. "I didn't mean any harm—what harm could a compass do? I thought it would come in handy."

"No wonder you always knew which direction we were traveling in," Tania said, remembering his comments about their routes both on the *Blessèd Queen*, and since. "I can't believe you could be so stupid!"

Connor's eyes blazed. "Stupid, am I?" he shouted. "I'm not the one who insisted we bring a voodoo junkie along with us." He pointed at Edric. "Remember what she had to say about *him* while we're at it!"

"We have not forgotten, Connor," said Rathina. "But do not seek to deflect your own blame." She had her hand out. "Give me that thing, which you should never have taken in the first place. Give it to me now!"

Shrinking back, Connor handed the compass to her.

She looked at it. "This thing of Isenmort should not have been removed from the Helan Archaia," she said. "I cannot return it—but we shall at least be rid of it!"

She twisted around and hurled the thing out over the river. It hit the water with a loud splash. A fluke of white foam rose and ripples spread.

"There let it lie," she said. "For all eternity." She glared at Connor. "And now for your other secret.

Your more dark and sinister secret." Tania saw her hand move to the hilt of her sword. "What is that, pray?"

"There's nothing else," Connor said. "Search me if you don't trust me. Go on—go through my pockets if it'll make you happy."

"A secret need not be a thing that can be kept in a pocket," growled Rathina. "You will tell us this secret, or by all the spirits, I will hold your head under the water till your mind is swept away on its dark flux." Her eyes narrowed. "Believe me in this thing, Connor Estabrook. I do not lie."

Alarm filled Connor's face. "It's nothing!" he said, his voice quavering. "I promise—on my mother's life—it's nothing bad."

"Tell us," said Tania. "We'll decide whether it's bad or not."

He looked at her, and she could see the conflict in his face.

What has he done? Oh god, what is it?

"I never meant to tell you this," he mumbled, his voice cracking. "I promised myself I would never tell you." A kind of desperate defiance came into his eyes. "Okay," he said, swallowing hard. "You want to know my greatest, darkest secret, do you?" He stared around at them. "All of you? You all want to hear it?" Now his eyes were back on Tania. "I love you," he stammered. "That's all it is. . . . I'm in love with you."

Tania stared at him. Appalled.

"Connor . . ."

"I hoped that if I helped you out and stayed with you . . . you might end up loving me back," Connor said. "And it was almost happening. . . . I know it was. And then magic boy turns up and—" He came to a choking halt. "That's my big bad secret. Happy now, all of you? That's what that woman was talking about!"

He turned away, releasing the reins of his horse, walking a few steps along the riverbank and then sinking to a crouch, his head down, his hands over his face.

A dreadful silence fell. Tania could hear the blood beating like drums in her head.

How did I not see this coming? How could I have been so stupid?

XXIV

Tania turned away from Connor. She could think of nothing to say to him.

Rathina stood with her eyes cast down and her lips a thin, pale line. Tania guessed she was thinking of her own unrequited love. She knew that black abyss all too well.

Edric looked into Tania's face. There was sadness in his eyes, and a kind of dull resignation.

She released her horse's reins and walked up to him.

"Thank you," she said softly.

"For what?" he whispered.

"For not enjoying what just happened." She flicked a glance over her shoulder to where Connor crouched under a willow tree.

Edric shook his head. "Everything's wrong. Connor is wrong—I'm wrong. The whole world is wrong." Anguish filled his eyes. "I'm going to fail you, Tania. You heard what she said. I'm too weak."

"She also said someone else would come to your rescue." She forced a smile. "That's me." She touched her fingertips to his chest. "Don't worry," she said, her heart swelling in her chest. "When the time comes, I'll be there for you." She lifted her hands to his face, tenderly tracing the contours of his lips, his cheeks, his eyebrows, her hands trembling. She could hardly speak now for the emotion that flooded through her. "I love you," she said breathlessly. "I *will* save you."

He gazed intensely at her, and she all but drowned in his eyes. She swallowed, pulling away, afraid of losing herself so completely to him that nothing else would matter.

Rathina had taken the reins of Connor's and Tania's horses and she was crooning softly to them. She lifted her head. "We have traveled far after a disturbed night," she said. "Mayhap we should rest here awhile and continue on the morrow."

"Yes, that's a good idea." Tania looked again at Connor. "I should go and talk to him," she said. "He must be feeling . . ." But she couldn't think of words to express how Connor must be feeling. Embarrassed? Devastated? His revelation certainly made her feel desperately awkward.

She walked over to him, crouching and resting her hand on his bent shoulder.

"How are you doing?" she asked as gently as she could.

He looked up at her. "Pathetic," he said.

She gave the hint of a smile. "I think you're being

a bit harsh on yourself," she said. He didn't respond. "Connor? We're friends, aren't we? We agreed."

"I lied."

"I don't feel . . . *that way* about you." She sighed. "Okay, for a few moments back in the tavern—you know when I mean—I kidded myself that maybe I *could* feel like that. But it wasn't real." Her voice became firm. "No matter what happens between me and Edric, this thing between you and me—it's never going to happen." He lifted his head, his eyes liquid and sad. "I need to know you understand."

He swallowed. "Okay . . ." he said, his voice almost inaudible. "Just friends."

"That's right." Tania sighed and glanced around. Rathina was with the horses; Edric had moved to the forest path and was staring into the darkness. "Maybe you should go now. Seriously. Just let me take you home, Connor. Back to a world that makes sense to you. Back to premed and a high-flying career as one of the UK's top surgeons or whatever it was you had planned before all this happened."

He gave a hollow laugh. "That's funny," he said. "That's really funny."

"Why?"

"Because I was failing," he said. "I was no good at it. It was too hard. That evening—the evening you turned up out of nowhere—I had finally decided to give it all up. Being a doctor was my dad's ambition for me; he's the one who pushed me to go for it. I've known for six months I'd never cut it. I was going to drop out of premed, Anita!"

She stared at him, not bothering to correct his use of her name. "You never said . . ."

"It's not the kind of thing that comes up in casual conversation," he said with a trace of bitterness. "I'd done a good job of keeping the truth hidden from everyone. No one knows about it. I was going to drop it on my folks that weekend—the weekend after you suddenly turned up. And then there *you* are . . . and . . . and . . ." He snorted. "Did you never once wonder why I was so totally up for all this?" He gestured to encompass the alien night. "One day I'm so sick of everything that I'm thinking of emptying out my savings and going AWOL for a year—the next I'm being invited to come away to a whole new world. Did it never strike you as odd that I leaped at the chance?"

"I thought it was just you being . . . impulsive."

"No." His eyes burned into hers. "It was you, saving me from . . . from . . . *everything*. Suddenly I wasn't this dismal failure anymore—I was a hero. I was in the middle of a totally unbelievable adventure. And on top of that there was the chance that I could stroll back home at some point with the secret of Immortality in my back pocket!"

"I never knew . . ."

"You weren't supposed to."

"Oh . . . *Connor*. . . ." It was disturbing to realize she had been deceived. *How do you trust someone who's that good at covering up? And the medical stuff had seemed to come so naturally to him. Was he really the dismal failure he wanted her to think? Or was this just another excuse to stay with her . . . in the hope that . . . maybe . . . somehow . . . ?*

Whatever was going on, she couldn't bring herself to force him to return to London. And maybe if he saw this quest through, he would feel less of a loser when he did get home.

She looked keenly into his face. "I won't make you go back," she said. "But the thing between you and Edric—that has got to stop. Right?"

Connor nodded. Then he lifted his head and sniffed. "Can you smell that?" he asked.

"What?" She sniffed, too. Yes—there was an odd smell on the air. Looking over her shoulder, she saw that Rathina and Edric were also alert, staring around themselves as the smell wafted through the trees. "I know it . . . but I can't place it." Tania stood up. "What is it?"

Connor also got to his feet. "Well, weird as this is going to sound, it's the same electric smell you get at . . . fairgrounds! With bumper cars."

"Yes. You're right."

The horses began to whinny and toss their heads, their hooves stamping uneasily, so that Rathina had trouble keeping control of the three sets of reins in her hands.

A soft droning sound filled the air, and Tania saw small points of light moving purposefully through the trees, blinking in and out as they glided behind the trunks and branches.

And then, in a moment, Tania and Connor were

surrounded by a swarm of tiny red flames, hovering and dancing all around them.

"They're insects." Connor gasped, his face ruddy from the light. "Like . . . like fireflies . . . but actually on fire." He reached out a hand then drew it back with a shout as one of the creatures touched his fingers.

Another of them brushed the back of Tania's hand. "Ow!" She snatched her hand away. "They burn!"

"Let us away from here!" shouted Rathina. "The horses are fit to bolt!"

Connor and Tania ran back, the fiery insects all around them. The droning was laced now with a spitting, crackling sound, like wet logs catching fire. And each of the insects trailed a thread of blue smoke, so that their flight left pale ribbons drifting in the air.

The horses were seriously alarmed now, their eyes rolling, their ears back as the burning flies gathered around them. Tania's horse reared, hooves striking so she had to duck aside to avoid them. The horse dropped onto all fours again, pulling away, dragging her along. She leaped for the horse's back, just managing to clutch hold of the saddle. Her feet left the ground and her arms were wrenched painfully. But then another horse came up close behind her, and a hand grabbed her and heaved her upward. She managed to get her leg over the animal's back and crash into the saddle. She turned—seeing Connor's face right behind her. "Thanks!"

"Don't mention it. Let's get out of here!"

Edric and Rathina were also in their saddles now,

surrounded by the thronging insects. Tania kicked hard at her horse's flanks, jerking the reins to turn the frightened animal's head toward the forest road.

"Go!" she shouted, ducking and twisting to avoid the fierce little flames. "*Go!*"

Her horse leaped forward under the branches, earth flying high from its hooves as it sped away from the riverbank.

"What were those things?" Connor asked as they rode at a steady pace under the endless trees.

"I think we just saw the first example of a land where magic has run wild," said Edric. He turned in the saddle and peered away under the tunnel of branches. "We outran them, thankfully." He sucked his wrist where one of the creatures had burned him. "It could have been worse."

"I trust this is not a sign of the welcome we are to encounter throughout Erin," said Rathina. "If flies can cause such consternation, what of greater beasts?"

Tania could still smell a faint tang of scorching on the air where the fireflies had singed their clothing. But Edric was right: It could have been a whole lot worse. Without horses the four of them could have been inundated by the burning insects, and then what? Burned alive?

The roadway led through the forest, the trees arching over them to form a roof; but now and then they would come to a place where the branches drew back, and then they could see the stars in the black velvet sky. They were the same stars and constellations that made their stately way across the Faerie sky—except that the night sky here was also streaked over and over again by shooting stars trailing silvery tails as they curved across the heavens, burning briefly before fading away.

Tania turned to Rathina. "Can you tell what part of the night this is?" she asked. She had lost track of the time, but she had the feeling they must have been following this roadway for several hours.

Rathina frowned. "I cannot, sister," she said, "and that vexes me. I know the stars, and I have oft times watched their progress across the night. But these stars do not move. I have observed for some time now; here, by my troth, 'tis always the middle of the night—as though we have come to a land caught and suspended in the place where one day ends and another begins."

"You mean it might be night all the time here?" asked Connor. "I mean—forever?"

"Anything is possible where an enchantress is in control," said Edric. "But how are we going to find our way through Erin if the stars never move and there is no sun? How will we know which direction we're heading?"

There was a worried silence, punctured by Connor, speaking in a soft voice. "I bet you wish you hadn't chucked that compass away now."

"Indeed, Connor," murmured Rathina. "Maybe we acted in haste." Her eyes shone darkly as she looked at Tania. "Mayhap it was ordained by the fates that we would need such a device to fulfill our quest. Maybe it was good spirits that compelled Connor to take it from the Hall of Archives."

Tania looked at her. "Are you suggesting we go back to try and fish it out of the river?" she asked abruptly. "Bearing in mind what Lord Cillian told us about the water?"

"No, I am not suggesting that," Rathina said, her voice subdued. "'Twould be pure madness to do so. But it may be that our choices are not so clear as we thought hereto. Perhaps more prudence is called for ere we condemn any of our number for perceived transgressions."

Tania didn't reply. What if Rathina was right? What if Connor was *meant* to have taken that compass? Not by Oberon, necessarily, but by some other benevolent power?

"Let us hope that this land offers more hope to the traveler than we have seen thus far," Rathina remarked. "Elsewise our quest may be marred by . . ." She stopped, sitting suddenly erect in the saddle. "Do you hear that?" she whispered.

XXV

Voices! Voices in the trees!

They brought their horses to a halt, all of them listening intently, staring through the dark forest, trying to pinpoint the direction from which the voices were coming.

So many different voices. Young voices and old. Happy and sad. Weeping voices and laughing voices. The voices of men and women and of children, too. Sometimes only a word or two could be picked up in the chorus—and sometimes entire phrases soared on the air.

. . . voices in the village street, smiling faces that you meet, dancing eyes and dancing feet, wonder all can share . . .

. . . the sharp winds of winter cut through to the bone . . .

. . . did we dance in the fire . . . ?

. . . fate moves a fickle finger in palaces of the moon, reflections on white water, that echo fluted tunes . . .

. . . the loss of love is such a sad, sad thing . . .

"Who are they?" shouted Connor, his eyes wide. "Who are all these people?"

"Phantoms, maybe!" called Rathina. "Chimera. Wraiths of the night. We should not listen."

"She's right," said Edric. "Don't listen to them!"

A new voice called from under the branches. An impossibly familiar voice. The voice of a dead princess, calling plaintively.

Tania-a-a-a-a . . .

Tania stiffened. "Zara, is that you?"

Ta-a-a-ania-a-a-a . . .

Tania urged her horse sideways off the road, heading toward the voice, seeing her lost sister in her mind: the wide blue eyes and the curling golden hair, her small slender figure and her sunshine smile . . .

"No! Tania, no!"

"But it's Zara . . . She's calling to me . . ."

"Zara is *not* here!" shouted Rathina.

"She is! She is!" Tears of joy were pricking in Tania's eyes as she stared into the beguiling darkness under the trees. "Zara, I'm coming!"

Come . . . come . . .

"Yes!"

"No!" It was Edric, suddenly close behind Tania. He leaned from the saddle and caught her arm. "Don't go in there!"

"I must!" She tried to shake his fingers loose, but his grip held her tight. "She needs me. Oh god, can't you hear her calling?"

"It's not Zara!" Edric cried.

"We have to get out of here!" shouted Connor.

And now all the voices were crying out in unison.

COME . . . COME . . .

Tania fought to get free of Edric. Couldn't he hear Zara calling for her? Didn't he realize she had to go to her sister? She sounded so lost, so alone. What was wrong with him? With all of them?

"Let . . . me . . . go!" she snarled, struggling to get her hand to her sword hilt. If he wouldn't release her, she'd have to cut his hand off. If he held her back from her sister, she'd plunge the blade into his heart. Nothing mattered more than getting to Zara. Nothing!

Rathina rode up to her side.

"Rathina!" Tania was desperate. "Help me!"

"Forgive me, Tania." Rathina leaned toward her, one arm raised. Her hand came slicing through the air, striking Tania hard across her face.

The pain was shocking, driving tears from her eyes.

"Now, Captain Chanticleer. Get her away from here!"

While Tania was still stunned from Rathina's blow, Edric lunged and dragged her from the saddle.

"No! No! No!"

She gasped as Edric hauled her across his saddle-bow, the breath beaten out of her. She hung gaping across his horse's back, held down by Edric's arm. He let out a yell and kicked the horse to a gallop, and suddenly all was wind and noise and violent movement . . .

. . . and bright, shimmering sunlight.

The voices had fallen silent. Edric reined his horse up. Hurt and angry, Tania squirmed down from the high ridge of the horse's back. She lost her footing and stumbled, falling into tall grass, smelling meadowsweet all around her, blinking in the sudden light.

They were a little way beyond the eaves of the forest, and it was noon. Dazzled and bewildered, Tania stared into the clear blue sky. Yes! The sun was at its apex, a burning ball of white, too bright to look at.

She staggered to her feet. Rathina and Connor were close by, their horses brought to a halt, their faces amazed as they stared around themselves. Rathina also held the reins of Tania's horse.

Connor was the first to break the silence, and he sounded as astonished as they all looked. "What just happened?"

"I think we have the answer to the question of day and night in Erin," Rathina said, leaning on her saddlebow, her eyes narrowed against the sunlight.

"But it's the middle of the day," Connor said. "How's that . . . ?" He stopped, his shoulders slumping. "I give up," he said. "I totally give up!"

Edric jumped from the saddle and stood in front of Tania. "Are you all right?"

"Yes," she gasped, her hand to her mouth. She stared into the darkness under the trees. The forest stretched into a blue haze in both directions. "I don't know what I was thinking." She stared at him. "I thought . . . I heard . . ."

"You thought Zara called to you," said Rathina.

"Yes. Yes, exactly. I was sure it was her . . . totally certain. . . ."

Rathina arched an eyebrow. "And I wonder what would have happened to you, sweet sister, had you gone in under those trees. Nothing good, that is for sure."

"It wasn't Zara," Tania said. "Why did I think it was her?"

"It was an enchantment put on you to prevent you from ever leaving the forest," said Edric.

"And it would have worked if you hadn't stopped me," Tania said, horrified to think she had come so close to abandoning the quest. "Thank you." She put her hand to her cheek, still stinging from Rathina's blow. "Thank you both."

Connor twisted in the saddle and glowered at the forest. "Is it still night in there, do you think?" he asked. "Is that how this place works? Perpetual midnight in the forest, midday everywhere else?"

"I'd not go back to test that theory, Connor," said Rathina. "Neither should you."

"Don't worry," Connor said. "I wasn't planning to." He squinted into the sky. "But I'd guess we're stuck with the same problem we had before. How do we know which direction to go in if the sun never moves and we don't have a compass anymore?"

Tania turned to Edric, looking into his eyes. He lifted his hand to lightly cradle her cheek.

"That was quite a whack Rathina gave you," he said softly.

She smiled, resting her own hand over his, trembling at his touch. "She doesn't mess around," she said. He took his hand from her face, threading his fingers with hers, leaning close and quickly kissing her cheek.

She reluctantly drew back. Part of her was desperate for this closeness, but she feared that if she let herself slip into Edric's arms, she would never want to let go again. And she really wasn't ready to allow herself to be that vulnerable. Not while he had all that bad magic inside him. Not with Coriceil's warning still ringing in her head. And not with Connor only a few yards away, pretending he wasn't watching them.

Untwining her fingers from his, she turned and walked toward her horse. She climbed into the saddle, gazing at the new landscape that surrounded them.

At their backs the dark forest stretched from horizon to horizon, but ahead of them the land spread out like a rumpled quilt, all hills and sudden valleys, and copses and woods that rippled away in a golden haze of warm summer sunlight.

The horizon was odd, though. Purple and mauve mountains curved on the edge of sight, but although they looked solid when Tania stared straight at them, she found that if she looked away and then back again, the distant outlines had changed—as if the mountains were in a constant state of unrest, flowing into one another, changing, mutating, only to become stable again when she fixed her eyes on them.

A land where magic has run wild. . . .

They had to get across both Erin and Hy Brassail if they were to fulfill their quest, but Connor was right: They had no way of setting a course. Tania knew they needed to head into the west—and it would be easy enough to guess that the west lay in the opposite direction from the forest—but what were they to do once they lost sight of the forest? What then?

"I see no sign of village nor farm," said Rathina, standing high in the stirrups and scouring the landscape, her hand shielding her eyes. "Should we seek for the folk who dwell here and ask their aid, do you think?"

"We don't even *know* if anyone lives here," said Connor. "Except for the enchantress, of course . . . assuming she really exists."

It was true: They had no idea what was waiting for them in this land and even less of what would be expected of them further down the line

"The kind of witchery we've already seen needs to be maintained by a keen and a strong mind," said Edric. "The Green Lady exists, I think we can be certain of that."

"But will she prove an ally or an enemy?" asked Rathina. "Should we seek her out in her palace of flowers—or should we avoid her?"

"That's a good question," said Tania. She looked at her three companions. "Anyone got an answer?" No one spoke. "Okay," she decided, "here's the plan. We'll ride on *that* way." She pointed away from the forest. "We'll keep going as far as we can. Then we'll see what we're up against."

"I suggest we trust nothing we see or hear," Edric warned. "I can smell sorcery thick in the air. We must keep close together all the time. And if anyone tries to ride away for any reason, the rest of us must stop them." He looked gravely at the others. "The chances are we'll be shown enticing things and be offered wonderful gifts, but we should believe none of it! We need to keep our heads clear and not listen to any voices that call to us—no matter who they seem to be. Remember all the time: We are in a land of untruth and fantasy!"

The sun never shifted from the top of the sky as they rode along. The light was golden and hazy. Not a cloud stirred to disturb the crystalline blue.

At one point they saw shoals of slender silver fishes moving through a grove of trees as though through water. And at the end of a far valley they saw huge beasts, like shaggy buffalo, passing in a herd, each of the humpbacked animals the size of a moving hill.

"Untruth and fantasy, indeed!" murmured Rathina, gazing wide-eyed at the massive creatures.

"I'd kill for a digital camera," Connor said under his breath.

As they traveled, they heard hoofbeats where there were no horses and laughing voices among the rocks. Many-colored butterflies swarmed around them forming the shapes of men and women, dancing in the air. In the distance they thought they saw citadels and towers, but they dissolved into mist the moment anyone's eyes tried to focus on them. They saw a waterfall that poured upward and a river that flowed through the air and beautiful figures who appeared in groves of trees, smiling and beckoning.

What is there to trust here? Tania thought. She had no idea.

Rocks rolled uphill, chiming like bells as they moved. Birds of glass flapped slowly by. Children made of flowers ran along the crest of a hill, towing a great kite in the shape of a lion.

Worn out, they paused and slept by a singing river, trying to find some shade from the sun, waking at noon. Lying under fruit trees heavy with clusters of rubies and pearls and diamonds.

They rode on again, coming suddenly upon a three-masted galleon plowing through a field under full sail. The mariners hung from the rigging waving and beckoning as the ship curved away and was gone, leaving a wake of new-turned earth.

"Awesome," muttered Connor.

"Don't look," warned Edric. "Ignore them!"

Tania stared at him. "How do we do that?"

Three times they slept, and three times they got back into the saddle, and each time Tania found it harder to carry on. The end of all hope came suddenly during a long, exhausting ride over a wide landscape of rolling hills. Edric was the first to come to the crest of the highest hill.

"No!"

Tania nudged her heels into her horse's flanks. The long, unwinding crest of the hill opened up to her—and revealed beyond, a great dark forest that stretched forever in both directions. It was the Gormenwood—Tania recognized the landscape immediately—they were back where they had started.

She heard Connor's voice. "All that time . . . all that way . . ."

"Can we be sure this is the same forest?" Rathina asked, but there was little optimism in her voice.

"Of course it is," said Tania, slumping in her saddle. She slid forlornly from the horse, her body aching.

"Riding on hope alone has failed us," Rathina said, suddenly at her side. "But if one way is closed to us, then we must seek another."

Tania looked despondently at her. "Such as?"

"Come," Rathina said gently. "Sit. Let us see what great need can accomplish. Let us try reaching out to Eden, or Oberon himself."

Tania hesitated, remembering Sancha's warning that she mustn't call on them again. But she saw no other choice.

They sat facing each other on the sun-drenched hilltop, in the middle of the land of magic and wonder, holding hands and closing their eyes.

Tania struggled to get a picture of Eden in her head—but the light was too bright through her eyelids, and all she could see was a flame red glow that pulsated and writhed in her mind.

"Eden . . . ?" She screwed her eyes tight, desperately trying to concentrate. "Eden . . . please? Oberon . . . ?"

She felt nothing. Not a glimmer. Not a shred of communion with her faraway family.

She opened her eyes, seeing the look of sorrow on Rathina's face.

"There's nothing . . ." Tania said. "Not a thing. Either we're too far away or they don't have the strength left to make contact," she said. "I think we're on our own."

She saw Connor standing close by, frowning deeply as he stared at the forest.

"Can I say something without being shouted down?" he asked.

Tania sighed. "Go ahead."

"We're stuck here because of some kind of magic spell, right?" He looked around at the three of them, but no one needed to speak. "So what we surely need is another magic spell to get us out." He looked at Tania. "That's what you were trying for just now, wasn't it? A bit of magic from Faerie?"

"Yes, but it didn't work," said Tania. "And Rathina and I don't have any useful magic about us."

"No, *you* don't," said Connor, turning now to look up at Edric, still in the saddle, his face impassive. "But *he* does."

"No!" Tania said, animated for a moment. "That's not an option."

"Excuse me!" demanded Connor. "How come you get to make that choice? We're all of us stuck in this place, running around like rats in a maze. We already *know* he's going to use the Dark Arts—that ferrywoman told us so. So why not have him use them to get us out of here? What difference does it make if he's going to fail anyway? Why not make use of him?"

Tania stood up, swaying a little. Light-headed from the effort of trying to contact her sister. "Because it could destroy him," she said angrily.

Connor held his ground. "Then give us an alternative, Tania," he said. "Tell us how else we get out of here—now that we don't have a compass any longer?"

There was a dreadful silence.

Rathina got to her feet. "We were wrong to throw away the compass. Let us not make the wrong decision a second time. If our quest fails, Faerie falls." She looked at Tania. "If Edric is our only hope, we cannot dismiss it so swiftly. Did I not say prudence should dictate our future decisions?"

"No!" Tania shouted. "I won't ask him to do that. I don't care. I won't!"

"I don't need your permission, Tania," Edric said, looking tenderly into her face. "Like Connor said—you don't get to make all the decisions."

She ran toward him. "No! Edric, no! We'll find another way."

"I don't think so."

"Edric!"

He looked away from her, and already she could see the sheen of silver floating across his brown eyes. He lifted his arms and formed shapes in the air with his outstretched fingers. And where his fingers passed, the air grew dark and clouded, creating a web of deep blue light that shone and throbbed all around him.

Tania fell to her knees, her head filling with the chanting of a voice that both was and was not Edric's voice. She could not understand the words, but she knew they held power and danger.

Edric and his horse were only shadows now in the expanding ball of blue light, and all around them the grass lay flat on the hill, as though beaten down by a great wind. Tania was thrown back. She heard the whinnying of frightened horses, Rathina shouting, Connor calling something that was swept away on the wind.

A voice came out of the darkness. "I see you!" It was Edric, sounding startled and amazed. "I *see* you!"

Tania opened her eyes a crack, fighting the blasting wind.

The ball of light was larger now, and it was no longer blue. It was green—and standing tall and slender in front of Edric's horse was a woman dressed all in green, with flaming red hair and a white face and ruby red lips.

Tania knew her in an instant. The Green Lady! The enchantress of Erin.

"And I see *you*, my fine horseman," said the Green

Lady. Her voice was strong and full of laughter. "Such powers you have, my friend, that I have not tasted in many a long age. I knew my nets would catch one such as you on a fine noontide day." She laughed merrily. "You will make a gallant knight at the court of Ashling dar Dair." She reached out her arms to him, and tendrils of green light flowed from her fingertips. "Say farewell to your friends, knight of the Dark Arts!"

Edric struggled and turned his head toward Tania. There was irrevocable loss in his eyes. His mouth opened as if he was about to speak, but then the hilltop was riven by a blast of emerald light that knocked Tania onto her back and sent her rolling helplessly away down the long slope of the hill.

Tania came to her senses in long grass under the noonday sun.

"Edric!" She clambered to her feet, staggering. The sight that met her eyes almost brought her to her knees again. The whole of the top of the hill had been blasted apart, the grass torn away, the earth ruptured to reveal the deep, dark bones of the land.

She ran up the hill, scrabbling with hands as well as feet.

She saw Rathina first—lying on her face at the very rim of the crater. Dropping at her sister's side, she turned her onto her back.

Rathina's eyes were closed, but she seemed no more than deeply asleep.

"Rathina! Wake up!" Tania shook her, leaning close to her face, stroking her hair, tears falling onto her sister's skin.

But Rathina did not wake up.

Tania got to her feet again. Connor? Edric?

Where were the horses?

Gone.

It was useless even to try and guess how long ago that happened. A few heartbeats, a day—whatever *that* meant in this mad Realm.

She stared down into the chasm, remembering the look on Edric's face—remembering the explosion of green light that had engulfed him.

She saw another figure, lying on the far side of the dreadful hole. "Connor!"

But when she came to him, she found that he, too, was deeply asleep and she was unable to rouse him no matter what she did. But at least he and Rathina did not seem to have been harmed by the eruption of sorcery that had engulfed Edric.

The Green Lady had taken him.

Tania sat in the grass, her face in her hands.

It was the Dark Arts. The moment Edric had summoned the Dark Arts, the Green Lady had pounced. What was it she had said?

I knew my nets would catch one such as you on a fine noontide day. . . .

Tania turned her face to the scorching sky. "Edric!" she howled. And then she opened her mouth wide and let out a scream of misery and despair.

Spent of all breath, she dropped onto her face in the long grass and wept. All hope was gone. The quest was over.

* * *

"Come now, it can't be as bad as all that," said a voice. A hand touched her shoulder. "Why, you'll break your heart with weeping."

Tania turned onto her back and opened swollen eyes. Two smiling faces floated above her.

"Michael . . . ?" She sat up. "Rose?"

"I am Rose Maguire, indeed," the woman said, but her face was puzzled. "Where is it you know us from?"

Tania pressed the heels of her hands into her eyes. "No. This is just a dream. That's all it is."

She opened her eyes again, and once the fog was gone from her vision, she found Michael and Rose gazing at her as before.

"You can't *be* here," Tania said.

"Is that a fact?" said Michael. "Well, now! And don't I feel the fool."

"Help the poor child up," said Rose, offering a hand to Tania. "Look at her, all bedraggled and woebegone."

Tania stood, taking a long, steadying breath. "Who are you?" she asked.

"It seems you know that already," said Michael with a beaming smile. "Two wandering minstrels sent to give a helping hand to a lady in distress." His black eyes twinkled. "Will you tell us your name?"

Tania blinked from one to the other. "Don't you remember me?" she asked. "Back in . . . in . . . Ireland. At the Iron Stone Tavern. We met you there." She gestured to where Rathina lay sleeping still. "You helped us." She looked into Rose's perplexed face. "Tania and Rathina. Don't you remember? You gave me a leaf that opened doors. . . ."

"Not I, Rathina," said Rose.

"No, I'm *Tania*." She felt like screaming. "Oh, this is crazy!" She stared around herself. "What's going on?"

"Calm yourself, Tania," Rose said gently. "We've been sent to tell you two secrets."

"Who sent you?" Tania demanded.

"That is not one of the secrets to be revealed," said Michael, catching hold of Tania's hand. Rose was still holding the other, and now she took Michael's free hand, so the three of them were standing in a ring on the hilltop.

Tania looked from one to the other. Two friendly faces in all the perilous madness of Erin. Was that why she had met them before—so that she would trust them now?

"Tell me the secrets," Tania asked.

Michael smiled. "They can be unlocked only by the right key."

Tania frowned at him. "You mean . . . I have to ask the right questions?"

"Exactly so," said Michael.

What two questions should she ask? Her duty was to find the Divine Harper—but her heart ached for Edric. She had to know what had happened to him—she had to know if he could be saved from the Green Lady.

Two questions.

The quest is all that matters—everything else is selfishness.

I don't care. I have to know what happened to Edric.

"Okay," Tania said at last. "Two questions. Question one is how do I get Edric back." She licked her lips, her mouth dry. "Question two is how do we get to Tirnanog."

Rose smiled. "Fine questions, Tania!" she said. "To seek for Tirnanog you must travel through Erin and over the pathless mountains of Hy Brassail to the shore of the Limitless Ocean. Tirnanog lies beyond that ocean, but there is no ship that can take you across that vast water, and even if a ship could be found, Tirnanog lies beyond the edge of the world."

Rose paused for a moment at the look of dismay Tania gave her. "But that is not the first of your tribulations," she continued. "For no common steed nor shoe can bear you safe through dragon-haunted Hy Brassail. Only the horses of the Deena Shee can safely make passage across that cracked and desolate land—and the Deena Shee do not part with their horses for love, nor magic, nor horded treasure."

Tania gaped at her.

"And there's the answer to one of your questions," said Rose.

"So, you're telling me . . . it's hopeless?" Tania choked out at last. "Even if I managed to find a way out of Erin, I'd never get across Hy Brassail. And even if I managed *that*, there's still no way to get to Tirnanog!"

"That, I cannot say."

"I think you just did!" Tania exclaimed. "You've just told me what I want to do is impossible."

"Nothing is impossible, daughter last of daughters seven," said Rose. "Not with your true love by your side, with honest hand in true love given."

"Well said, my darling girl." Michael laughed. "And now for your other question, Tania. The Green Lady has a will that has never been thwarted. She has sought for a thousand years for a worthy consort to share her throne—"

"A consort?" declared Tania. "You mean . . . like . . . a husband? Oh no! No way is that happening!"

Michael laughed. "The fury of love burns bright in you, Tania, and that's all to the good. But listen to me carefully now if you'd win him back." He turned, an arm coming around her shoulders so that she was turned with him. He pointed into the distance. "You must walk in a straight line till you come to a place where twilight rules. There you will find a high ring of grassy earth taller than the tallest tree, turfed and grassed and overgrown with night phlox and moon-flower and evening primrose. Do not seek to pass over the ramparts of that place without first saying these words, and these words exactly: 'Ashling dar Dair, I am come for my true love. Hear me, Ashling dar Dair. I will not depart without him.' The words have great power in them. The enchantress will be forced to respond to your challenge. She will have to let you into her citadel—and what comes next, you must face alone."

"What do you mean, 'what comes next'?"

"The ancient laws allow the Green Lady to present you with two challenges," said Michael. "Two ordeals. If you survive, Edric will be yours once more. If not she keeps him for all eternity."

His arm slid away from her shoulders and he stepped back, leaving her gazing out over the hills and valleys of Erin with the sun beating fierce on her head.

"I can do that," she murmured. "But . . . but what will I have to do once I'm inside? If she's been waiting for a husband for a thousand years, she's not going to just hand him over because I say so. What kind of ordeals will they be?" She paused, waiting for Michael to speak.

She turned. "I need to have a better idea of . . . what . . . I . . . might . . ."

She was alone on the hill.

The messengers were gone.

Tania was still unable to wake Rathina and Connor. Their sleep was as deep as ever and nothing she did came close to rousing them. But before she set off to follow Michael's instructions, she was determined to make sure they were as comfortable as possible.

She knelt at Rathina's head, smoothing her hair back off her face, gazing fondly at her.

"I'm going to try and rescue Edric," she whispered. "If it all works out the way I hope, I promise we'll be back as soon as possible." She paused. "If not, I hope you wake up and find your way home without me. Connor will help, I'm sure. You can keep each other company, huh?" She leaned forward and kissed her sister's forehead.

She knelt briefly at Connor's side, straightening his clothes a little. "You make sure you look after Rathina, hear me?" she said, her voice cracking. "She could use some of that love you've got bubbling away inside you."

She stood up. "A place where twilight rules," she murmured to herself, settling her crystal sword at her hip. She took a deep breath. "Okay," she said to no one at all. "Here goes nothing!"

As Tania walked, she began to notice that the countryside around her was no longer teeming with strangeness.

The air still had that distracting golden haze about it—but towers and palaces and gateways were no longer appearing and disappearing from the corner of her eyes, and no voices called enticingly from woods and caves. The sun was still nailed to the roof of the sky, and the circling mountains still rippled and changed when Tania wasn't looking, but it was as if much of the magic of the place had gone to sleep. Or maybe it was that the enchantress had other things to occupy herself with now.

Edric, for instance.

Tania never saw the twilight coming. One moment she was walking along under the noonday sun, the next she was in the cool of a summer evening surrounded by drowsy shadows, the air filled with the sweet aromas of evening primrose and night scented herbs.

A high, steep sloping rampart rose almost at her feet, grass-covered and mantled with flowers of pink and white and yellow. She halted in her tracks, remembering what Michael had told her to do.

One hand gripping the hilt of her sword, she took

a deep breath and called into the silent gloaming. "Ashling dar Dair, I am come for my true love! Hear me, Ashling dar Dair. I will not depart without him!"

She was aware of a faint shivering all around her, as if the land was trembling with suppressed laughter. She drew her sword, comforted by the way it sparkled in the dusky light.

The ground quivered under her feet, and a sound filled her ears like discordant music. The music reached a shrill pitch, and her sword shattered in her hand. She stumbled back, gasping for breath. The air sparked, stinging her skin. Then the rumbling beneath her grew to a roar, and the hill split open in front of her as though cloven by an invisible ax.

She stared into the dark gulf, expecting some horror to emerge. But there was nothing. The land had become still and quiet again and the music was gone.

A voice sounded from beyond the cleft. A woman's voice, powerful and ringing with amusement. "Come, then, child. Take back your love . . . if you are able."

No sword. No one to back her up. Nothing to cling to but courage and love.

It would have to be enough.

As Tania walked into the sinister gap, her legs trembled and her stomach was a ball of stone. Darkness wove sinister webs in her mind.

She stepped into an enclosed area as round and steep-walled as a bowl. There was grass under her feet, and ahead of her was a ring of rowan trees laden with red berries. In the center of the circle of trees the

Green Lady sat on a throne made from intertwined branches and twigs.

The Green Lady leaned back, her hands resting idly on the arms of the throne, her head against the high, arched back. One leg was stretched out, a bare foot revealed beneath the hem of her long, green gown.

Edric was crouched in front of her, washing her foot with water from a wooden bowl.

The enchantress cast a languid, sleepy-eyed look at Tania and smiled—and Tania saw that she had pointed teeth, like the teeth of a lizard or a snake.

"Edric—we have a guest," the Green Lady drawled, half lifting a limp hand.

Cradling the Green Lady's foot in his lap, Edric turned to look at Tania. She fought to stop herself from crying out as she saw the silver sheen that coated his eyes.

"This girl has come for you," said the Green Lady. "Would you like to go with her?"

Edric bared his teeth at Tania and snarled, then turned his face away again and continued to wash the Green Lady's foot.

Subduing her fear, Tania walked through the trees, her head high, refusing to be daunted by the enchantress. She stood behind Edric, avoiding the Green Lady's eyes, stooping to touch Edric's rounded shoulder.

"Edric? Listen to me. She's put a spell on you. I need you to stop doing that and pay attention to me." She shook his shoulder, but he shrugged heavily, trying to dislodge her hand. Still he lifted a cloth from the bowl and continued to wash the Green Lady's foot.

Tania knelt, bringing her hand down on his. "Look at me!"

He turned his head again, his face utterly blank, his eyes like silver moons.

"Come with me, Edric," Tania said. All the while she was waiting for the Green Lady to do something, all the while she was bracing herself for some sorcerous attack.

"He will not go with you, child," said the Green Lady. "He knows now the bite of a deeper, stronger love."

Tania held Edric's face between her two hands, looking into his eyes, trying to see the brown behind the silver. "I love you, Edric—and you love me. Can you keep that in your mind? We need to leave here now; we really do. Right now."

She saw the lips of the enchantress moving silently, conjuring a spell that came from her mouth as a thin green vapor. Moments later Tania felt a pressure building around her—as though the air was congealing into fists of iron and closing on her head like the jaws of a vice.

She looked into Edric's expressionless face, holding his eyes despite the feeling that her brain was about to explode. As she came to the last shred of endurance, a thread of music came gliding into her brain. Familiar music, a melody, slow and sad, but filled with a mournful hope. A music of fiddle and drum—music that she remembered from the Iron Stone Tavern. And as she thought of Michael and Rose, the pain lessened and she was almost herself again.

She heard an angry snarl. The enchantress was leaning forward on her throne, her eyes blazing, her sharp teeth bared.

"Do not seek to bring that maudlin ditty into my domain, child!" she hissed. "It will serve you nothing!"

Tania looked at her. "Is that right?" she countered. "Why does it bother you so much?"

The enchantress opened her mouth and Tania saw her tongue flickering like that of a serpent. And then a heavy green mist came spewing out of the Green Lady's gaping mouth, and the world vanished in a flood of poisonous venom.

There was no Green Lady.

There was no land of Erin.

There was no quest and there never had been.

Tania and Edric were in Camden Market in London, standing facing each other while oblivious crowds went bustling by. All that Tania knew was that she was out enjoying some retail therapy with her best friend, Jade, and that she was finding her split life a real trial, and that her mum and dad were on her case about her badly explained three-day absence, and that Edric had just said something cruel and hurtful to her.

"I don't like being told I'm stupid, Edric," she

snapped, glaring into his face. "I'm doing my best. You have no idea how hard this is for me."

"And is it easy for me?" he asked. "Trapped in this benighted world, knowing that I can get back home only with your help?"

"Is that *my* fault?" she retorted. "If anyone deserves to be wound up here, it's me! I never asked for you to come and totally mess up my life! I never asked for you to pretend you liked me just so you could drag me off to your own world to marry your boss!"

"I explained that to you," snapped Edric, his eyes blazing. "I didn't have any choice in the matter!" His face grew stiff. "Do you really think I'd have wasted all that time with you if I could have helped it?" He rolled his eyes to the sky. "Have you any idea what a self-centered, whiny little pain in the neck you can be, Tania?"

"Stop calling me that! My name's Anita!"

"Yeah—whatever, *Anita*!"

"And if you detest me so much, why don't you just get lost?" she spat. "My life was fine till you came along."

"Oh, was it?" A sneering note came into his voice. "Kind of odd, then, that you've been all over me like a rash for the last couple of months, telling me how you couldn't live without me."

"My mistake!" hissed Tania. "I didn't know you so well then! I thought you were different." Her voice choked, stopping her.

"Oh, what's this now?" Edric crowed. "Going to

squirt a few tears, are you?"

Tania would not let him see her cry! She would not let him know how much pain she was in. Never!

She spun on her heel. Jade was still sitting at the wrought-iron table sucking Coke up through a straw, peering at Tania over the round blue lenses of her new sunglasses, her eyes cynical and caustic.

"Go away, Edric," Tania said icily, not even looking back at him. "I never want to see you again." She took a deep breath and walked to the table. She sat down and picked up her paper cup, hearing the ice rattle as she sucked at the straw.

"Problems?" asked Jade.

"Nope," Tania said. "Not anymore."

A wide grin spread across Jade's face. "I see," she drawled. "Trouble in paradise, eh? Well, if *you* don't want him anymore . . . can I have him? He's kind of cute in a dumb blond way."

Tania shrugged. "You want him, you can have him," she said. "I'm done with him."

"Excellent!" said Jade, her teeth as white as pearls. "That's exactly what I wanted to hear!"

There was the scrape of iron on stone as Jade got up from the table. She was about to walk past Tania, making for where Edric was still standing, when a snatch of melody came into Tania's mind, quite different from the calypso music that was being piped into the small eating area alongside the Stable Market.

A melancholy tune played on a fiddle and accompanied by a slow drumbeat. The music opened a door in her head and let a great burst of clear white light flow into her mind.

This wasn't real! None of it was real!

"No!" She snatched at Jade's wrist as she was passing. She looked up at her best friend's face, the eyes triumphant behind the blue lenses. "Nice try!" she said. "But you don't get to keep him that easily."

The market and the sunshine and the calypso music all fell away like a discarded skin, and she was back in the rowan grove in the twilight citadel of Ashling dar Dair. The Green Lady was glaring at her, and Edric was kneeling at her feet.

"A strong mind you have, my child," said the Green Lady, and although her voice was steady and smooth, Tania could sense the anger seething behind it—she could see it flickering like flame in the eyes of the enchantress. "But that will not be enough, I think. Not by a long way."

The Green Lady stood up, stretching her arms out and throwing her head back.

"Come to me, my Deena Shee!" she shouted into the sky. "Come to me, three by three. Come from your mounds, I call to thee! Come and do your duty to your Queen!"

A memory. Sharp but distant. *Three by three?* Where had she heard that before?

The ground began to shake under Tania's feet, and the air was filled with a groaning noise.

Edric threw himself forward, clutching at the Green Lady's gown.

Tania stared around, trying to control her mounting fear as mouths opened in the grassy ramparts of Ashling dar Dair: three dark mouths that yawned and stretched till they were as wide as castle gates.

Tania heard the thud of hooves. Then she saw a flickering red light in the central chasm.

Three red horsemen rode from the hill. Weird and uncanny, they were like figures formed of firelight, wearing armor of red leather and carrying spears of red wood. Flames danced on the points of their spears, played among their long red hair and beards, and glowed in their red eyes. Their horses were also red, their manes and tails and eyes brimming with fire.

The leading horseman lifted his spear high. "We come," he called, "the flame-lords of Culann, to do our duty to the Faerie Queen!" The flames shot from his spear and burned the sky.

Then Tania saw three more horsemen come riding from the second hole. But these were green, green to their skin and their hair and their spears, and they rode upon horses as green as poison.

"We come," called the leader, lifting his spear, "lords of malachite, to do homage to our Queen!"

I know this! I've heard this before! But where? When . . . ?

And finally three horsemen all in yellow rode from the last of the mouths in the hillside, and everything about them was yellow, and their horses were yellow from withers to hooves, and a burnished yellow light leaped from their spearpoints.

"We come, lords of the amber sun, in fealty to the Queen of Erin!"

The nine riders entered the ring of rowan trees, their movements slow and stately as they circled Tania and Edric and the Green Lady and came to a halt. Their horses turned, facing inward, and nine spears were leveled, pointing toward Tania.

"This child would take my young knight from me," called the Green Lady. "What would you do, flame-lords of Culann?"

"We would turn him to fire!" replied the red lord who had spoken first.

A shiver of fear ran through Tania. *Turn him to fire?*

The Green Lady looked at Tania, her eyes gleaming. "Hold him close, my child, and never let go—for if you do he is mine for all time!"

The Green Lady stepped back from where Edric knelt at her feet, and a second later flames leaped from the points of the red spears and poured down over Edric.

His mouth opened in a scream of utter agony as he writhed in the fire. Tania threw herself at him, on her knees, pressing him against her, enveloping him in her arms. She held on for what felt like an eternity.

Edric struggled against her, screaming. Tania's eyes filled with acrid black smoke. It clogged her lungs, but still she clung onto him—refusing to surrender him to the Green Lady. The pain was appalling, but she would not give in.

I'll never let you go! Never!

And then it was over and the flames were gone. She panted with shock, gradually realizing that there was no sign of injury to Edric's face or body—that they were both whole and unhurt.

Before she could make a move, she heard the Green Lady's voice, hissing like adders. "Burned to the bone and yet you cling on!" she spat. "There is great heart in you, child. But I am not done with you yet." Her voice rose to a shout. "What would you do for your Queen, lords of malachite?"

"We would make him a serpent!"

There was a flare of green light, and suddenly Edric was a great writhing snake, his body as thick as Tania's waist, his coils already tightening around her, squeezing the air from her lungs. And the worst of it was that, although the face of the serpent was distorted and hideous, it still bore traces of Edric.

The head reared; the eyes filled with malice. The snake opened its mouth wide and struck, its long fangs sinking into her neck.

Tania cried out as she felt the venom being pumped into her veins. Every instinct in her mind and body screamed for her to tear herself free of the squirming monster, but she would not.

It's Edric! It's my true love!

A coldness began to spread from her neck, a deadening coldness that crept across her shoulder and down her chest, burrowing deeper, moving toward her heart. Her heart stopped beating as the coldness surged around it. Her blood turned to ice, the air to stone in her lungs. Still she would not be overcome.

No! I'll never let go. Never!

And then the snake was suddenly gone from in front of her eyes. She gasped, staring around, amazed to find herself alive and still holding Edric in her arms.

The Green Lady's voice seethed with surprise and anger. "And still love endures!" she snarled. "But no more! Now I will have done with you, and death shall be your reward." She lifted her voice in a commanding cry. "Lords of amber sun, do fealty to your Queen!"

"Become a savage beast!" shouted a voice. "Rend her to the bone!"

Fear struck Tania as Edric jerked and thrashed in her arms, his head twisting, his face stretching and distorting. His jaw stretched unnaturally toward her, the teeth snapping. Wiry hair began to bristle from his skin, and his eyes grew wild and yellow. With a sudden surge of power he threw her onto her back. He was on top of her; and he was a werewolf, huge and shaggy and stinking, but still with a face that was half wolf and half Edric. The monster fought her wildly as she tried to defend herself, its bared fangs striking against her cheek, its open maw spraying foul spittle over her face. She cried out, feeling the raw power of its limbs as it reared over her, the mouth a gaping red hole, the eyes slithers of vicious yellow light.

An arm rose and fell, claws raking across her face. Pain and terror. The feel of her flesh being torn. The roars and snarls of the beast above her, filling the night, the hot breath pouring down over her. Again it struck her, the claws slicing deep into her skin, tearing at her clothes, gouging her arms as she tried to defend herself.

Edric, no! Please, no!

She screamed, lost in agony and terror, forgetting everything.

Through a red haze she saw her shredded gown, blood blossoming across the fabric. And above the roaring of the werewolf she could hear the mocking laughter of the Green Lady.

She choked, her arms falling limp as the beast straddled her and roared its triumph, its weight crushing down on her, making it impossible to draw breath.

She struggled weakly, swamped by darkness. Losing consciousness.

She lay still. Dead, surely.

The werewolf clambered to its feet and turned, dropping to all fours and running to where the Green Lady stood. It rubbed up against her, fawning at her feet.

Tania could do nothing. She was dead. Dead, *surely*? She saw the Green Lady smile and pet the werewolf as the light faded from her eyes.

No . . . not . . . dead . . .

Struggling to hold on to consciousness, Tania did not know where she found the strength—she did not know how she endured the pain and the deathly cold to lift herself and hand over hand, her legs dragging, to crawl to where the werewolf was nuzzling its snout into the Green Lady's hand.

With her final breath she caught hold of the werewolf's forepaw and closed her fingers about it. "I'll never let go. Never."

Then the dark took her.

Tania felt herself lifted to her feet, a hand at her throat. She opened her eyes and found herself staring into the Green Lady's fearsome, enraged face. She hung in the grip of the enchantress of Erin.

"Had I known the power of the love in you, I would not have brought you into this place!" the Green Lady spat. Her voice was half choked with rage. "I would have slain the boy where he stood rather than have him taken from me!"

Tania stared at the enchantress, her head gradually clearing as she looked into those bitter, hate-filled eyes. She realized that her hand was tight in another hand. Her head was held fixed by the Green Lady, but she swiveled her eyes and saw Edric standing at her side. He looked exhausted, but there was a smile on his face as he gazed at her. And his eyes were brown.

"Take the boy and take with him the curse of my heart on you!" hissed the enchantress, her fingernails digging into Tania's skin. "You will never know true happiness, child of the riven soul," she spat. "Any happiness you do find will be nothing but an illusion!"

The fingers loosened on Tania's throat and she staggered and would have fallen over if Edric hadn't caught her.

"It's all right," he said, his arms around her. "You've beaten her. . . . You won!"

The Green Lady turned and swept away, her gown sliding across the grass in her wake as she walked away. Tania saw that the nine riders ringed them still, their spears pointing inward, their horses immobile, their faces unreadable.

The Green Lady lifted her arms and before her the hillside split open with a sound like thunder. With neither word nor gesture she walked into the hill, and the lips of grass closed at her back, solid once more.

Tania turned in Edric's arms, clinging to him, pressing her face into his neck, feeling him holding her. "Is it over?" she said gasping.

"Yes."

"Truly?"

He laughed, his arms tightening around her. *"Yes!"*

She looked into his face. "Don't ever leave me again!" she said.

"I won't."

"You'll never be taken away from me. Not ever! I'll come for you, no matter how far you go."

"I know."

She looked into his face, into his wide brown eyes, and for a few moments Edric was all that existed in the world.

XXIX

"Be gone from this place!" howled an angry voice. "There is no welcome for you here! The Faerie Queen of Erin curses you."

Tania pulled away from Edric to see the foremost of the red horsemen towering over them, his fire-barbed spear lowered, pointing at her face.

A line of a song came like an arrow into her mind. *Where the horsemen nine, beyond all time, pay homage to the Faerie Queen . . .*

That was it! That was the music she had been hearing! It was the song that Michael had sung in the Iron Stone Tavern. The song about the Faerie Queen and the nine horsemen she held in thrall.

"We will go if you'll give us leave," said Edric to the horseman, his arm coming around Tania's shoulders. "We have no wish to linger."

"Then depart, and an ill grace go with you," said the red horseman. He pulled on the reins and the red horse stepped aside, and there was a clear path to the cleft that divided the ramparts of Ashling dar Dair.

"No!" Tania slid away from Edric's protective arm. She had only heard the words of the song that one time—she was desperately trying to remember how it went. "Wait!"

"What is it?" Edric's voice was puzzled.

She screwed her eyes shut, cudgeling her brains. "Give me a moment," she said. "I have to get this right." She began falteringly to sing . . .

"*An apple tree grows on the Faerie Queen's hill that bears the fruit so round . . .*" She opened her eyes. "Red apples and green apples and yellow apples—all together on the one tree. Yes, that was it!" She stared up into the uncanny red eyes of the leading horseman. "Where is the tree?" she demanded. "Where is the magic apple tree?"

"You cannot approach it," declared the rider. "None can, on pain of death!"

"Yes, I know that," Tania said. "Just tell me where it is."

The horseman lifted his spear and stretched out his arm. Tania turned, following the slender, pointing finger of the spear.

At first there was nothing—just the dusky sky over the green hill. But then, like a hidden picture that reveals itself only if it's stared at for a while, Tania suddenly saw a tree growing directly above the place where the Green Lady had walked into the hill.

An apple tree. And even in the twilight she saw that it had red and green and yellow fruit!

"Edric—we have to get to the tree," she said. "We have to pick one of each color apple."

He nodded and caught her hand. Together they dived between two of the horsemen and began to run for the steep slope.

Tania felt such love for Edric that it almost burst her heart. He had not asked why; he had not hesitated for a single second. He had simply taken her hand and gone for it!

But even as they were running up the hillside, she heard the thud of hooves and the rattle of harnesses as the nine horsemen went galloping full tilt up the hill, speeding past them.

Before they came halfway up the ramparts, the nine horsemen had surrounded the tree, facing outward, faces grim, spears at the ready.

Tania and Edric slowed, walking now, still hand-in-hand, till they were only a few feet from the first horseman.

"I don't think they're going to let us past," said Edric.

"Listen!" Tania called to the statue-still horsemen. "You're under the Green Lady's spell." She paused. "Do you get what I'm telling you? You don't have to do this. Let me through. If I pick the apples, you'll all be free of her. Trust me!"

Trust me! I heard it in a song. . . .

"None may come nigh the tree," boomed the red horseman. "None may pass, neither by magic, nor by stealth, but they shall come to their death."

None may pass . . .

Save she whose step is an airy dance, and she who can thwart the Faerie Queen's will, with her true love at her side . . .

An airy dance . . .

Tania smiled and tightened her grip on Edric's hand.

"How many paces, would you say, to get to the tree?" she asked him.

"Ten . . . maybe twelve," he said.

"Okay, then—let's do it!"

She focused her mind and sidestepped.

They found themselves on a windy hill under the soft light of a new day. Trees shivered in the breeze and yellow bushes whispered.

The apple tree and the nine horsemen of the Deena Shee were gone.

Tania turned, the wind cool in her face, making her hair fly as she gazed over fresh, green countryside to a horizon where a white sun rose among bands of orange cloud.

A picturesque village huddled at the foot of the hill, stone houses with gray slate roofs. Streetlights and tarmac roads and the odd car on the move as the sun came up. Sleepy and timeless and . . . *normal.*

She turned to Edric, overcome by an urgent need. She took his other hand, drawing him close. They kissed, clinging to each other, freed for the moment from danger, able to hold each other briefly to forget everything but their rekindled love.

Breaking the kiss, Tania pressed her face into his neck, breathing him in, circled in his arms.

"Is there time to tell me why we need the apples?" Edric asked, his fingers still laced with hers. "I don't mind if not."

"It's a song," Tania said, pulling reluctantly away. "Pick the apples and break the spell." She looked at him and smiled. "We need those men to loan us horses to get across Hy Brassail; there's no other way. Ordinary horses won't do it. And the only way to get them to help us is if we free them from the spell that the Green Lady has put them under. At least, that's my theory."

"Sounds good to me," said Edric.

She frowned. "Edric—is my gift—you know, my ability to walk between the worlds—is it magic?"

"No, not magic," said Edric. "It's something else."

"Good. That's all I needed to know. Come on—what was it—twelve paces?"

"More or less."

Side-by-side they carefully paced their way up the hill.

"Okay," Tania said. "We'll need to be quick once we go back—otherwise we're going to get perforated before we can make a move."

"I'll go for green and yellow—you go for red."

"Done!" She took a steadying breath. "Ready?"

She took a last longing look at the peaceful Irish

countryside—wishing she could stay, wishing things could be different.

"Go!"

"Oh!" She pulled her head back, startled to find herself only inches from the trunk of the apple tree.

"See! They are returned!" roared a ferocious voice. "Pierce them through!" It was the red horseman, twisting in the saddle, his face fierce with anger.

Edric released Tania's hand and jumped, snatching at the low branches. He came down with a yellow apple in one hand.

"No!" This was one of the yellow horsemen. "I am Finbarr, lord of Cragg Nagore. I am no witch's slave."

It was working! Tania leaped for a low-hanging red apple. A swift-thrown spear grazed her shoulder, sending her sprawling, but as she lay gasping in the grass, she saw that she had a red apple in her fist.

She heard cries from all the horsemen, and when she turned, Edric was standing close by with a green apple in his other hand.

She stood up, feeling the land shudder around her as the magic of the enchantress melted away.

The men were no longer all green and all red and all yellow. They were clad in dark leathers and sweeping cloaks. They had dark wavy hair and brown, waking eyes. Only their horses had not changed, and Tania realized that, although the nine men had been under an enchantment, their nine steeds were magic still.

The men jumped down from the saddle, shouting and greeting one another like friends long separated.

"Cailtie and Cumhal, hail! By the powers, it was a fearful dark spell we were under, my brothers."

"Aye, like a living death it was, friend Midhir."

"Like lying awake in your grave!"

"Is the foul woman gone? The stink of enchantment is in my nostrils yet."

"Aye, a dark and dreadful dream has been upon us! How long have we been captive in this place?"

"It's been a hundred years times five, friend Lugh!"

The nine men gathered, embracing one another, slapping hands on leather-clad backs, laughing loud enough to crack the sky open.

"Were we under the Green Lady's spell for so long?"

"Aye, it was a monstrous long time, my lords, and I am glad indeed to be free of her dark deceits!"

"Well, that certainly worked," said Edric, tossing a yellow apple as he came to Tania's side. "Do you know who these men are?"

"I think they're the lords who ruled Erin before the Green Lady appeared," said Tania. "Part of the song says that if the nine horsemen could be freed from the spell, 'great lords again would they be.' I think that means they used to rule here. And I think we just liberated them."

The man who had led the red riders came striding up to Tania, his hands outstretched. "Maiden, young sir, I am Finn of the Open Heart. You have done us a great courtesy by freeing us from the foul enchantments of that evil creature!"

"Our pleasure," said Tania as his great, strong hand gripped hers. "Are you sure she's really gone?"

"The enchantment is broken," said Lord Finn. "The Green Lady must weave new webs in her dark den under the hill ere she shall snare us again—and the more wary will we be. Nay, I think she shall not do us more hurt. Neither to us nor to our fair land."

"I think the magic is gone," said Edric, lifting his head as though searching for an elusive scent.

"Aye, 'tis quite gone!" said Finn.

"But it's still twilight," said Tania.

"Aye, maiden—the twilight of a new day!"

Tania realized that the light was different. It was no longer the endless oppressive twilight that had hung over them ever since they had come to Ashling dar Dair; it was dawn! And away over the hills there was the silvery shine of the rising sun.

"How may we repay you for your service?" asked Lord Finn, his face glowing in the slowly building light. "Ask, and if it is in our power, you shall have whatsoever you wish."

Tania grinned. "Actually," she said, "there is something we need. Something really special."

Part Five:

The Land Beyond the World's End

XXX

The horses of the Deena Shee galloped tirelessly as the sun rose behind them, kindling the spikes and horns of the mountains of Hy Brassail so that they shone like polished brass.

For the first time since Tania had embarked on this quest, she felt elated and full of confidence, riding through the foothills with Edric at her side and Connor and Rathina close behind. Some benevolent power was watching over them—of that she was now certain. It had sent Michael and Rose to her when all had seemed lost; it had guided her footsteps when she was faltering.

"Who is it doing this?" Tania wondered.

"Our benefactor is indeed mysterious," Rathina observed. "Our father has great gifts and potencies at his command, as does our sister Eden—but surely they are too consumed by the burden of the Gildensleep to offer us such aid."

"And if it is Oberon, why the secrecy?" added Connor. "It doesn't make sense."

"Could the Dream Weaver be behind it?" Tania asked.

"From what you've told me, the Dream Weaver's power faded while you were crossing the sea," said Edric. "No, some other mystic force is at work here, although I cannot say what it is."

"How about someone using the Dark Arts?" Connor asked.

Edric shook his head. "I don't think so. It feels like some power over and above all the Mystic Arts. But I have no idea what."

"Then it must remain a conundrum," said Rathina. "Let us seek not to pierce its veil but be glad of its succor!"

Tania assumed there had to be some reason for the secrecy; their guardian angel must have some purpose in not revealing him or herself. They had no choice but to trust that all would be revealed in good time.

"Whatever it is, let's hope it keeps helping," she said. "Because if it stops now, we're in big trouble."

Events had moved quickly since Tania and Edric had freed the nine lords of Erin from the Green Lady's enchantments.

They had been given four of the magical horses: two red, one green, and one yellow. The strange animals seemed to need no guidance: no pull of reins or bridle, no urging on with knees and heels. The moment Tania and Edric were astride their high backs, the two red horses had galloped out through the cleft of Ashling dar Dair and were away like the wind, the green and the yellow horses following.

They had found Rathina and Connor sitting together on the blasted hillside—newly awoken, dazed and bewildered in a land now lost to magic, a land over which the morning sun was rising like molten gold. A land cupped in a horizon of purple mountains that no longer shifted and changed.

"Saddle up!" Tania had shouted gleefully as Rathina and Connor had stood up, staring at the horses of the Deena Shee. "The enchantress is gone." Her horse had reared, neighing loudly and striking at the air with its red hooves. "Quickly! Nothing can stop us now."

Connor had been stunned by the appearance of the extraordinary steeds.

"Did they *come* in those colors?" he had asked in amazement.

"They're not ordinary horses, Connor," Tania had called down.

"You don't say?"

Rathina and Connor had climbed into the saddle, and the four horses had turned to the west and run as though to outdo the shafts of golden sunlight that came shooting out of the east.

* * *

As the morning grew, so the pathway to the west became steadily steeper and narrower. There was no clear border between Erin and the western mountains, but Tania guessed they were well into Hy Brassail by now. Crags and buttresses of stone towered all around them, and the sound of the horses' hooves echoed between the peaks like an endless growl of thunder. But the horses of the Deena Shee were not daunted by the dangerous passes. They threaded their way confidently between the pinnacles of the mountains. And Tania trusted them, despite the narrow ravines and the dark gulfs. After all, what other hope had they in this bleak land but these supernatural steeds?

Tania looked back from one lofty aerie—a brown wall of rock to her left and a fathomless drop to her right. Behind them the land of Erin lay green and serene in the midday sunshine. The Gormenwood and the land of Alba were lost in a powdery blue haze.

They had come so far!

And yet . . . Now that her euphoria had faded she couldn't help but remember what Rose had told her.

To seek for Tirnanog you must travel through Erin and over the pathless mountains of Hy Brassail to the shore of the Limitless Ocean. Tirnanog lies beyond that ocean, but there is no ship that can take you across that vast water, and even if a ship could be found, Tirnanog lies beyond the edge of the world. . . .

She hadn't told the others about this. They had come all this way, overcoming so many obstacles and dangers together—they didn't need to know that she had been told Tirnanog was beyond their reach. Besides, Rose had also told her that nothing was impossible. . . .

Not with your true love by your side, with honest hand in true love given . . .

Edric was at her side now, and they would never be parted again. The Dark Arts still seethed behind his eyes, but together they would find a way to rid him of them. The Dark Arts would not split them up again. Nothing would ever do that.

They were in a deep canyon, and the sun was in the high afternoon sky, hazy above the towering peaks. So far in all this craggy land they had seen no living thing except for a few straggly bushes and trees and the occasional clump of tough, spiky grass.

Waterfalls pounded down from the high escarpments, looking like streaks of silver ribbon hung from the tall cliffs. A white haze rolled out over the floor of the ravine, engulfing the four riders, misting their clothes and bedewing their faces.

"Do you see that?" called Connor. Tania turned in the saddle. He was pointing up high. "Some kind of bird, I think," he said. "A big one. Except . . ."

She followed the line of his finger. Yes, there was something up there gliding among the peaks on wide, still wings. A bird, obviously, but an oddly shaped bird: a diamond-shaped bird with a huge head, crested and heavy-beaked, so that its head and neck reminded Tania of a pickax.

"A strange bird," said Rathina. "It has no feathers or my eyes play tricks."

There was silence as the four of them watched the creature circle between the mountaintops. Then they noticed that with each lazy loop the bird was dropping a little deeper into the chasm.

"We should get out of here," Connor said, his voice strained. "I don't like the look of that thing's big beak."

"It's huge," Edric said. "And Rathina is right: It doesn't have feathers. The wings are just stretched skin, like a bat's."

"It's getting closer," said Connor, sounding panicky now. "And there's no way that thing is a bat!"

The horses sensed their alarm. Tania was almost torn from the saddle as hers broke into a sudden gallop.

Along the narrow path they stormed, clinging to their horses as they sped through the waterfall mist, half blinded by the spray, drenched and gasping.

Tania heard a ghastly leathery flapping. A shadow filled the gorge and the air was torn by a high-pitched shrieking. She glanced up. The thing was immense—gliding now only a few yards above them, its membranous wings blotting out the sun, its claws reaching down.

"Get you gone!" Rathina shouted. Tania saw a flash

of gray light through the mist: Rathina's iron sword cleaving the air.

The monster screeched again, its beak opening wide, revealing rows of sharp teeth.

Tania had no weapon, no way of fighting the creature.

The iron sword flashed again in Rathina's grip, and this time its keen edge found a mark, severing a claw from a groping foot. The creature screamed in pain, jerking up, pulling away, flapping its vast wings.

The last Tania saw of the monster was a pale shape above them, fading away to nothing among the peaks.

"What was that?" said Connor, gasping, his face white.

"Some abomination from ancient times, mayhap," said Rathina. "But where one such fiend dwells, others must surely have found a home!"

"Then let's get out of this valley before they come for us," said Tania.

Their encounter with the flying creature had been frightening but mercifully brief. How would they fare if they were attacked by a whole flock of them? Tania did not want to find out.

The deeper they traveled into the barren mountains of Hy Brassail, the more the shadows gathered.

But it was not the shadows that disturbed Tania most. More alarming to her was a growing weariness that she fought to keep hidden from her companions. It came over her in wracking pulses, making her limbs feel leaden and aching through every sinew of her body. She gritted her teeth when the exhaustion was at its worst, noticing how Rathina's shoulders slumped—knowing that her sister must also be suffering.

They saw no more of the flying creatures, but they heard bellowing and roaring from afar—or so they hoped—and they were startled by the occasional uncertain glimpse of a skulking shape among the rocks or the clatter of claws on stone as something scuttled out of sight.

As she was the only one still bearing a weapon, Rathina took the lead, her iron sword in her hand, her head turning as she scanned the rugged landscape for any sight of the beasts.

But none showed themselves.

As the evening came down and the night began to gather in black pools all around them, Tania saw eyes staring from out of the darkness. Eyes that reflected the fading light. Green eyes and yellow. Slitted eyes that watched and waited.

It was almost full night when they rode up onto a plateau and found themselves on the brink of a wide, dark lake, hemmed in on two sides by steep walls but offering a slender path around and a flat, open space at the far shore.

"This is as good a place as any to spend the night," Tania said. "At least here nothing will be able to creep up on us without being seen."

"How far to the coast, I wonder," mused Rathina as the horses picked their way past the inky lake. "I was hoping we would set our feet in Tirnanog before this day died."

Tania was also uneasy about having to spend the night here—but the growing tiredness was becoming too oppressive and she was desperate to rest.

As they made their way along the lakeside, the exhaustion welled suddenly through her body, invading her mind, draining her of energy and resolve. She toppled from the saddle, only just managing to clutch at the reins and get her legs under her as she slid from the animal's back. The horse stopped, turning its head as though in concern.

Edric leaped from the saddle and was at her side in a moment, catching her.

She heard Rathina groan and saw her fall from the saddle and drop to her knees, her hand dragging on her horse's reins. Connor was off his horse and by her side in an instant.

He looked apprehensively at Tania, his hands under Rathina's arms, holding her upright as her head lolled on his shoulder. "How are they able to do this to you from so far away?"

"The bonds of family are not severed by the count of miles, Connor." Rathina gasped, raising her head and gripping his shoulders. "The dire need of the House of Aurealis knows no limits."

"But they're going to bleed you white!" Connor said savagely. "Don't you get that? If this goes on, they're going to kill you."

Tania looked dizzily at him. "They won't do that," she said. "It's temporary. We'll be better soon. Just give us a moment."

"Tania?" Edric's voice was full of concern.

She looked up into his worried face. She faked a smile and touched her fingers to his lips. "Shh! Don't say anything. I've been feeling bad for a while now. But I'm sure it'll go soon."

Edric looked anxiously at her. "You never said."

"There's nothing you could have done about it," Tania replied. "Just help me up. I'll be fine."

Edric's lips were a thin, pale line as he brought Tania to her feet. Her legs felt weak and her head was swimming, but she was just about able to walk.

Her face contorted with the effort, Rathina also clambered to her feet, leaning heavily on Connor.

Supported by the two men, they came to the far end of the lake. The horses followed faithfully behind them and gathered together in the lee of the cliff, as though content to wait until they were needed again.

Tania bent over, kneading the aching muscles of her legs, feeling the weight of exhaustion lifting a little. She straightened up, breathing hard.

"There," she said, resting her hand against Edric's chest. "The worst is over."

"For the moment," he said.

Rathina also seemed to be recovering. Connor was

standing close beside her.

Tania looked at them, wondering whether it was time to tell them that she had no idea how to get to Tirnanog, wondering how much farther they could go before the truth had to be revealed.

XXXI

Tania dreamed of snakes and woke in darkness. The stars were a powdery blur, as though the air of this place was too dense to allow their light to shine down clearly. A cool breeze blew. She turned over, rising on one elbow, expecting to see either Connor or Edric standing guard.

That had been the agreement: that the two men would take turns to watch through the night so that she and Rathina could rest.

There was Rathina curled up on her side, deeply asleep. And Edric was close by, too—his face toward Tania, his eyes closed in sleep.

She gazed drowsily around. Where was Connor?

Alert now and uneasy, she sat up. The four horses were gathered together by the cliff wall—awake and watching but not obviously nervous.

Tania got to her feet. It was so hard in the deep dark of the mountains to know which lump of gloom was a rock and which might be a lurking beast. The lake was a sheet of pure black, reflecting nothing.

Something moved. Tania crouched and picked up a sharp stone, her eyes fixed on the creeping hump of shadow. She thought she heard the rattle of claws, the clack of stone on stone. And then two luminous green eyes opened and she knew she was not imagining things.

"Edric! Rathina!"

The beast came for her, hissing and spitting. Wide, leathery wings opened and a sinuous neck stretched forward. The head was like the skull of a horse, the teeth like daggers.

She threw the rock and snatched up more. There was a ringing sound as the stone bounced off hard scales.

The monster was almost on her now. She fell back, stumbling on the uneven ground, throwing stones, aware that Edric and Rathina were scrambling to their feet.

The monster had only two limbs: two great, powerful, ostrichlike legs that ended in stark, spreading claws. Its thick tail swung, long and barbed.

Edric gave Tania a desperate glance, as though guilt-ridden to have slept. He sprang between Tania and the beast and threw up his arms, shouting. "Get back! Get away from us!"

It was a brave but empty act.

The monster lunged at him with clashing teeth, its wings beating him to the ground. It lifted a huge leg to stamp down on him and rend him with its claws.

Rathina ran to Tania, snatching hold of her arm, dragging her out of danger as the monster's claws swiped at Edric, missing him by mere inches.

"No! Edric!" Tania cried as she saw the long neck stoop and the dagger teeth snap at Edric. He just managed to roll to one side as the jaws closed on air, but a clawed foot rose and came down hard on his chest, pinning him to the ground.

"Edric!" Tania screamed in panic and terror. "Use the Dark Arts. *Use them!*"

Pinioned beneath the monster's massive claw, Edric reached up and called in a deep voice. A shield of dark blue light rose from his hands, beating back the roaring and shrieking creature.

Edric staggered to his feet, both hands stretched out to keep the blue shield between him and the beast. But it only fell back a few steps before it surged forward again. Its head plunged and its beak snapped, and the shield was torn open from top to bottom.

The beast lumbered on, the riven shield writhing like smoke as it flapped its wings. The monster rose into the air, its claws reaching for Edric. He threw himself onto the ground just as Rathina leaped forward.

Tania saw the gray length of her sword vanish into the creature's chest. There was screeching and thrashing as the monster came crashing to the earth. Shouting aloud, Rathina yanked out the sword and gave a great two-handed swing. She severed the monster's head from its neck, and it became still, black blood oozing thickly onto the ground.

Edric staggered to his feet, his eyes wide, his chest rising and falling.

Tania ran to him. "Are you all right?"

He stared at her in despair. He gasped. "I used the Dark Arts!"

"I *told* you to," said Tania. "That thing would have killed you otherwise."

Rathina looked into his face. "An understandable lapse, Master Chanticleer," she said. "But a lapse nonetheless." A grim smile touched her lips. "Seek not to do it again. And do not attack such foul fiends with but your bare hands."

"I didn't think. . . ." said Edric. "It was coming for Tania . . ."

"All is done," said Rathina. "It is dead and we have come to no harm."

"But what is it?" said Tania, trembling as she looked down at the hideous creature.

"A wyvern," said Rathina. "I have seen pictures of them in Sancha's old books—but I never thought to encounter one. Stand back, sister: The blood of a wyvern is envenomed."

"Is it alone?" Tania asked, peering anxiously into the night. "Will there be more?"

"They are solitary creatures if memory serves," said Rathina. "But its death knell will alert every monster within earshot. I think we would be wise to quit this place."

Now Tania remembered! "Connor!" she cried. "Where's Connor?" Had the wyvern killed him? Would they find his dead body among the rocks?

"The last I saw of him was in the middle of the night," said Edric. "I woke him to relieve my watch."

"Connor!" Rathina called into the darkness. "Connor!"

A figure came running toward them from behind. "I'm here! What happened?" Connor was breathless and flushed.

"Where were you?" demanded Tania.

"It was a call of nature," Connor said, panting. "I'm sorry." He grimaced as he saw the dead wyvern. "I was only gone a minute or two."

"You should not have left your post!" Rathina chided him. "We would have been attacked as we slept if not for Tania's watchfulness."

"What's that in your hand?" Edric asked.

"Nothing." Connor slid his right hand into his pocket. "It's nothing."

"Nothing, forsooth!" hissed Rathina. "Then you'll need no pocket to keep it in, Connor." She lifted her sword, steaming and thick with the wyvern's blood. "Show us this *nothing*, or I'll beat you black and blue with the flat of my blade."

Tania hadn't even noticed that Connor was holding anything. She couldn't believe he was keeping yet more secrets from them.

Connor brought his hand out of his pocket. Something round shone darkly in the frail starlight. "It's nothing," he repeated.

Edric strode forward and grasped his wrist,

bringing the object close to his face. He let out an angry snarl. "It's metal," he said. "Isenmort!" He flung Connor's hand away, and the metal disk fell out of his fingers and went bouncing away through the stones.

"From the Helan Archaia, no doubt!" growled Rathina. "Is there no end to your perfidy, Mortal?"

"Oh, give it a rest, Rathina!" Connor said angrily. "It's just a piece of metal. I found it with the compass, but it's nothing." He looked sharply at Tania but was unable to hold her gaze for more than a few seconds. "I'm sick of being judged by you people," he said. "You didn't make such a great job of it last time if you remember. Dumping the compass just when we needed it."

Tania looked uncertainly at him. Perhaps he was right. Perhaps they shouldn't make too much of this.

"For what purpose have you kept it from us?" asked Rathina.

"Because you'd have taken it away from me if you knew about it," said Connor. "I liked to have it with me—I used it as a mirror, if you must know. Sometimes in all this craziness I just liked to see my own face—just now and then—to remind me who I really am. To remind me that I'm still *me*!"

Tania looked at him, unsure what to make of this new revelation. *What is he thinking? What kind of person needs a mirror at a time like this?*

There were times when she didn't even recognize this person as the Connor she had always known. Had the quest changed him so much?

A low, guttural roar ripped across the lake, silencing any response to Connor's words.

Rathina spun, her sword ready.

A large humped and spined shape was moving toward them along the lakeside. Huge, red slitted eyes stared. A snarl rumbled.

"Something comes to feast on the dead," said Rathina. "And on the living if we remain!"

"Rathina's right—we have to get out of here," said Edric.

Snatching up saddles and trappings, they ran to where the four horses stood waiting. The animals showed no fear, but they were clearly eager to be gone: their eyes staring, their ears pulled back.

Tania's fingers fumbled with the leather straps and the small crystal buckles. She had seen that Connor had stooped and picked up his metal disk as he'd run. Well—why not? If it gave him any comfort.

There were more eyes in the night, and dreadful shapes, horned and ridged, came creeping forward on bent limbs, claws scraping and hot breaths rattling.

Then the four of them were all mounted up, and their horses turned to the west and raced through the mountains, leaping away as fangs snapped and claws raked and voices bellowed.

Although the monsters were shrouded in the night, Tania was just able to glimpse terrible shapes as they fled. Most of the creatures seemed reptilian, encrusted and plated with hard, shining scales—things like crocodiles and huge lizards, snakes with plumes and crests and flickering tongues, and things like the wyvern: dragon things with snapping jaws and burning eyes. And among them Tania saw things that looked like the Great Salamander, lunging at them with gaping jaws.

But the horses of the Deena Shee trod a dauntless path through the swarming monsters, never faltering, galloping so fast that Tania could barely keep in the saddle. Moving as surely as though the way before them was lit by the noonday sun.

Tania felt exhausted and sick to her stomach. She did not resent her family's need to draw on her energy, but it made things so hard for her and Rathina. *Just let me find the strength to finish the quest—that's all!* But moment by moment the infirmity grew worse. Not even the sunrise and sight of the western extremes of the mountains could rouse her spirits.

They were moving at a walking pace, as though the horses knew that she and Rathina didn't have the strength to keep in the saddle at a gallop.

Edric rode at Tania's side, constantly watching her, his face tormented by anxiety. She wanted to say something to reassure him, to let him know that she would be all right, but it was too much effort. She needed every ounce of her remaining energy just to keep upright on the horse's back, to keep from giving up and allowing herself to fall.

And she could see that Rathina was faring no better. Connor rode with her, talking to her to try and keep her awake. But her head was bowed and her long black hair hung over her face.

"It can't be far now," came Edric's worried voice. "I think we've left the reptile things behind. We could stop. Rest awhile."

"No." It was such a dreadful effort to speak. What dire straits must Oberon and her family be in that they needed to draw on so much of their spirits? Was the Gildensleep shield failing? Was the plague on the move again? It was as though an artery had been opened in her body, as though her life was draining away moment by moment.

"Please, Tania—let me protect you from this," Edric beseeched. "It's killing you."

She lifted her head and looked at him. "No, they must need it. . . ." She swallowed, her head throbbing. "Maybe it won't . . . last too long. . . ."

Connor looked back. "Do you know how long the human body can cope with the kind of stress you're under?" he asked, his voice strangely cold and detached.

"No, Connor, I don't." She sighed.

"At this rate I'd give the two of you a couple more hours at most," Connor said. "Then you're finished."

"Connor! Shut up!" snapped Edric.

"Just telling it like I see it," said Connor. "I thought you guys wanted me to be more honest with you."

Tania looked into his face. Something about him had changed since their quarrel in the mountains. It was as if a wall had come down behind his eyes, shutting him off from them. It was as if he didn't care anymore.

Or maybe he's just stopped pretending.

He held her eyes for a moment, as though defying her to challenge him, then he turned away and the tension lessened.

"I wish they could use my power instead," said Edric. "I'd gladly give them all they wanted if it would stop this happening to you."

"Dark power?" murmured Tania. "I don't think so. . . ."

Edric's voice was angry. "Don't they realize what this is doing to you? Don't they understand how hard this journey has been? And now they're making it impossible."

A faint smile touched her lips. "Nothing is impossible. . . ." she whispered. "Not with you here. . . ."

He brought his horse even closer, reaching out and brushing her hair off her face. "I love you," he murmured.

"I know. . . ."

"Love never dies in Faerie."

"So I'm told. . . . And is that a good thing, do you think . . . ?"

"It's a powerful thing, I know that."

Rathina's voice rang out suddenly. "The sea!" she called. "We have reached the sea!"

Tania lifted her head.

Yes! There was the ocean at long last.

They had come out of a long, sloping valley to see

the land falling rapidly away in front of them—down and down in green slopes to a wide-mouthed bay with a rocky shoreline and beaches of coral. The waves came in like white lace on the olive green ocean. Seagulls drifted across the sky, their voices calling through the brine-laden air.

The wind was from the west, brisk and cool in Tania's face, breathing new life into her, giving her the strength to sit upright in the saddle.

Rathina, too, pulled herself together and gazed down at the welcoming bay. "There is a ship," she said. She looked at Tania. "Do you think it awaits us?" she asked. "To bear us to Tirnanog?"

Tania stared down at the ship. It was a three-masted galleon, its sails furled as it rode at anchor in the middle of the bay. Two dark rowboats were drawn up on the beach, and she saw several figures moving over the pebbly surface.

A ship to take them to Tirnanog! Rose had told her there would be no ship! Yet here it was. Tears pricked behind Tania's eyes.

Thank god!

Here, at the end of the world, she was being given the means to take her quest to the Divine Harper. But why? Was it a reward for all her efforts so far? Had the benevolent power decided they were worthy of this final gift? Tania's spirits soared as she gazed out at the wonderful vessel.

It must be! It must!

Weak still but now full of hope, she rode with her

companions down the steep terraces that led to the bay. The way the land folded on itself meant that after a while they could no longer see the rocky coastline—but there was a path of beaten earth that led down through the ridges and furrows of the falling hills. They rounded a shoulder of grassy land and saw the pebbly beach once more, shelving down to the rippling water.

A new wave of pain and weakness swept over Tania, making the sky go dark, filling her head with thunder. She heard Rathina cry out in pain.

And then, with the whole world growing dim around her, Tania saw several dark figures step from cover. One of them held an iron chain in his fist, and the chain led to a great white salamander.

A voice came into her mind like a black storm cloud. "Well met, Master Estabrook," it called. "You have served me well—and great shall be your reward!"

The pain overwhelmed her and the world fell away.

XXXII

Voices were talking in the darkness.

Connor's voice was one . . . and the other?

The other was the deep, cruel voice that she had heard booming up from the torture chamber of Dorcha Tur. Lord Balor's voice.

"You promised you wouldn't hurt them." Connor sounded angry and afraid. "You gave me your word!"

"Silence, fool!"

"No! I won't be silent. We had a deal." Connor sounded desperate now, his voice cracking. "When I agreed to take the iron mirror so you could use it to find us, it was on the condition that no harm would come to them."

The iron mirror? Tania's senses were beginning to return now. This wasn't a dream; this conversation was happening in the world outside her aching head. But what was the iron mirror? Oh! The disk Connor had? It didn't come from the Hall of Archives at all—it belonged to Lord Balor! It must be a magical device, some kind of tracker—like Edric's black onyx pendant. *Let me go and I'll find them for you. I promise. I'll bring them to you.* Oh, dear lord, what had Connor done to them?

"You knew my desire," growled Lord Balor. "Very well, you knew it, boy! Did you think that I would shrink from doing whatever was necessary to secure from those women the secret of Immortality?" He gave a grating laugh. "No, boy, I will have it from them if I have to tear their bodies to quivering shreds to find it! And when I hold it in my palm, then will you get your reward—then will I share the knowledge with you as you wished. And then will I aid you to return to the world from which you came, to use the secret for whatever ends may please you!"

Tania opened her eyes. She was lying on her back in half-darkness, bound tight at the wrist and ankle. She turned her head. Rathina and Edric lay close by, both of them unconscious, it seemed. They were in a low cave, and beyond the mouth she could see a sunlit shore. Connor and Balor were nowhere to be seen; their voices carried to her from somewhere outside the cave.

"Listen! Please listen to me," said Connor. "They don't know the secret. I'm absolutely certain of that. If there *is* a secret to how they can live forever, they don't know what it is. No matter what you do to them, they won't be able to tell you!"

"*Tell me*, boy?" There was a trace of vicious humor in Lord Balor's voice. "I don't expect them to *tell* me the secret. I have better ways. I shall bind them to the Wheel of Sortilege and I will rend their bodies with such sorceries as they have never known! I will rip them apart and dip my fingers into their hearts' blood. Let them then keep their secret from me!"

"No! I won't let you do this!"

Tania heard the sounds of a scuffle followed by a heavy blow and a cry cut short. Then there was a low, rumbling growl.

"No, Salamander, leave him be!" said Balor. "He may yet be of use to us." His voice rose in triumph. "Immortality is within my grasp at last. When my men return from the *Reaper* with the Wheel of Sortilege, we shall begin! Well it was that I chose to track them by sea, Salamander! It would have been hard work, indeed, to seek to bear that heavy engine of sorcery over land."

The *Reaper* must be the galleon Tania had seen at anchor in the bay shortly before she passed out. It was not a vessel sent to take them to Tirnanog—it was Lord Balor's ship.

They had come so far, so close to journey's end, and all for nothing.

No!

She turned her head from the light. "Rathina?" She projected a hoarse whisper. "Rathina?" There was no response. "Edric? Please—Edric—wake up!"

But his eyes remained closed, and Tania saw that there were bruises and cuts on his face. He must have fought hard to try and protect them from Lord Balor.

But perhaps even with the Dark Arts he had been overwhelmed.

Then Tania saw something that gave her hope.

Rathina's iron sword had been thrown into the cave with them. It was lying about a yard away from Tania. She began to writhe, digging into the floor with her heels, arching her back, using her shoulders to edge closer to the sword.

As she came closer, she could feel the poison of Isenmort like an itch under her skin. She knew how much worse that sensation would become once she made contact with the iron blade. She tipped herself onto her side and lifted her bound wrists toward the sword. Gritting her teeth, she began to saw her arms to and fro, pressing the ropes against the sharp edge.

The sword kept shifting, and every now and then her skin would come in contact with the metal and she'd feel a pain like lightning go crackling up her arms and into her body. She clamped her lips together to stifle her cries of agony.

But at last the ropes began to fray, coming away strand by strand. Tensing her shoulders, she tried to force her wrists apart. The rope snapped. Gasping and sweating, she sat up and worked at the knots on the rope that was wound around her ankles.

She would free Edric and Rathina next, and when Balor's men came for them, they would find them ready and waiting. Only one sword between them, for sure, but the men would enter the cave unawares and surprise would provide Tania and Edric weapons of their own. Then they would make such a fight of it!

She heard the crunching of boots in the beach outside.

"Good! That is good!" Balor's voice, a little way off. "Set the device there with its back to the cliff. You, Kirhan, and you, Leannan—go into the cave and bring out one of the women. I care not which. I will have ample sport with either. Make sure the man has not awoken. He has powers I do not trust. I'd kill him now for safety's sake, but he is one of the Immortals, I deem, and he may serve us yet."

No time to cut the others free! Tania had to act quickly.

Bracing herself against the pain she knew would come, she got to her feet. She reached out and closed shrinking fingers around the hilt of Rathina's Isenmort sword.

The pain was blinding. The sword was like fire in her hand, and the anguish of it sent razors slicing through her veins. Every fiber of her being screamed for her to let the sword drop.

But in the torture of her mind a clear point of reason and purpose managed to survive. Panting and dizzy, she carried the sword to the cave mouth and stepped out into the open.

With a howl of anger and pain she stood there, the sword raised.

She saw everything in a flash. The two men who had been approaching the cave fell back at the sight of the sword, shouting and cursing. Connor was lying facedown on the beach. A huge wheel of heavy timbers two yards across, spoked and fitted with iron manacles, was leaning against the cliff face: the Wheel of Sortilege. There was no sign of the horses of the Deena Shee. Fled, Tania guessed—back into the mountains.

Half blind with pain and her movements jerky and uncoordinated, she stumbled toward where Lord Balor stood with the Great Salamander at his side. She saw surprise and rage on his face. She saw the Salamander's jaws open wide as it surged forward on its iron leash.

In full sunlight the creature was even more terrible and awe-inspiring than Tania remembered. White as snow, its lithe body shone like oiled marble as it glided low toward her over the beach, scimitar claws chiming on the stones. Its eyes flared golden, its tongue flicking between serrated teeth.

"You'll not escape me a second time!" roared Balor, groping for his sword.

Tania lifted the Isenmort blade high, closing her other hand around the hilt. She lurched up to him, and screaming wildly, she brought the iron sword down with all her might. His arm lifted to ward off the blow, the iron hand balled into a fist.

She felt a moment of resistance, then her sword sliced clean through his arm, severing the iron fist from his flesh. He roared in agony, staggering back, clutching the bleeding stump of his arm. The iron fist came crashing into the beach like a thunderbolt, the long chain rattling.

There were shouts of fear and alarm from the nearby men.

While Tania was still reeling, the Great Salamander let out a piercing roar. Its claw lifted, scratching at the iron collar, breaking it open. Then it turned, and with one leap it drove Lord Balor onto his back. The jaws snapped. Blood sprayed high. Lord Balor's legs twitched for a moment and then became still.

"That, for all those years of imprisonment, tyrant!" howled the Salamander, and his voice was like a fire, crackling and spitting.

Tania fell to her knees, the Isenmort blade tumbling out of her deadened hands, her palms and fingers red and raw and stripped of skin.

The Salamander whipped around, its eyes on the men who stood confounded close by. "Depart or perish!" hissed the Salamander, its fangs dripping gore. "Your lord is dead—you have no reason to stay and die with him."

The men fled, kicking up the beach as they ran for the boats.

"And you, engine of evil, you shall not survive your lord!" hissed the Great Salamander, rising and smashing its claws down on the Wheel of Sortilege, breaking the timbers, sending splinters flying.

Tania was in a daze, so consumed with suffering that she hardly knew where she was. She held her hands to her chest, trembling.

The Great Salamander turned to her, its protruding

yellow eyes sharp as gemstones. Slowly it advanced on her, white as ghost light, sinuous and deadly. She was mesmerized by its gaze. She couldn't look away.

It is said that a day will come when a champion will arise to sever Balor's iron hand from his arm—and on that day the Great Salamander will reveal a fantastical secret that will shake the skies!

The Salamander stood in front of her, its tongue flicking in and out between bloodied jaws, its eyes shining with inhuman wisdom.

Tania tried to speak, but her mouth was parched. She swallowed and attempted again to form words. "What . . . is . . . your . . . secret . . . ?"

The yellow eyes glittered. "Would you know the way to Tirnanog?" said the Salamander, hissing.

"Yes . . ."

"Then turn your eyes to the sky, child, and see wonders beyond the world."

Tania looked up. The sky was suffused with gold, shining like a glorious summer sunset—although she was certain that only a few moments ago the sun had been at her back and the day only a few hours old.

The sky-fields stretched away from her like an endless beach of golden sand studded with cloud-rocks banded with amber and saffron. And far away, high in the distance, she saw a cloud that looked exactly like a long, white rock. And at the end of the rock stood a small stool and a harp, as though waiting for a celestial musician to come and play.

"How . . . do I get . . . there . . . ?"

"Through pain and transformation," hissed the Salamander.

"I don't understand. . . ."

"Oh, but you shall," hissed the Salamander. "You *shall*!" It rose and lifted a claw, its jaws widening, its mouth red and deep. It roared and the breath was like a furnace on her skin.

Tirnanog is heaven! The only way to get there is by dying!

Crying out, she threw her arms up to shield her face. She felt a blow on the side of her head as the Salamander's claw struck hard. She fell onto her side, knowing that the Salamander was towering over her.

The claw came down on her shoulder, pushing her onto her face on the beach. As she sprawled helplessly, she felt the great claws come raking down her back. As dreadful as the pain of the Isenmort sword had been, this was worse still. Far worse.

This was a pain that would kill her.

XXXIII

Tania huddled on the beach waiting for the deathblow. She could hear the Salamander's rasping breath; she could feel it hot on her wounded back.

And then she felt a new and terrifying sensation that grew from deep within the long wounds of her back. Her whole body contracted in a spasm of agony. She drew her knees to her chest, her fists beating the pebbly beach as she let out a scream of fear and anguish.

Things were growing from the slashes on her back—things that stretched and reached upward and slowly unfurled. They burgeoned and expanded, filling with potency, surging up until she was weeping with the intensity of it.

Wings!

She crouched, panting, hardly able to breathe. She felt strange new sinews and muscles working. She twisted her head and saw the gossamer wings spreading out from her bent back, the golden light sparkling and glittering on filigrees of silvery filaments as the wings slowly flapped.

The Salamander's sizzling voice broke into her astonishment. "Fly to Tirnanog, Princess of Faerie!" it hissed. "Fly!"

Tania gathered herself. The pain in her back was gone. She got carefully to her feet. Her hands still hurt—they were raw and bloody. She stumbled, a little dizzy. The wings flapped, helping her to keep balance.

She began to gasp out laughter as tears ran down her flushed cheeks. Of all the ends she had considered to her quest—this had never been one of them. That she should grow wings—not in a dream, not in an illusion, but in the real world. Wings!

"I have to free Edric and Rathina," she said, gasping, wiping the backs of her bleeding hands over her face.

"There is no time," growled the Salamander. "Fly!"

She frowned. "No. I'll release them first."

"The path to Tirnanog is fleeting, Princess of Faerie," hissed the Salamander. "Hesitate at your peril. Go now or the way will be closed. I will free your companions." The long, wedge-shaped white head turned to Connor. "And I will slay the traitor!"

Tania looked to where Connor lay unconscious from Lord Balor's blow. What had Coriceil said? That he bore a secret too dark to speak. He had convinced her that his dark secret was that he was in love with her. *Liar!* And ever since they had rescued him from the dungeons of Dorcha Tur, he had rejected every suggestion that he should return home. Now it made sense. His reasons for staying were also lies! Lies to cover up the fact that he had gone over to Lord Balor's side—that he had sold them out in the hope of learning the secret of Immortality. He was weak and he was selfish . . . but if not for her, he would never have been put in this position—he would never have set foot in this world. If anyone was to blame, she was. Why should he die for her mistake?

"No! You can't do that," she said firmly. "You mustn't touch him."

"He betrayed you, Princess of Faerie," said the Salamander. "For the promise of wealth and fame he gave you up to Lord Balor. He deserves death."

"No! It wasn't just for those things. He wanted to prove himself—he wanted to be a hero. He thought that was the way. He never meant us to be hurt, I'm sure of it."

"So be it," hissed the Salamander. "He shall not die at my hand. But go, Princess of Faerie, before the pathway fades. Fly into the golden void!"

Tania paused, staring back at the cave mouth—desperate for a final word with Edric, a final touch.

"Fly!" roared the Salamander. "Already the way grows faint."

The creature was right—the golden light was diffusing, the strewn stones melting back into cloud, the harp and the stool already no more than a blur.

"Edric!" she shouted, hoping he could hear. "I'll

love you forever!" She sprang up and her wings caught the air and lifted her high into the golden sky.

But oh, the joy of it! The air rushing in her ears, the long beach falling away beneath her. The golden light enveloping her. The power and the glory and the sheer freedom of climbing the endless sky, of swooping and gliding, of shedding the burden of gravity, the sublime and heartrending perfection of it!

I was born for this!

She laughed, her eyes brimming with golden tears.

She looked down. The Great Salamander was a sinuous white streak on the coral beach. The ocean was a dark green cloak trimmed with white lace.

Then she turned her face into the impossible golden sunset. Her wings flapped and she surged even higher into the heavens, surrendering herself to the honeyed light.

She came down feather light to land on an endless beach of golden sand that stretched away forever. A great blue ocean lapped the shore. There were white cliffs and distant green hills. There was birdsong. There was peace and contentment.

And there was a long, high white stone that jutted out into the sea. Upon its furthermost end there was a wooden stool and a waiting harp.

Two figures were walking toward her across the sand. They approached hand-in-hand, Michael Corr

Mahone and the dark-eyed gypsy woman named Rose.

Tania felt a rush of affection to see them again.

Michael smiled widely. "You made it, then!" he called. "I'm glad to see you, Tania. For a while I doubted you, but Rose said you had the strength to reach journey's end."

Rose broke hands with him and ran toward Tania. "I am never wrong!" she said, her face shining with joy. "Ah, but your wings are a wonderful sight! How I envy you them." A cloud crossed her face as she came to a halt in front of Tania. "But your poor hands! You are injured. Come, give them to me. I'll see if I have a panacea for your discomfort."

Dazed still, Tania offered up her hands. Rose took them, bowing over them and breathing on them.

"Ow!" It was an odd sensation, almost like pins and needles—sharp and astringent—but then Rose released Tania's hands, and the injuries inflicted by the Isenmort sword were healed and her palms and fingers were whole again.

"Thank you," Tania said. Michael was with them now, still smiling, his dark eyes filled with humor. "Who are you?" she asked, looking from one to the other. "Can you tell me now?"

"We are messengers," said Michael. "Our master sends us forth when our help is needed for some momentous event that threatens the balance of creation."

"Oh. I see. . . ."

"We didn't deliberately keep our true selves from you, Tania," Rose continued. "Only here on the Golden Shore are we whole and complete."

"Is this Tirnanog?"

"Some name it that," said Michael. "It is a place that has many names, but for you it is Tirnanog."

"You are at journey's end!" said Rose. "Come, walk awhile with us."

They each linked arms with Tania, leading her over the soft sand toward the white rock.

Tania looked at Rose. "Can you tell me now," she asked, "are you the Dream Weaver?"

Rose smiled. "No, that was never me." She squeezed Tania's arm. "But you will meet her again." Her eyes glowed with mystery. "And I think you will be surprised!"

Steps had been carved in the landward end of the white rock, and Rose and Michael led Tania up and onto the high summit.

"Am I to meet your master?" Tania asked as they approached the stool and the harp.

"Let us hope so," said Rose.

"Your master—he's the Divine Harper, right?"

"He is that," said Michael.

Tania frowned. "I'm sorry if this is a stupid question, but *what* is he?" she asked.

Michael chuckled. "My, but there's a halfway remarkable question," he said. "What is he? Rose—do you have the words for it?"

"He is balance," said Rose. "He is harmony and symmetry and proportion. He keeps all of creation in tune with itself. He oversees the melody of nature."

"So . . . so he's *good*, right?"

"He's neither good nor bad," said Rose. "The virtue of balance is constancy."

"He plays his tunes for all of creation with equal devotion," added Michael. "For him there is no conflict, there is just *life*, in all its diversity."

They had come now to the harp.

"Sit," offered Rose. "Play."

"Play what? I don't know how to play a harp."

"Oh, but you do, Tania," said Michael, taking her arm and guiding her to sit on the stool. "Play the song that has no ending. . . ."

"Play the song you know so well," said Rose.

"Okay, I'll give it a try," said Tania.

They stepped back from her. She wavered a few moments, her hands poised over the strings.

What song? What should I play?

She touched a string and a pure note rang out. She smiled, touching another. It sounded sweet and clear. A simple melody came into her head. She tried the strings, fumbling, getting it wrong, seeking out the correct run of notes.

And then, quite suddenly, she was playing the melody that was in her head.

A deep, rich voice began to sing at her back.

"I am the song that sings behind the eyes of poets
and thieves
No music of the mind can leap lest it rises from
the black blood that seethes
I am the secret of the oyster shell and the
strength of the supple grass
Is it not I who colors the spearhead with blood?
No splintering of moonlight that strikes from a
shield is not mine
No glaze on the eye of the dead and unborn
No sheen on the sea or ice-becloaked mountain
is free
Of the music that is turning and burning
within
I sing dragons in Hy Brassail and crystal lakes
in Alba
I sing shining palaces in Faerie and dark towers
in Lyonesse
I sing dreamers and madmen and angels and
heroes
I sing lovers and cowards and ghouls
I sing killers and weepers and dancers and
sleepers
I sing actors and demons and fools."

Tania turned to look at the singer. Her fingers faltered on the harp strings and the song came to an abrupt end.

It was the man she had briefly met seated at the bar in the Iron Stone Tavern—the round-faced old man with the gray beard and swept-back gray hair, the man with the impossibly blue eyes set deep in brown-skinned laugh lines.

He stood close behind her although she had not heard him approach, and now he was wearing robes that shimmered with an iridescent light.

He smiled. "Well met, Princess of Faerie," he said, his voice melodic even in ordinary speech. "Did I not say we would maybe meet again . . . one fine day?"

"You . . . ?"

"I indeed."

A tangle of thoughts and questions and conflicting emotions went crashing across Tania's mind.

In the end she blurted out a few incoherent words. "You could have saved me . . . saved us . . . so much . . . so . . . *much*—" She came to a choking halt, unable to articulate the chaos in her mind. "Why?" she cried. "Why didn't you tell me who you were? Why did you make us do all those things . . . all those impossible things?"

"The journey is as important as the arrival, Tania of Faerie," said the Divine Harper. "You had your path set before you. I could not deprive you of all that you needed to suffer and to learn. And your journey has touched not you alone. Have you not been the downfall of Balor, the tyrant of Alba? Have you not released Erin from baleful enchantment?"

Tania stared at him. It had never occurred to her that her quest might have purposes beyond the needs of Faerie. "But . . . but if you weren't there in the tavern to help me—what was the point of being there at all?"

"Curiosity, perhaps," said the Harper. "I wished to see this seventh daughter of Oberon Aurealis—this half-Mortal child who would risk all, who would go beyond the ends of the world to save the people of Faerie." His warm hand rested on her shoulder. "And I helped as I was able, Tania of Faerie. I sent my minstrels to light your path when I could."

Tania gazed beyond him to where Michael and Rose stood at his back.

"May I play now awhile, Tania of Faerie?" asked the Harper.

She rose awkwardly from the stool and moved aside so that he could sit. His hands came up unerringly to the strings, and a melody flowed from his fingers, intoxicating, passionate, strong, and subtle. A song that was like all of creation.

"So?" he said, his eyes on the strings. "Tania of Faerie, what would you have of me? And before you ask, understand this: Balance is all, my child; for everything given, something must be taken. For each question answered there must be a forfeit." His sky blue eyes turned to her, and there was compassion in them, but a cold resolution, too. "And for the great question," he said, his voice almost a song against the music of the harp, "for the great thing you would ask of me, the forfeit must be the uttermost wish of your heart." He paused for a moment, his head bowed, as though thinking. "So?" he said, looking at her again. "Do you still wish to ask your question of me?"

What is the uttermost wish of my heart? My very dearest wish . . . ?

To be with Edric for always.

Yes, when all else was discarded, the thing that remained was her love for Edric. To get the answers she came here for, she would have to give up Edric's love.

She had always known her sacrifice would need to be immense, but a whole Realm full of people was depending on her. She could not let them down, no matter how much it hurt her. And it did hurt—it wounded her to the very core—the thought of losing Edric hurt so deeply that she was sure she would die of it. To be forever without the one she loved. It would be *worse* than death—far worse.

Edric . . . oh . . . my love . . . my love . . .

She trembled as she spoke, riven to the very soul, hardly able to believe the words she heard herself saying. "Yes, I do want to ask," she said, "and I will give up the uttermost wish of my heart."

"Then ask your question."

"My father, King Oberon . . ." she began hesitantly. "He came here a long time ago. He came to save the people of Faerie from a plague . . . an illness that was killing them. He made a covenant with you. He traded their wings for Immortality. And the plague went away." She licked parched lips. "The plague was sent by someone called Nargostrond, but I don't know who he was . . . who he *is*. . . ."

A dark, dissonant tone came into the music now.

"Then know this, Tania of Faerie—Anita of the Mortal World. Know this!" The Harper's voice was like thunder, and even the sky seemed to darken as he spoke. "The creature known as Nargostrond is the older brother of Oberon Aurealis. His name was once Lear—Prince Lear Aurealis—and he was next in line to the throne upon which sat his great father, King Rafe."

Tania let out a gasp. This was impossible! Oberon's own *brother*?

"Prince Lear had cruelty and avarice stamped deep in his soul," said the Harper, and as he spoke the sea rose and came crashing in cold foam over the white rock. "He had ambitions that went beyond the rule of Faerie. He had a mind for conquest and warfare. He wished to forge an empire—an empire that would take his armies even into the Mortal World!"

Tania shivered, suddenly terribly cold, aware that above her head the sky had clouded over. The wind bit at her skin.

"Prince Lear raised an army against his father, meaning to murder him and usurp his throne," said the Harper. "But Oberon learned of the plot, and Lear and his forces were defeated. King Rafe could not execute his firstborn son, but he sent him into distant exile—beyond even Ynis Maw—to the bitter cold of Ynis Borealis, there to live out his life in misery and remorse. And yet the King did not know the extent of Lear's undying malice, for his son called upon the Dark Arts and he brewed evil in that place, and sent the evil upon the north wind to Faerie."

"The plague," Tania breathed. "He sent the plague. . . ."

The Harper nodded. "And now he has returned, slipping through the rift in the covenant that was created when the Sorcerer of Lyonesse sat briefly upon the throne of Faerie. And Prince Lear's power and his ambition have not lessened over the millennia. Indeed, they have grown ever more fearsome."

"Oberon's own brother is killing the people of Faerie?" said Tania. "His own *brother*? Does he know this?"

"No, Tania of Faerie, all memory of events before the Great Awakening was taken away at the forging of the covenant. King Oberon knows nothing of this. None in all of creation knows of it, save you and I."

"Help me!" Tania cried. "Help me to put things right."

"What would you have me do, child?"

"Renew the covenant!" Tania shouted, fighting against the sudden howling of the wind and the rasping crack of the gathering thunder.

"There are but two ways for this to be done," said the Harper. "Either Oberon must come to me—or I must go to him. But I cannot enter Faerie, and the King must not leave his Realm, for if he does he will lose his throne to Lear for all time."

"No! That can't be right!" Lightning forked across the blackened sky, striking at the hills, swift lizards' tongues, poisoning the air. "That's impossible!"

"It is not impossible," said the Harper, his voice strangely clear through the violence of the arid thunderstorm. "Nothing is impossible." His eyes flashed as though reflecting the lightning. "Your question is answered, Tania of Faerie, Anita of the Mortal World. Now you must give me that which was offered. You must render up the dearest wish of your heart."

"Wait! It's too soon. I need to know more!" Her voice was all but drowned by the thunder now and by the raging of the sea. "I need to know how to . . ."

The Harper reached out his hand toward her, the forefinger outstretched.

His finger touched her forehead and her mind flooded with light. The last thing she remembered was what the Divine Harper said: *the dearest wish of your heart . . .*

XXXIV

Anita sat up on her bed, blinking and disoriented.

She felt drowsy and woozy, but outside the open curtains she could see that it was still daylight.

And on top of that she was fully dressed.

What had she been thinking, napping in the middle of the day? What was she, a doddering old granny or something?

She got up, dizzy for a moment. "I've got to tell Jade about that dream!" she said, grinning and heading for the computer. "She'll freak out."

She sat down, still rubbing the sleep out of her eyes as she turned on the computer and connected to the internet. And Evan—she'd have to tell him, too. He'd be well impressed; he was totally up for freaky things like that: legends and mythology and all that kind of . . . strange . . . old . . .

"Now that's bizarre," she said, the chat room open, her fingers poised over the keyboard.

The dream had gone. It had been so vivid—but

now she couldn't remember a single thing about it.

Weird!

She yawned and stretched, her head still foggy. She looked at the time display at the bottom of the screen. 11:09.

Midmorning. But what day was it? Saturday or Sunday?

"Oh great," she said. "Now I don't even know what day of the week I'm in! Losing my marbles or what?"

She got up and wandered out of her room, still feeling odd. She clattered down the stairs and turned in the hall, heading for the kitchen.

Her mum was there, at the table, packing her handbag.

Yawning still, Anita strolled in. "Hi, mum," she said. "What's up?"

Her mother jumped—then stared at her—a huge smile breaking out across her face. "Tania!" she gasped, running and throwing her arms around her. "Oh, sweetheart, it's so wonderful to see you! And your dad will be so pleased. We thought we might never see you again!"

Anita stared at her, taken completely aback—half stifled by her mother's frantic embrace.

"What are you talking about, mum?" she asked. "I was only upstairs." She stared at her mother, completely baffled by this sudden display of affection. "And who on earth is *Tania*?"

Follow Tania's quest to save Faerie in

Book Six of The FAERIE PATH

Tania wakes up in the Mortal World with no recollection of the past seven weeks. Memories of the Faerie Realm, her princess identity, and her true love, Edric, have vanished, and all recollection of her quest to save Faerie has been lost. With the help of an unexpected ally, Tania learns she must reawaken her Faerie self—but how?

By the light of the Pure Eclipse, a thrilling final battle is waged that affects not only the fate of Faerie, but Tania's final destiny. Loyalties are tested, true love questioned, and nothing is what it seems. . . .